THE GOATSKIN COAT

By
Reed Lovac

MAPLE
PUBLISHERS

The Goatskin Coat

Author: Reed Lovac

First Published in 2025

ISBN 978-1-83538-703-0 (Paperback)
    978-1-83538-704-7 (E-Book)

Book Book Cover and Layout by:
    White Magic Studios
    www.whitemagicstudios.co.uk

Published by:
    Maple Publishers
    Fairbourne Drive, Atterbury,
    Milton Keynes,
    MK10 9RG, UK
    www.maplepublishers.com

CONTENTS

This book is written to show my appreciation for my daughter, Nya Rachelle Coverdale, who supports me in every project I do. I'm extremely proud to be your dad, so I hope you like what I've written.

Story One
Seduced by a Cult

Foreword

Over a period of six months, eleven children from across six different counties have disappeared from home. Rumours of a cult and the name Fabian Le Vor, the supposed cult leader, are flung around by town folk, but nobody can say for certain that this cult actually exists. The eleven missing children are all the same age: fifteen and all girls. A troop of Neighbourhood Watch Officials keep a vigil over all the children in the town of Boundford, in case the cult heads their way. Judging by recent patterns, this is the next place in line for a visit.

Chapter One

The Meeting

It is 1993 and all over the news, all those missing girls; no reasons why; they were all doing well at school. They hadn't any family troubles; yet they're not here to explain what is happening. The police, the media and the parents of each missing girl had appealed in vain to a mysterious person called Fabian Le Vor. He is believed to be responsible for their disappearances. Several of the missing girls had put coded references about Fabian in their diaries, so the police hadn't much to work with. If the girls left of their own free will, to be with this Fabian, then the only advice the police can give is hope they come home safe and well.

In the town of Boundford, Max Keeble, a fifty-five-year-old former police officer and chairman of the local Neighbourhood Watch troop, is busy organizing this month's meeting, always held at his house. He's on the telephone with his Vice Chair, Serendipity Wilkes.

"We need to call on everyone to attend, these events can't be ignored anymore, Mrs Wilkes."

"I agree, my son saw a convoy of caravans arrive today in the north of the town. Leon seems to think they are from this cult, which has been on the tele recently, Max."

"Then ring around every member and make sure they get to my place; we must keep our children safe." Max ended his call to check on his wife, Teresa who was busy organizing the food, their daughter Peri would be due home from school soon, so they needed to find somewhere for her to go whilst they held this meeting. Peri is a straight A's student, with a normal life. She has blond hair and a mature, shapely figure for a girl of fifteen. She attends Boundford High School.

"Hello darling, almost ready, are we?"

"Yes, my love just about. What are we going to do about our Peri then? She really shouldn't be here when we are planning her safety. She'll be embarrassed." Teresa asked.

"Yes, I know. If Seren Wilkes brings Leon with her, maybe we can send them to the movies or something," suggested Max, as he went to change into more appropriate clothing. Max went upstairs just as Peri came through the side door of the kitchen.

"Hello Mum," Peri kissed her mother's cheek and then went to check on her pet cockatiel called Boffin.

"Peri darling, we are having a meeting tonight, so your father and I thought it would be best if you went to the cinema for a couple of hours. Leon Wilkes may come over, maybe you could go together?" Her mother called after her.

"Yeah, whatever Mum." She was preoccupied with pulling faces at Boffin. Leon Wilkes had spent all of the school day leering at her and now she'll be sitting next to him at the cinema. Not the most comfortable night she had planned, but she wouldn't defy her parent's orders, so she agreed reluctantly. Leon had a crush on Peri for about a year now. He was always taking photographs of her, which made her feel ever so awkward. He would know what she did the night before, really uneasy stuff, almost stalker like. She once threw out a bag of clothes that no longer fitted her, and the next day, Leon was carrying some of it and showing his friends at school, very odd behaviour. He is mostly a loner and dresses in black Gothic clothes, not Peri's type at all.

Seren Wilkes at forty-seven is a likable woman. She is a more popular person than Max among the Watch troop members. She is single now, so some of the men were jockeying for her affections you could say. Seren is extremely attractive, the exact opposite of her son, extrovert and bossy. She was busy with the last- minute touches to her make-up when the phone in her room rang.

"Seren Wilkes!"

"Hello, this is Teresa Keeble, we felt it would be helpful if you brought Leon over as company for our Peri. She feels very uneasy when we have our meetings here at the house. Would it be okay for you to bring him? They can go and see a movie or something."

"Okay, I'll ask him. See you at seven Mrs Keeble, thank you."

Seren finished off her lipstick and pursed her lips one last time in the mirror, now she was ready, just a quick correction to her hair and she made her way to Leon's room. He was listening to his favourite music, 'Death Metal' it made him feel connected to something. Although he had a few friends at school, they weren't what you would call best friends they just talked to Leon at random moments of the day, otherwise he was on his own a lot. Seren knocked on his door.

"Hello Mother, what's wrong?" He asked quietly.

"Nothing Leon, the Keebles would like it if you could accompany Peri to the cinema, so that they can discuss her safety without her being present. Would you do that for me?"

"Okay, of course. When are you ready to go?"

"In about half an hour or so. Thank you, Leon." Seren left him; Leon smirked to himself. A whole evening with Peri was his most favourite fantasy. He leaped out of his armchair and instantly got ready for his 'date'.

Max was finally ready for his meeting, his keynotes were organized, the food was laid out and covered over. Peri had changed from her uniform into a casual plain attire. She didn't want Leon getting the wrong idea. Her father gave her £20 for the fare and film, and her mother gave her a further £10 for treats, whilst Max wasn't looking. The Keebles are a close family. Max and Teresa are both fifty-five and, they have been married for twenty years. Max used to be a policeman but now sells insurance for a living. Teresa works at a cafeteria in the town centre. Peri has an older brother Corbin, who is twenty-two, but he's left home and is now married to his wife Katie. Peri spends one weekend a month at his place, and this weekend she was due for a visit. The lounge looked like a conference room, two dining tables stood lengthwise and twelve chairs surrounded this. It was a quarter to seven. Max was rubbing his hands nervously, and Teresa stepped in to calm him. The doorbell rang and the first members had arrived.

"Mr and Mrs Player welcome; do come in and have a seat" greeted Teresa as they filed in and met Max with handshakes.

"Thanks for coming William. Heather welcome, please sit down" They were the eldest of the troop. William used to be in security before he retired, and Heather was a secretary. Both their skills come in handy at these get-togethers. No sooner had they sat down, the bell rang again, and this time Max greeted the visitors.

"Mr and Mrs Goodwin, thanks. I am pleased you made it over."

"Thank you, Max. We just want our daughters to be safe here. That's why we're all here, aren't we?" replied Robin Goodwin.

They were eagerly ushered in to the lounge and they chose to sit opposite William and Heather. Robin and Freda Goodwin had both been in the military, Robin was in the Marines and Freda had a career in the Navy. Again, very useful people. Four people, plus Max and Teresa made six people, now all they needed was the final six chairs occupied, and then they could begin.

At exactly seven o'clock the other six arrived, Seren had brought Leon, behind them was Floyd Gant, Mr and Mrs Jeffries, John Sobers and Vivienne Leeson. Floyd is Treasurer, he works in banking, Allan and Poppy Jeffries both work at the school; they are ideally placed to watch the children. John Sobers is the local Clergy and Vivienne Leeson is the Community Police Officer. Leon stepped past the group and found Peri waiting for him to take her out. Teresa faced her daughter and demanded she be back by eleven o'clock. Peri felt awkward with Leon standing beside her, but she didn't show it outwardly.

"Have a lovely time, Peri; be careful won't you Leon?" said Max. Leon nodded and they left so that the adults could have their meeting.

"Good. Now that they are out of the way, we can begin with the meeting." Max poured out drinks and then sat down to host this important social gathering.

"Welcome everyone. The first item on the agenda, our children's protection from this so-called cult." Seren began.

"We should insist that all girls aged fifteen, not necessarily boys, if they want to go to places, then they do so in pairs. Reports on the news said those eleven girls were taken singularly, and without witnesses," suggested William.

"Good point William, we'll make sure that happens from today onward." Max ticked his first paragraph and then issued his own suggestions. "I think it makes sense that we know where the children go so that they can be watched, especially when they're not in school. How do we approach this?" Max focused on Allan and Poppy for the answer.

"I think that if they want to go somewhere, we as parents take them, and they call us to be collected. Any responsible parent would do this. That way we minimize any threat of getting taken," offered Allan. Max scribbled this down and then sought extra inputs from Poppy, who was nodding next to her husband.

"Poppy, anything to add? Everyone must have at least one suggestion?" He queried.

"Yes Max, I do have a suggestion, but it's a bit extreme. My brother Barley, he's an electrical engineer. He can generate some devices that can be fitted to our daughters, and then we can monitor their movements, kind of like a tracking device."

"We haven't quite entered a Big Brother state just yet Poppy. Our children aren't criminals," Mrs Goodwin chipped in; she has two daughters, and didn't fancy getting nosy with either of them.

"It's an option - that's all I'm saying Freda. How else are we going to protect them?" Poppy replied.

"Yes, we can vote on the key points at the end. Let's continue. Anyone else have ideas?" Seren pitched in.

The meeting went on and by nine o'clock they had a complete table of suggestions for every possible event. Like chaperoning, behaviour studies, in case the cult had contacted their children, supply each fifteen-year-old girl with a pager, so that they can call if they feel threatened. As there were a couple of hundred fifteen-year-old girls in Boundford, Floyd offered to bankroll this small extravagance and offered to loan the committee money to buy this equipment, so long as his bosses agreed with him. By then, the food had been eaten and the drink quaffed. Max returned all the smokers to the lounge and initiated the final part of the meeting. It was voting time.

"Right, you've heard all the suggestions. Now you can vote on every issue. Just yes or no, so let's begin." Max passed around pieces of paper and they began to formulate their votes. This would take most of the remaining hour...

With the movie over and the discomfort of having Leon beside her the whole time, Peri was a relieved young lady.

"Did you enjoy the film, Peri?" Leon asked.

"It was a bit long winded in places for my liking, the plot was loose and predictable, just like when I knew you'd put your arm on my shoulders. If it wasn't a full house, I'd have moved to a different row." Peri made it clear where Leon stood with her.

"Alright, let's go back home then?" Leon didn't force the issue, he wanted her to like him, and knew the shoulder trick was a bad move.

"I need the loo first, please excuse me!" Peri left to do this, and Leon stood fidgeting as he waited for her to return. She reached the ladies toilets, and she was the only person in these facilities. She finished and tidied herself and unlocked the cubicle to find a man leaning against the sinks.

"Hello! Listen, I think you're in the wrong toilet," she tried to be helpful. The man was very charismatic, he had long black silky hair, he was wearing an animal skin coat, which was deep tan in colour and lined with fur on the collar and cuffs. There were symbols all over it that made her curious. "What are those markings on that jacket?" Never mind he was a man in the ladies' toilets anymore.

"So, these interest you, do they? "Asked the man. He was young looking, mid to late twenties, but he had wise eyes. "Well, if they do interest you as much as your eyes are telling me, then visit me here?" The man offered a card. Peri moved towards him, and he laid a card down on the sink and then casually walked out.

"Wait! What's your name?" she called after him.

"They call me Fabian, Fabian Le Vor." Peri hadn't watched the news lately; otherwise, this man's name would automatically be ringing alarm bells. She stared at the card he left; it was a hand drawn map of where he was staying. The markings on Fabian's coat did seem to interest her, but it was late, and she'd have to find this place tomorrow. She slipped the card into her bra cup and found Leon again, still waiting for her.

"Let's go home then Leon."

They took the bus home and always the gentleman; he offered to walk Peri to her front door. As they reached the house, all the Watch members began to pour out and walk to their vehicles. His mother was the last person to leave, but she spent several minutes talking with Floyd, much to the annoyance of Leon. Peri went inside and straight to her room. Leon left the rabble and walked around the back of Peri's house. He stood and gazed up at Peri's bedroom window, he watched her undressing. From her bra cup, she plucked out a white card. This made Leon curious, Peri gazed at it for a few moments and disappeared from the window, then returned and looked out. She was not surprised to see Leon staring up at her. She raised her left middle finger and then drew the curtains in a display of temper. Leon then smirked to himself again and returned to his mother. Max and Teresa tidied up the house until it resembled their living room again; they then went to see Peri before retiring to their own bed.

"Did you have a good evening darling?" Teresa asked her.

"No Mum, that Leon gives me the creeps, he's always watching me. I'd pay money for him to go blind, just so that he couldn't see me anymore." Peri was already in her pyjamas and settling down for bed.

"At least you're home safely. Goodnight, dear," added Max.

They closed the door on their daughter and went to their room. Peri lay there thinking of that man, and tomorrow she would pretend to go to school as usual but was determined to find out about those markings on that strange coat, he was wearing. She rolled over and began to sleep deeply.

⸺◆⸺

Chapter Two

The lure of Fabian Le Vor

Friday morning arrived. Peri showered and got herself ready for school, but under her uniform she wore casual clothes. These she could change into, once she was out of form room registration. Max had already left for work and Teresa was busy fixing some breakfast for her daughter in the kitchen.

"Morning Mum!"

"Hi Peri, want some toast?"

"One slice please, I ate quite late last night." Peri checked on Boffin and fed him some popcorn, which she conveniently saved from her trip to the cinema. Following that, she got her school bag ready, then returned to eat her toast. Teresa stood and sipped at her lemon tea; she stared out of the window and could see the top of a boy's head. Teresa leaned forward and opened the window.

"Whoever you are, clear off from my garden!" She shouted. Peri stared over and saw it was Leon. She tutted with displeasure.

"See Mum, I bet he's been there most of the night, the creep!"

"Sorry Mrs Keeble, I was waiting to escort Peri to school," Leon said, and he walked around to the front of the house.

"I think that would be a good idea Leon," replied Teresa. Peri fetched her coat and made her way to the front door, no sooner had she opened it, Leon was beside her again.

"See you later on Mum," she shouted back as they left. She still had that uneasy feeling about Leon, but also apprehension about what she had planned.

As they got to school, Peri now felt safer, some of her friends were waiting and if Leon didn't want to be bullied by them, he'd have to beat a hasty retreat. Luckily Peri is more intellectual than Leon, which means they had to separate for different classes. This was her chance to get away from the school, without any creepy boys following her. Leon had noticed a difference in Peri's behaviour, and he was keen to get to the bottom of it. Nothing escaped Leon, when it comes to Peri Keeble. They reported for assembly and then form registration. Peri's first lesson was double maths, Mr Highgate was her teacher, and he was a gentle chap, easy for Peri to manipulate, so she could skip class. If she was back for afternoon registration, the school wouldn't miss her. As the class settled down for the lesson, Peri approached Mr Highgate.

"Sir! I have period pains, could I be excused for a few moments, please?" Peri pleaded.

"Make it quick please Miss Keeble. okay?" He replied, Peri moved quickly out and through the department block to the toilets.

Leon's lesson was technical drawing; he noticed Peri skipping out of class; he also asked to be dismissed for the toilet. His teacher allowed this; Leon hid out of sight and waited for Peri. But he'd be waiting for a while, because she had changed her clothes and squeezed out of the toilet window. She very quickly made her way out of the school gates and across the road to the bus stop. Peri still had money from last night and caught the bus to town. Leon had sussed the ruse that Peri had made for him, and headed for the main gate too, just in time to see her bus was pulling away, at the very least he knew she was heading for town. Another bus would be along in five minutes, so Leon waited for this. The five minutes went by and right on time the next bus came. He boarded and knew that Peri would disembark from her bus just before the main bus station, because her mother worked there in the cafeteria. Leon needed to catch up with her and find out what she was up to.

Peri left her bus at the usual stop, she reached for the map inside her bra, and the roads were drawn in the shape of the capital letter Q, except it lay on its side. Fabian had marked the tail as to where his position was. Peri knew that a new Retail Park was being built there, not much progress had been made though. She headed towards this place, as she walked down, Leon's bus passed her, he quickly called the bus to stop as soon as he'd seen her. Leon got off behind her, hoping she couldn't see him. Peri crossed at the traffic lights and skipped quickly down to this little road that led away from the ring road. Leon did the same only a few metres behind her. As Peri reached the bottom, she saw a column of caravans parked there, but nobody was seen around them. Leon hung back to see what she did next. He hid behind a tall stack of iron girders and peered around. Suddenly one of the caravan doors opened and Fabian stretched out of it.

"I see your curiosity got the better of you, welcome to my temporary abode."

"I really want to learn what those symbols mean, it's all that's been on my mind since last night," Peri replied.

"What's your name girl?"

"I'm Peri, Peri Keeble, that's who I am."

"Well then Peri Keeble, step this way and you shall be enlightened."

Fabian opened the door, stepped down so that Peri could enter, Leon's heart was racing, because he felt concerned for her safety. He stood and watched helpless to rescue her; she won't forgive him ever for following her. The caravan door closed, and Peri sat down; that marvellous coat was resting on the back of a chair.

"Are you going to hurt me?" She had to ask him.

"Of course not, you are my guest, you can leave whenever you like. I just thought you wanted to learn about my coat and the symbols?" Fabian replied. He was offended that she thought of him this way.

"I do sorry, but nobody knows I'm here and if I disappear that would break my parent's hearts." Peri added.

"Well, that boy who keeps following you knows you're here, so you needn't worry." revealed Fabian.

"Bloody hell Leon!" She cursed, but she was also a bit relieved to know this.

"Right, we have two hours, but then I have to go back to my camp. If you want to learn more after today, you will find me here." Fabian handed Peri one more card with another map on it. Peri instantly put the card in the same place; Fabian didn't even flinch at the motion. Then Peri sought to know about those markings.

"What if I told you that the theory of God was all wrong, when in fact he was the bad guy and not Beelzebub, as you would know him.

Sorry I should say her, because if man were created in the image of God, then the opposite equation would be that the Devil is a woman. That's right, a woman and the ultimate temptation to all men." Fabian began. Peri wasn't shocked at all, she also added to the conversation.

"Yes, I know the Garden of Eden story, Adam was tempted by Satan disguised as a serpent in the tree of knowledge, to seduce Eve into eating the forbidden fruit, that made God angry and banished them from the garden."

"Yes, and God found out that Satan had done this. She was thrown out of Heaven, and bound forever to roam the underworld, which we all now know to be a place called Hell. You see, God thought Satan was trying to force all women folk to side with her, against all men. God put up these barriers and fed lies to mankind, making us think that Hell was a bad place. Heaven is the resting place for all good souls, but Hell is a realm where many souls live on and their fantasies are fulfilled repeatedly, for eternity." Fabian paused for her reply.

"Are you trying to tell me you are a Satanist?"

"Not trying Peri, I am one, but if you want to learn more then come with us. We can show you the truth, what these symbols represent." Fabian's eyes looked through her and she felt a belonging but couldn't just get up and leave without telling anyone.

"Tell me a little bit about those symbols. I want to learn more." Fabian knew that once Peri learned these, she wouldn't be able to resist joining him.

"These symbols represent every temptation known to all humankind, throughout the ages, whatever you desire will be fulfilled. The skin of a goat is the purist animal that Satan can occupy. There are rituals and gatherings to celebrate her wisdom, and each time we meet, a new symbol appears on this coat. The wearer must earn the right to its use. We have initiations and tests. Once you've passed these, you too can wear it, and you will get what you wish for." Fabian now held Peri's attention and began to explain a few of the markings.

"How did you come by a coat such as this?" Peri asked, she felt the coat for the first time, and it was soft, almost velvet in texture.

"You don't come by it; the coat picks you. I was just like you. A teacher showed me, and I took on the mantel of leading the next generation, calling themselves 'The Disciples of Lucifer'. Just like Jesus, there are twelve in number; if you were to join us; you would be that twelfth disciple. Think it over carefully." Fabian spread out the coat so that Peri could see the marks clearly.

Across the shoulders sat a picture of a long stretched out star, upside down with five points, it was a pentacle without the circle and when Peri looked a little closer, she could make out it resembled the head of a goat. On the sleeves were various pictures, the markings for male and female origins. On the elbows were more etchings, these were spirals and when Peri looked for long enough, they seemed to hold her in a trance... Peri blinked and the spirals stopped oscillating; she felt giddy for a few moments.

"This is fascinating Fabian, I would like to learn more, but I'm running out of time today." Peri knew she had to be back at school, before they missed her.

"Then come to the camp at the weekend. I won't be here later. I can tell you want to learn. There are others like you willing to be enlightened." Fabian offered.

"Okay, I am supposed to visit with my brother this weekend, that would provide me with the opportunity to get over to you."

Peri smiled and Fabian opened the caravan door. As Peri jumped down this time Fabian didn't appear at the door. He knew Leon was waiting to capture him on his camera.

"How old are you, Peri?" Fabian asked from the gap of the door.

"I'm fifteen, my birthday is on the 6th of June, in three weeks."

"That's interesting, we'll look forward to seeing you on the weekend." Fabian waved at her as she walked away, Leon crouched down so that she couldn't see him, but as she passed, she called to him.

"You can stop hiding now Leon, I'm safe as you know too well."

"What were you doing with him?" Leon asked, running after her, but Peri wasn't in the mood to tell him.

"Just talking that's all and if you tell my parents we've skipped school, you're done for, got it?" She threatened.

"Then make it worth it" offered Leon.

"Oh! hell Leon!" Peri grabbed him by the blazer, pulled him closer and kissed him on the mouth. "Let's get back to school, before we're caught." Leon had a stunned expression, but Peri hadn't realized what she started, he would only follow her all the more from now on.

They both caught the same bus and returned to school, Peri would have to shake this pest off, if she wanted to visit Fabian's camp at the weekend, so she thought of a perfect way. She kept these ideas to herself for now and trotted quickly away to class. She had been gone for two hours. When Mr Highgate realized that she was longer than usual in the toilets, he went to investigate. Peri climbed back through the window and quickly changed back into her uniform. As she came out of the toilets, she could see Mr Highgate striding down the corridor.

"Class is over. Feeling better now, are we Miss Keeble?" He asked.

"Yes Sir, I'm sorry, but I feel fine." Peri then applied herself for the rest of the school day. All the time Peri thought about what Fabian had told her. She couldn't determine whether he was telling the truth or bullshitting. The longer she was away from him, the worse her feelings got.

As the school day ended Peri was now at the mercy of the weekend, she quickly spoke with some of her friends, not once saying anything about Fabian, but Leon knew she was up to something, and Peri was going to keep the creep from pursuing her. She was discussing ways for them to make a diversion, so she could get away clean. After this little gathering, she headed for home, with her head full of images and feelings from this day of escapades.

⚜

Chapter Three

The camp.

It was Saturday morning and Max was waiting for Peri to get up. He had the pager for her, which was discussed on Thursday. He could hear faint rumblings from upstairs and started preparing breakfast. Teresa had an early start as was usual on a Saturday, so it was up to Max to warn Peri of a possible danger looming over the town. Peri came down and straight away fed Boffin, then joined her father in the kitchen for breakfast.

"Morning Dad! I thought that I should visit Corbin and Katie this weekend. Would you be able to take me over there?" She asked.

"Of course I can, but there are a few things that I need to discuss with you first, then I'll take you, okay?" Max replied.

"What are they?" Peri sat at the dining table and Max sat beside her. He brought out the pager and he also had one for himself.

"I want you to have this please Peri, you see there is a rumour of a cult around the town, taking young ladies your age. It's a safety precaution that's all. I know you will be safe at Corbin's, but if you go into the town centre, then be sure to go with a friend, promise me?" Explained Max. Peri took the pager from Max and promised. Did this cult that he was talking about have anything to do with Fabian? That was one thing she was going to ask later. "My number is already put in, your mother has one of these pagers too, she's also on it. You can reach either of us." Max allowed Peri to finish her breakfast without any more fuss. He went outside to do some mowing before taking Peri to Corbin's house.

Leon woke up and he was keen to find out what Peri had planned for the day. He skipped breakfast and went straight out, taking his bicycle with him. He rode to the back of Peri's house and waited for her to come out. She was on the phone with one of her best friends,

Andrea Watson. Peri could see that Leon was already waiting and told Andrea about her plan to stop him following her.

"Right Andrea that creep is waiting for me, head straight over so that he can't see where Dad is taking me."

"Righto Peri," she replied and went across to distract Leon. She only lived around the corner from Peri, but she walked through the back alleys to where Leon was waiting. He could hear footsteps coming and when Andrea appeared he jumped a little as she usually teased him about his strangeness.

"Oh Andrea, you scared me!" He said.

"Look Leon, I'm sorry that I pick on you at school. If I don't, then my friends won't speak to me. I like you really, but you do understand, don't you?"

"But I like Peri, if only she would like me back."

"It's difficult for her to trust boys right now, since she split up with Callum. He tried it on with her but she wasn't ready, and you just creep her out a little." Leon seemed to take this explanation well. "But I like you Leon we could do something together?" She offered.

The distraction was working; Max had finished his mowing and collected Peri in the car ready for her weekend at Corbin's. Leon missed this and now was disturbed that he didn't know where Peri was.

"Oh Andrea, you spoiled it. She could be in danger. She met with a man yesterday, and I'm her only hope that she's safe. Now

get off me!" Leon pushed her away and Andrea suddenly felt bad. If Leon was telling the truth, then she'd played her part in

this.

"Wait! I'll come with you, and we'll find her together." Andrea was trying to help.

"Get your bike then and we'll head for town," Leon said, hoping that he would see Peri there.

Max pulled the car outside of Corbin's and Peri waited for him to help her in with her bag. Max stood by the car as Corbin came out to greet them, Katie was stood at the front door, Peri waved to her, and she responded.

"Good morning, Son!" Greeted Max.

"Dad, Peri, I'll take your bag. Here for the weekend are you, Sis?" Corbin picked up the bag and with a strong arm around her shoulders they walked straight inside. Katie kissed Peri as she got there.

"Bring her home on Sunday about eight, okay Corbin?" Max ordered, Corbin waved and then closed the front door; Max felt at least she'd be safe at her brother's house. He drove home for some much-needed rest and relaxation.

Once inside Corbin's house, Peri quickly went to their spare room. She began planning her journey to the camp. She got the map out and tried memorizing it: **Out of the town using the number eighty-three bus, get off before the large roundabout and head for three quarters of a mile down the public footpath, just off the main road. After the small white cottage, turn right and walk down an old muddy path until you find the camp.** This was written on the card and arrows over it showing Peri the way. She spent a small amount of time with Corbin and Katie before making her mind up to go out. Peri told them she'd be back at teatime.

"Who is going with you Peri? Dad says you should go to town with a buddy. If you are meeting someone, please let us know, okay?"

"Yeah, of course. Andrea's coming to town and I'm meeting her." She lied to her brother for the first time in years. She just wanted to see this camp and then she would come back.

"Okay then Sis, so long as we know, we'll see you later."

Corbin was now satisfied with Peri's answer. Peri went straight out and headed for the bus stop. The number eighty-three came on time, and she hopped aboard the bus which drove her to the stop on the map.

Andrea and Leon rode the cycle path to the town centre expecting to see Peri shopping at her favourite places, but she wasn't there.

"What do you think she would be doing this weekend?" Andrea asked Leon.

"Well, if she is planning on seeing that man again, then that was over at the new retail centre being built."

But Leon didn't know that the caravans wouldn't be there either. They headed there anyway and realized that it was a wild goose chase. The caravans were indeed gone.

"You should have let me follow her, now she could be hurt or something." Leon blamed Andrea for this, but she defended herself.

"It's not my fault; she asked me to distract you. Peri hates you following her, but I know where she is this weekend. She's gone to Corbin's house, I bet she's there with him right now."

"Right then, let's make sure she is there," suggested Leon. They rode over to Corbin's place.

As the bus stopped, Peri checked to see if she was being followed, before walking anywhere. Once she knew that her distraction techniques worked and Leon was nowhere to be seen, she began to walk towards the camp. She reached the footpath, clambered over the difficult, but elegant stile and headed for the white cottage as she remembered. Three quarters of a mile later she reached the cottage and saw the muddy path. Peri slipped off her shoes and slowly but carefully navigated this tricky path. Peri thought that someone had deliberately made it boggy, so that any curious person wouldn't go down it. The path was quite long and very sticky; her feet sunk down deeply, the bottom of her skirt, almost touching the mud. All these obstacles had better be worth it, she thought to herself as she managed it; the path was at an end, thankfully. Right at the end on a tree was a large sign saying, **CLEAN YOUR FEET AND HEAD THIS WAY FOR A WONDEROUS EXPERIENCE.** Peri obeyed the sign and did clean her feet; she thought maybe it was an offense not to. Once her feet and legs were free of mud, she put her shoes on and headed for a clearing, and there right before her was the camp. There were at least twenty tents here, plus the four caravans she had seen back in town. She made it! Just then right on cue, Fabian appeared from one of them.

"Welcome Peri Keeble everyone!" He called out. All four caravans opened straight after. and eleven girls went towards Peri. "Bring her to the main tent, please" Fabian ordered. The girls surrounded Peri and inspected her before obeying him. The girls then flanked her and walked with her to the tent that Fabian had just gone into. "Are you ready to learn more then, Peri?" He asked.

"I am ready Fabian, please teach me more" She sat down with the rest and Fabian began to teach.

Back at Corbin's house Andrea called at the door. She made Leon wait at the end of the road whilst she did this.

"Andrea, what are you doing here? She told me you were meeting in town." Corbin said with surprise.

"Peri said she was staying here, but she didn't say she was meeting me in town, sorry." Andrea replied. She looked at Corbin and knew she had just got her friend into trouble with him for lying.

"Well Dad has just given her a new pager, so let's call it and hope she responds." Suggested Corbin. He called the number of the pager, and it went off, but they could both hear it beeping in her room. They went up to look and found the pager on the side table.

"I'd better tell Dad she's gone without it," Corbin said and left the room briefly to do this.

Andrea saw the screwed-up card in the bin and stooped to pick it up. She saw it was directions to some camp and quickly stowed it into her pocket before Corbin returned.

"Right, Dad is furious, if you do find her, give her this back and tell her to get home." Corbin looked angry, Peri had used her brother to cover this up and he wasn't pleased. Andrea left the room to go back outside again. She gave Corbin a promise.

"I'll find her for you Corbin don't worry." Andrea then went back to find Leon and she showed him the map.

"Let's go and find her, then bring her back. What do you think Andrea?" Leon knew this would excite her.

"The Keebles are properly pissed off with Peri, so make no mistakes, okay Leon?" He nodded in reply, and they started riding towards the camp to find Peri.

While they were traveling, Fabian was explaining more of the purpose for the camp being here.

"Do you know why we chose Boundford to rest for his weekend, Peri?"

"No, I don't, but I would like to."

"Right, I'll explain. These young ladies lived in six different counties nearby and as I searched for them, they were as keen as you are to learn about The Disciples of Lucifer. My travels formed a pattern, and each girl here celebrates her birthday on exactly the same day as you, 6th June." Peri put her hand to her mouth as he made this revelation.

"On the 6th of June 1977, we were born and now we wait for her to rise again!" The eleven girls chanted together.

"That's right Peri, the digits of your birth coincide with the number of our Mistress '666'. With you here now, we have our twelve Disciples. Don't you see? We now have the power to revive the soul of Satan herself." Fabian looked serious and Peri seemed a little concerned.

"You're not a cult, are you? Because if you are, I have no wish to join you," she made her point clear.

"This is no cult, a cult believes in something that doesn't exist, this is real; none of these girls were forced to come here. Just like you they volunteered, once you've experienced what this coat can do, you will want to join us." was Fabian's response to that. Again, he was offended by her comments.

"I'm sorry, but the people at home have been saying it, that's all." Fabian's expression changed to a more peaceful mood.

"Those people care for you and want to keep you safe; they use the word 'cult' to frighten you, it's all part of God's rich tapestry of denial, that our 'Lady of the Darkness' actually exists," explained Fabian.

"It's true, it's true!" The eleven chanted again, and Fabian nodded at Peri softly.

"I will stay, I want to know more." Peri was keen again.

"Right then, we will have supper and then at night fall, we'll show you some magic." Fabian concluded the meeting, and Peri joined the other eleven girls, staying here.

Andrea and Leon had reached the stile where Peri had crossed and walked down, this was an obvious no cycle zone. Leon had a chain on his bike, and they hoisted the bikes over and locked them both together and then walked the rest of the way. As they got to the white cottage they noticed the sticky, muddy footpath.

"Shoes off Leon, we need to go down here, look."

Andrea showed the map to Leon again and she was right. They both slipped their shoes off and just like Peri walked carefully down to the end. When Fabian left the girls, he had taken down the sign, leading Peri into their camp. So, when Andrea and Leon got there, they were stuck not knowing which direction Peri took. The path was dry again and there were no trails to follow. Their feet were dirty from the short walk along the path. They found the same clearing, and they were faced with the same twenty tents as Peri had, but they had to hide out of sight until they saw her and what she was up to. They didn't know how much danger she was in, and they might cause even more for her if they just rushed in.

"We will just have to wait now and see what they are doing here," insisted Andrea.

As they sat crouched behind some bushes, both Andrea and Leon felt sharp pricks hit their backs and, in an instant, felt completely incapacitated. They slumped over and lay paralyzed; Fabian had anticipated this and planned to ambush their rescue mission. He dragged each one to his caravan and locked them in. He then went hunting for something to eat. As Fabian left, four burly men stood guard outside the caravan, just in case their uninvited guests caused mischief. These were Fabian's security, and nobody could mess with them as they were skilled in martial arts. As the darkness drew nearer, some beacons were lit so that the girls could walk from one tent to another. Soon Fabian would return, and he would be ready to perform the group's first ritual. The sacrifice of an animal to welcome Peri. The girls formed a circle just in front of the tents. They knew what was coming and they began chanting a verse.

"We thank you Master Fabian for the vessel from which we will feast! Gracious Lady of the Darkness, hear our thanks and bless our travels this night!" Peri was curious to know what Fabian had brought. Across his shoulders was a medium sized Billy Goat, about six years old and in the prime of its life.

"Before we begin with the sacrifice, please provide Peri with the appropriate clothes for which we are to receive this vessel" Fabian asked the two girls to Peri's right to give her a robe to put on and escort her to a tent, where she changed into it. Fabian did some more chanting. "Disciples of Lucifer, hear my command. Tonight, the sisterhood is complete, and the initiation process can begin."

Peri came back out of the tent in her robe, now she was the same as the others, all dressed in white, except for the crowns they were wearing - they were the tops of goat's heads. Fabian beckoned her over. He had hung the goat by the hind legs above a table, and it was still alive; Fabian had only stunned the animal. There were thirteen goblets that stood in a line waiting to receive the blood of this blessed beast. The girls then stood in a circle again. Fabian started the initiation of Peri Keeble. He called to each girl in turn.

"Elaine, Jenna, Diane, Kristen, Marie, Elizabeth, Susan, Louise, Joanna, Belinda and Amy, help Peri to become enlightened." Fabian then beckoned Peri forward; she took three steps and waited. Fabian turned his back and tipped powder into each goblet before continuing. He turned and held out a dagger, handle first for Peri to take.

Chapter Four

Strange goings on:

"Am I supposed to kill the goat? But he's still alive!" Peri wasn't sure she wanted to continue.

"The sacrifice must be made, the blood must be consumed, for then you will have the power to command my coat to do your bidding," Fabian tried to make it sound like a good idea. He took the dagger back again and showed Peri where to cut. "Just cut across the throat like this and then down the vein, in an L shape. See?" The goat shook and bleated as the blade touched him. "So, if you are ready, take my coat and this dagger, become a disciple." Fabian passed the dagger back and slid off the goatskin coat. He turned Peri around and hung it onto her shoulders. She slid her arms through and far from feeling heavy as she thought it might, it was light as if it was another layer of skin. It shrunk to meet her slender frame, and she felt an immediate warming comfort. The crown of course was to come, once the animal was offered to their Lady of the Darkness.

"Peri please, the animal, do not let it suffer, make it quick." Fabian needed this to happen. Peri hesitantly moved towards the goat again, she hid the dagger way from its line of sight and stroked the neck gently.

"I'm sorry, please go swiftly my friend," she whispered. The goat shook one more time, and the others began to chant again.

"Lucifer, Lucifer, Lucifer!"

Peri then pushed the dagger into the throat and sliced along; the blood began to flow down to the goblets below. She finished the cut across and then sliced up as shown by Fabian. Peri stood with the knife pointed to the ground as Fabian guided the goat along each goblet dividing the blood equally. Once the goat was still and the blood had stopped, Fabian held aloft the first goblet. He was to have the first drink, and then it would be Peri's turn.

"I drink to you, oh Lady of the Darkness, please accept this vessel and guide her well." Peri knew that Fabian was referring to her. Fabian then passed the second goblet to Peri, and she closed her eyes and thought of strawberry milk as she drank. "You must drink it all Peri," Fabian insisted. She did as she was asked, then waited as all the rest of the girls had their drink. Nothing weird was happening yet. Fabian then signalled for one of the burly men to come over and they took the goat away. "I want a crown made for Peri and then cut the meat so we can eat at last." The men carried the goat away as requested, and Fabian then prepared to guide Peri through her second initiation stage.

"How many of these must I go through?" Peri asked; she started to feel funny as the rest of them just stared at her. Suddenly they were chanting again.

"Rise up, rise up, rise up!"

Just as they were saying this she began to float straight up, she could feel herself rising. Another strange thing happened as she looked at her hands. Her right hand was larger than her left and at the end were talons, not fingernails. This was a strange experience, then as quickly as she rose, she was down again. She stared at the sleeve of the coat, on the cuff a letter P appeared, and another one lying down on its back and facing the other letter at a 90-degree angle. Peri looked at the rest of the sleeve and noticed there were twelve letters exactly like hers, just different capital letters for each girl here and then just at the top of the cuff a large letter F appeared.

"You are ready now Peri, what do you desire the most? The Lady of the Darkness will grant your request," Fabian invited her to reveal her thoughts.

"The first thing I hope for is that this town can't find this camp, and only I can find the way here." Peri thought out loudly and no sooner had she said this, a dense fog began to rise from the coat and into the night sky. Within minutes the whole of Boundford was covered in this mist. The townsfolk were puzzled by this event, and Fabian then explained the next part of the process.

"This will only work for you here, once you are back at home the fog will clear, but the camp will not be found. What do you want next?

Please ask." All this time that the ceremony was going on Andrea and Leon were stuck, locked in the caravan. Leon had got himself free from the ropes and was busy untying Andrea. Then Peri made her second request.

"There's this boy who keeps following me, he's always looking at me and I hate it, I want it fixed so that he cannot see me ever again."

Leon had finished freeing Andrea when he suddenly fell to the floor, bent over with his hands over his eyes. Leon started screaming and grasping at his face. Andrea looked on helplessly as she could see blood coming through his hands.

"Leon, are you okay, what's happening?" She asked.

"I can't see, there's too much blood, help me!" He pleaded. Peri's request was working; Leon was going blind. The others could hear Leon's screams, and Fabian knew that Peri's request was successful.

"Well done, Peri, he can't follow you anymore. Congratulations! You are now part of us. If you choose to leave tonight, then please return to us in three weeks, on the eve of your birthday, because now, we can truly bring Satan back from purgatory."

Fabian took the coat off her again and put it back on himself, and Peri felt normal again. During this time the man who took the goat had returned with her crown and some cooked meat, Fabian placed the meat on the table and then gathered the girls around for the final part of Peri's initiation.

"This crown symbolizes the passing of a noble animal, and the completion of the Lady of the Darkness circle." Fabian placed the crown on Peri's head and then invited the others to join them. Each girl kissed Peri and then Fabian on the right cheek; they then went away to do their own thing; the meat was eaten and Fabian then walked with Peri to his own caravan.

"What will happen to me now?" Peri asked.

"After tonight the fog will lift, and you can return home. If you don't return to us when we call, you will know it because the fog will return. We will discard you and that won't be pleasant for anyone."

Fabian gave her this warning, that she had made a pact with the Devil, and she must now honour it. "As for Leon, he has been punished by you for his undesirable pursuit of you. He will never be able to look at you again." Fabian then opened his caravan door and Leon fell out screaming, again with hands to his eyes. Andrea came out and tried helping him up. Fabian then left the three of them and returned to his camp.

"We have to get him to the hospital, please help us, Peri?" Andrea was actually begging her to help Leon. She did help of course; they were firm friends. They both walked out of the small woodland to the main road again, they flagged down a taxi and got Leon to a hospital. He was still holding his eyes and crying. Peri had done this, but she didn't feel guilty. Andrea wouldn't have known, and Peri wasn't going to tell her.

"You should call his mother and tell her Leon is here," suggested Peri. She then left the ward and walked out of the hospital. Andrea did call Seren, and she raced to be by Leon's side. Peri returned to Corbin's place. He was displeased for being used by her. "Sorry I'm so late," was all she could say. She was still wearing the white gown and there was blood all over her.

"How did you get blood on you Peri? Why are you dressed like that? Dad is going to lose it for sure, when he hears about this." Corbin vented his concerns and then gave her a big hug for being in one piece.

"Leon started bleeding and we had to take him to the hospital, that's why I'm covered in blood," she lied again to Corbin, but by now she was used to it.

"Get in and have a bath, I'll tell Mum and Dad you're okay." Corbin then went to the telephone. Peri did have a bath, and she couldn't stop thinking about the others at the camp or Fabian. That dominated her thoughts the most, not what happened to Leon. She wasn't paying attention to that. She had been enveloped in some malevolent force protecting her from harm. As she lay there in the bath, she began to fall asleep.

At the hospital Seren had spoken to the doctors, trying to get some sense of what happened. Speaking to one specialist, Seren was told this:

"Your son suffered from a progressive embolism, which had been building up behind his eyes, this ruptured and the blood trailed along his optic nerve and I'm afraid it has done some considerable damage. He may be blind for the rest of his life." Seren went in to see Leon. He had bandages over the top part of his face, and he couldn't see her pretty face anymore. Andrea knew they had gone somewhere they weren't supposed to be but couldn't hide this from Seren.

"All this didn't happen until we visited that place!"

"What place Andrea, where?" Seren yelled a little.

"Peri had gone there, we followed her, but we were knocked out and tied up in a caravan. Leon got free and helped me get free too, then suddenly he collapsed. and he was like this."

"We need to know where this place is." Seren wanted to see for herself. Andrea gave her the map that they had taken from Peri. Seren planned to visit this place in the morning. She was going to bring Max along too. Right now, she wanted peace and quiet with her son. Andrea left and returned home. She was puzzled as to why Leon was struck down and not her, one minute he was fine and the next he was bleeding through his eyes. One thing was for certain; it was something odd that Peri had said before.

"If Leon was blind, she would be so pleased, because he couldn't follow her anymore."

Had Peri really wished for this? And why didn't she stay at the hospital with her? These questions were going to be asked. Somebody had knocked them out, because they didn't want her and Leon finding out what was going on there. Was it the man that Leon had mentioned? Her friend had been manipulated, and she was going to discover why. She caught a late bus home and went straight to bed.

Chapter Five

Finding the truth.

It was Sunday morning and Corbin was eager to confront Peri again about last night. Peri was just lying still and staring at a blank wall. This went on for several minutes. Fed up with waiting, Corbin went up to her room, to have it out with his sister. He shook her awake.

"I want to know what the hell happened yesterday?"

"I already told you what happened. Leon collapsed with bleeding eyes. It wasn't anything to do with me, so I left the hospital. What else do you want to know?" She replied in a cold manner.

"Well, it went all foggy last night, really dense, we couldn't see in front of our own faces. This happened for about two hours. Then you come back home with blood all over you and a different dress." Corbin was convinced Peri was involved with something sinister.

"I don't know what happened. I got to Leon and Andrea; he was bleeding all over his face. I wish I can tell you more. Now take me home, I want Mum and Dad." Peri demanded.

"I've already told them about the state you are in; they'll be asking the same questions as me." Corbin tried calming her down; she had definitely been subjected to something against her will. At least he thought so. Corbin conceded the argument and took Peri home as requested.

Andrea woke up and knew she was going with Seren to find that camp; her bike was still chained to Leon's at the footpath. She called Seren on the phone, and they arranged to meet at Max's house. He had just called to tell her Peri was home from Corbin's. Now they'll get some answers. She's the only one who knows the truth.

"Dad, I can't get any sense out of her. She's been like that since the accident, so maybe you can get to the bottom of it?" Corbin said. He then drove home and away from this nonsense.

Peri was almost comatose. She didn't even say hello, instead she went straight in without even looking at Boffin. Out of habit that was the first thing she always did, speak to him and feed him. Teresa stood between the kitchen and the lounge. She just stared at her daughter, thinking that there was something different about her. She was withdrawn and quiet, unobtrusive in nature, when normally she was the exact opposite. Peri sat on the sofa, Max and Teresa sat with her until Seren and Andrea came over. Seren knocked at the door and Max called out.

"It's open Seren, do come in." Seren opened the front door and together with Andrea walked into the lounge. Almost instantly Seren knew what Peri had done.

"She's been taken in by that cult Max, look at her and you can tell. Has she said anything?"

"Not to us, but Corbin says she keeps on saying she was with Leon and Andrea and then his eyes started bleeding," replied Max.

"That's not right, Leon's eyes began bleeding before she got to us. When she did get to us, the bleeding became worse," corrected Andrea.

"What were you two doing there anyway?" pressed Teresa, she knew how Peri felt about Leon.

"Leon saw Peri meet a man on Friday. He was sure Peri was in danger, so, when he explained this to me, I went with him to get Peri out of there." Teresa was appalled Peri had skipped school.

"Right, I'm calling Vivienne, she can investigate what has happened to Peri. We can go and see this camp." Seren was eager to find the answers. Seren called from the Keeble house and then they waited for Vivienne to arrive. Twenty minutes went by, and Vivienne finally came to the house. She took one look at Peri and knew that she had been drugged; her symptoms matched the pattern of somebody withdrawing from an LSD trip.

"She's been lured in by that cult. Sorry Max but they've already got to her." Max wasn't too surprised with Vivienne's findings.

"We've got to find that place and stop this, they're not taking our Peri!" He said. Max then walked Peri to her bedroom and asked Teresa to keep an eye on her. Vivienne called the station and discussed the incident with her colleagues. Her friend in CID offered to investigate this cult that they suggested.

"I'll stay here with your wife, to make doubly sure Peri is safe, okay Max?" Vivienne said.

Max, Seren and Andrea then left to find the camp. Seren drove her car out to the main road and left it tucked up on the embankment. Leon's bike was still lying chained to Andrea's. Seren felt sad, because he would never be riding it again; she needed this to be done quickly so she could be with her son at the hospital. All three climbed over the stile and down the same path taken by Peri. As they reached the white cottage and turned right, the muddy path had changed to a smooth hard surface.

"No, this path was so boggy your feet sank right into it," remembered Andrea.

"It looks fine to me Andrea," replied Seren. They took the path all the way down and reached the clearing. There weren't any signs of a camp there either.

"Nobody's been here for years. What are you playing at Andrea, where is the camp?" said Max.

"It was here I swear! The path was boggy, there were tents and caravans, we were knocked out and Peri was with them." Andrea defended herself with such conviction that they couldn't disbelieve her.

"It's just a trick Max, now you see us, now you don't; these people know how to cover their tracks." Seren added. Now all they had left was Peri, and she wasn't telling anything to anyone.

"We should go home, let's put the bikes in the car and get away from here. We will keep an eye out and protect Peri, if this cult returns for her as I'm convinced they will. We'll follow them and end this once and for all." Max promised. They all trudged back to the car empty-handed and drove back to Max's place. Seren dropped off Andrea and Max, she then drove to the hospital.

"Please wish Leon well and pass on my love." Andrea spoke with sympathy, as Seren reversed out of Max's driveway. Seren nodded and then she was gone.

As they came back inside the house, Vivienne had just got off the phone from the station. She had a puzzled expression, as Max and Teresa came. They all sat down ready to hear what she had to say.

"That was DC Webster from my precinct. He's been looking into the name Fabian Le Vor for us, and the cult that he is supposed to represent. I'm afraid that Fabian Le Vor isn't a cult leader at all, because he is currently residing in a psychiatric hospital. He is delusional, he suffers from schizophrenia and believes that Satan is a woman who has been contacting him to collect her disciples. The doctors treating him at the hospital say that he believes in a theory that God 's bad and lies to us and is convinced that the Devil should rise and thwart God's work. He daubed in blood just last night these words; 'the battle between good and evil will happen on 6th June 1993'. The counsellors working with him say when he was admitted to the hospital sixteen years ago, he was covered in blood and drugged out of his mind, screaming and chanting out all the names of the Devil, - Lucifer, Beelzebub, Satan, Hades. His mental state hasn't improved at all despite medication, nor has it got worse, except say for that recent blood smearing." Vivienne paused so they could take it all in.

"What about that fog yesterday, how was Peri found in the same state, if he is in that hospital? What about the eleven missing girls? They're real, aren't they?" pressed Max.

"I don't know; that is what DC Webster says, I'm just repeating it. The man met by Peri yesterday was not Fabian Le Vor, it couldn't have been." Vivienne adamantly replied.

"We looked for the camp, it was gone, everybody had left," said Andrea.

"No one was there, you just heard Vivienne say," corrected Max.

He needed to know why Peri would make up all this. Did she hurt Leon? He did hear Peri say that she found him creepy. It could be possible that she wished for that to happen to Leon, and it did, but there wasn't an alternative explanation. Andrea had heard her wish for the same. It could just be coincidence. Nothing else was mentioned about it. The police had to conclude that they had helped as far as they could; without proof or leads, they were unable to pursue the investigation.

Peri eventually came back around to her normal chirpy self. Maybe where they went was some sort of lay land, and a psychic event happened. It would explain a few things, the mud they had walked in could have triggered a hallucinogenic substance on to their skin, and the events happened in their minds. It didn't go far enough to explain Leon's horrific accident though, unless he already had the embolism and the excitement caused it to rupture. They would never know for real what did happen. Peri could not remember beyond reaching the camp, but she explained that she cleaned her feet and then entered the camp. This could explain the difference but didn't outline why Peri lost her memory for about two hours. The obvious answer was she was drugged with a potent hallucinogenic, which gave her the state of an alternative reality. Peri told her parents that she had met Fabian Le Vor at the cinema. When they explained that she couldn't have because he was in a hospital, she began to cry. She was convinced it was true, the coat, the girls, the ritual, the slaughter she made, the fog, the levitation, her hand swelling and looking like a claw, her wish and Leon lying bleeding, she did wish it. They were all real, but only in her mind. This to her felt unbearable. But still they couldn't explain away the fog that lingered for two hours over the town.

Things calmed down for a while, Peri returned to school on Monday and Andrea felt strange. Her best friend was different. The police visited the hospital and confirmed that Fabian Le Vor was indeed there, and they heard his rhetoric first hand. Max still kept an eye out just in case the cult came back for Peri. He wasn't entirely convinced of this story from the police, and his daughter wouldn't willingly take drugs either, so somebody slipped it in while she wasn't looking. The incident was put to bed by the following Friday with nothing else strange happening. The town was peaceful again, except for Leon. He was sad, he wouldn't be able to look upon Peri ever again, and she was beautiful in his eyes. He was angry that Peri hadn't even visited, but Andrea did a few times, and they became closer because of it.

⋯⋐⫩⟨◊⟩⫪⫪⋯

Chapter Six

Two weeks later.

It was Friday the 4th of June, a usual day in the Keeble house. Somehow, they had put recent events behind them. Peri felt normal again and didn't long for Fabian anymore. She did keep a diary of what she could remember but wrote in code so that her mother couldn't read it. The history lesson on code breaking came in handy for Peri. This school day was the last day of her exams. After this, she would be leaving school for a career of her choice. She was feeling good and ready for the maths exam. Downstairs Teresa and Max were talking about their daughter.

"You know Max, the day after tomorrow, our Peri will be a young adult." whispered Teresa to Max, as he stroked her hair while they sat on the sofa.

"Yeah, sweet sixteen, she's certainly shot up quick. I wonder if her growing up and those weird events are linked in some way?"

"Oh Max! You've spoiled it now; we were having a peaceful time until now."

Teresa moved away and went to the kitchen. Peri came down and fed Boffin, she went straight to the kitchen and sat at the table. Max just watched her walk past without a word, she must have been listening and heard him say that stuff. He prepared to go out, wanting to call around to some of the other Watch members, hatch a plan just in case those people came back for his daughter. He wasn't convinced about this Fabian being secured in a psychiatric hospital. He called on Floyd Gant first. Frank knew somebody in the neighbouring town, who had a missing daughter because of this cult phenomenon.

"Morning Floyd, could I have a few words please?"

"Of course, Max, come on in. I'll fix us some coffee." Floyd escorted Max inside and poured a cup of percolated. "What's wrong Max? Is Peri okay now?"

"For now, yes. You had a friend whose daughter was taken by that cult. Just give me the low-down on what she said to you please Floyd"

"Yeah, Olivia Hansen, she works at the bank. Her daughter Amy was a bright kid, just like Peri, no bullying at school, just like Peri, and then she went out one weekend. Amy had met somebody called Fabian. When she returned Amy was wearing a white robe and she was covered in blood, just like Peri, but that wasn't the end of it. Olivia read her daughter's diary and found references to Satan and sacrificial rituals. Amy had been led there, and when she wore that coat, it obeyed whatever she desired. Olivia's boyfriend had made a lurid, disgusting pass at Amy. She made it happen so that he couldn't make advances to any woman ever again. Grant said he was driving home from work when a telegraph pole started sparking and then began falling towards his car. He swerved but the telegraph pole crashed through the roof of the car. He thought he was dead right there, at that moment. But he wasn't, one of the foot spikes had landed on his groin and severed his wedding tackle. Yeah, I know; he won't be able to use those again, right? Now he wears a prosthetic penis. Was it just an accident? Strange how there were references to it in Amy's diary. Then it gets worse; two weeks later Amy disappeared without a trace, Olivia thought maybe she felt guilty for making it happen. While Amy was gone, the boyfriend died from an infection brought on by his injuries. That was very weird, but Amy hasn't been seen since." Floyd explained. Max's coffee had gone cold, but he drank it quickly anyway.

"That isn't going to happen to Peri, never!" Max was keen to get going. After that revelation he was even more pressed to protect Peri. He decided to pay a visit to Robin and Freda. Before Max left, he asked Floyd for a favour. "If I need you to help me, can I count on you?"

"Max, we're friends. Of course, you can, when you need me, I'll be right here."

"Thanks!" Max shook hands with Floyd and then headed over to the Goodwins. He needed them to help infiltrate the cult should a need arise and stop whatever was happening to Peri. Now that he knew what was going on with those other girls, he needed to stop this cult from taking his daughter fully. With their military background and Max's own prowess as a police marksman, they planned to take down whatever might be coming for Peri. Thirdly Max visited Poppy Jeffries. He wanted one of those tracking devices for Peri and planned to fit it that night.

Max rang the bell on the door and Poppy came through to answer. She was taken aback by his abrupt visit but invited him in anyway.

"Hello Max, what can I do for you this afternoon?"

"Poppy, can you ask Barley to make me a bracelet? I'll pretend it's an early birthday present, when Peri wears it, we can monitor her movements. Secondly could you tell me how long making one would take?"

"Max they're already made, he made thirty-six for the fifteen-year-old girls at our school. I'll fetch you one tonight and bring it over." Poppy went to the phone to ring Barley; she waved Max out on the way there.

"Thank you, Poppy. Could you keep an eye open for Peri at school for us please?" Max pleaded, before he left for John Sobers' vicarage. Max would want his divine wisdom; it was the only reason for going to see John.

"You didn't need to ask that Max; she'll be fine there." Poppy called after him. After a visit to John, Seren was his next location; she would be as keen as Max to help stop this cult from ruining their lives. Now that Max's little band of liberators was assembled, he could have a peaceful Friday afternoon.

Peri had gone to school for her final maths exam; she was waiting for Allan, the examiner to order them to turn over and begin. They waited a few moments more for other students to arrive. Peri's mind began wandering. She felt the same floating sensation as two weeks ago. She looked across to the window and saw what looked like Fabian standing there. She waved and then the examiner disturbed her.

"Are you okay Peri? Who is it you are waving to?" Allan Jeffries inquired.

"Yes, for a moment I thought I saw... Oh forget it, just nerves playing tricks I think." Peri reasoned.

"Okay, Peri." Allan then gave the order for the exam to begin. "Alright everybody, turn your pages over and you can begin in your own time."

Peri then read the first question of the exam. It read: Q1) how are you going to get over to us tomorrow? Peri wrote her answer, A1) when the fog comes, I will follow it. Question two then read like this: Q2) do you still believe in what I told you? Peri answered again, A2) yes, I do. The next question was a request. Q3) then bring your robe and join us at eleven when the fog rises? Peri answered A3) okay then. The next question was a basic maths question. Q4) what is the cube root of 125? Peri wrote the answer A4) 5, showed the working out and then breathed a sigh of relief, that she could continue the exam without further distractions. Fabian's hold over her had returned. Peri finished the exam, and they were excused. She had to go to reception and sign the leaving certificate, then she was free to do as she pleased. On the way over, she stopped for the toilet. Again, she was the only person there, it was like the cinema incident. She finished and then just like before, Fabian was leaning against the sinks.

"That was an easy exam for you wasn't it Peri? Your biggest test comes tomorrow night. Here is where we will be staying." He placed the card down again and stepped away from her as she went towards him.

"Why can't I hold you?" She asked.

"We cannot become intimate Peri, it is forbidden, there is too much to lose. She will guide you down the right path, come see on the Sabbath Moon," he replied. Fabian then walked out and as Peri followed, a crowd of students met her; Fabian was nowhere to be seen.

"I must be going nuts," she muttered to herself. Peri felt she was falling in love with Fabian, but she wasn't supposed to. He was hard to resist and soon she would be sixteen and able to lay with him anyway; maybe that is what he must have meant. She continued to the reception office and finished her school day. On the way out she caught up with Andrea.

"Hey Andie! Want to do something later?"

"I am doing something later. Going to see Leon, remember him, do you? Now if you'd excuse me, I must be going." Andrea shrugged away Peri's hold and walked off. Peri just stared at her.

"You hated him too, you know!" She screamed after her. Andrea just kept walking.

Peri made her way home and said hello to her mother, but not to her father. She fed her pet and then went to her room for a while, she reached for her diary and began writing: **Finished my exams, sailed through it, strange thing happened though, the first three questions were from Fabian, then he appeared in the loos like before, I love him, it hurts so bad and I am going to be with him tomorrow night. Fabian you are my light. Can't wait to be with you again.** All this was coded of course so that her mother's prying eyes couldn't see. She spent a while in her room and then Max broke her peace.

"Hello dear! Listen if you heard me going on this morning then I apologize. I brought you this to make it up to you, here?" He said.

"It's okay Dad, don't stress about it. What is this?" Max unwrapped the paper and then opened the box; he showed the specially made bracelet to his daughter.

"It looks beautiful Dad, but it's not my birthday until Sunday."

"That's fine, you can have it now. Go on, you can wear it." He slipped it on to Peri's wrist. "Never forget we love you and only want to protect you." That was a weird thing to say after giving her such a lovely gift, but she didn't cotton on to the bracelet's true purpose. Max left her alone again and returned to be with Teresa. All that trouble Max had gone through, setting this up seemed a waste as nothing else happened. Saturday came and the five informed Watch members were on standby. Max made his excuses to Teresa and went to Floyd's place first. They then went over to Allan and Poppy's. John and Seren were already waiting at the Jeffries house. Once inside Poppy relayed the instructions about the bracelet, made for them by Barley.

"Peri is wearing the bracelet; we can see that because of the red flashing glow on this device. It is a small key chain, like a locator or central locking device. Now on the other side is a small- scale map and we can see that she is at your house now Max, which is four hundred yards across the estate. So long as we stay within that four-hundred-yard area, we'll be able to track her. The closer we get the faster the red light blinks." Max looked more closely at the device and then began to plan what was to happen next. The five members wouldn't be able to predict when this cult would strike, if at all, but at the very least they were prepared now.

"As soon as Peri moves, we will follow her. Wherever she goes, we will know about it. When she does move, I'll call Robin and Freda, then our group will be eight," Max reassured them all.

"Why haven't you called on Vivienne?" Poppy asked.

"I don't fully believe what she told us was true. They couldn't find any feasible answers and probably made up the mental hospital bit to distance themselves from all this. If that's the case, we don't need her; we will have Robin and Freda, and you've got me." Max explained.

"You're going to take down that cult once and for all aren't you?" Allan realized. Now he knew why Vivienne won't be needed. "I want to stay here, sorry Max." He added stubbornly.

Chapter Seven

The shroud of evil.

"Okay so we're seven, that's a lucky number; at least it was the last time I checked." Said Floyd.

They settled down and began playing cards, just to pass the time. If nothing happened that evening, they agreed to go home and wait. They had a few drinks except the two abstainers, John and Allan. But on reflection maybe they should have, because they would all remember that night for the rest of their lives. Time ticked on to ten o'clock, and still nothing happened. But at Max's house Peri was preparing to leave; soon the fog would come, and she would have to go, or she would suffer terribly. She slipped on the clean gown again but threw on baggy trousers and a sweatshirt to cover this. Next, she wrote in the diary the last entry she would make but this time she didn't encrypt it. It was this: **Tonight, I am going to be with the man I love. Then from midnight we will be joined, as is my right. Mother and Father, if you don't see me from tonight onward, I'm sorry, but the lure of what is promised to me is too strong for me to allow its passing and for tomorrow, as I become a woman, I want to thank you for bringing me into this world.** She wrote the letter P and then drew another one, like she saw on the coat sleeve, lying on its back facing at ninety degrees towards the standing one. She left the diary on her pillow, and then she went downstairs to see Boffin. Peri scooped him out of his cage, and he danced on her finger and nibbled her lip as she kissed him. She went to the window and opened it and put Boffin out. She didn't want him pining for her after she'd gone. Peri knew she wasn't coming back again and so she softly said her goodbyes. Boffin then flapped his wings and flew towards the trees. Then she laid his cage down and went back upstairs. It would look like Boffin's cage had fallen over and broken open, with Boffin getting out of the window. Teresa was filling the dishwasher and minding her own business. Peri returned to her room and read the card Fabian had given her. There weren't any directions it just read; you will know when it's time. No sooner had she read it the fog began rising again. This was her sign, and she opened the window to climb out. The Watch members noticed the fog again too, drifting across the sky towards their window.

"Shit she's on the move look!" Said Max, the red light was flashing. "I'll follow her, you call Robin and Freda, they'll bring their van, and you can catch up with me. We need to stay within that four-hundred-yard radius." He added and then ran out to keep up with Peri. She wasn't walking quickly, just pacing towards a destination, which was unknown at this point. Max decided not to alert Teresa, she would only call her friend Vivienne. Peri waited for the bus to take her to town. It was the last one out of the district tonight. Max stood and waited for the rest to join him. The fog thickened considerably and soon he couldn't see very much, as the van came by to collect him.

"She's waiting for the bus, we can follow it and see where she goes, just hang around here for now. I hope you're able to drive in this Freda?" said Max as she reached him.

"I've driven in worse Max," she replied. Peri's bus came and she got on board. Her red light began beeping again.

"Right okay, the bus is moving, let's try and keep up?" Instructed Max.

The thickening fog restricted the van's speed, but it was still able to keep within the limited boundary of the bus. A couple more metres down the road and Peri requested the bus to stop and she got off. She walked more briskly towards Fabian's camp. The fog was leading her in the direction of the psychiatric hospital. As Peri approached the gardens of this hospital, she could just about see the four caravans again, plus the twenty tents and this time a massive bonfire in the centre. Max and his gang were right behind her. Peri began to undress the top layer of her clothes, so that she was only wearing the white robe. Then with purpose she headed for the central caravan. She paused expecting Fabian to lean out and greet her but he didn't. He wouldn't appear until eleven o'clock and so Peri had to wait. Freda parked the van close enough for them to still get a signal from the device. Robin then went to the back of the van; he was fetching the rifles needed for Max and himself.

"This rifle is for you, when we see Fabian, we take him out, rescue the girls and then get the hell out of here," briefed Robin.

Max nodded; then they organized the rest to provide a distraction. Two of Fabian's burly men were busy scouting the area. Under Fabian's instructions they were ordered to stop anyone entering the camp, capture them and tie them up on the stakes around the fire. Floyd led the rest towards Peri's position while Robin and Max moved around the outside. Max found Peri's discarded clothes and scooped them up in his arms. He still had the tracker, and Peri began to move again. It was a quarter to eleven by this time. Peri went to the middle of the camp; the fire was warm, and she waited there. As Peri stopped, the fog thickened even more, as if it was covering the camp from uninvited guests. Just then a tent to the left opened and it was Marie, one of the other disciples.

"Quick Peri in here, Fabian knows you are here, but you're being followed," she whispered. Peri didn't know who was following at this point, just that somebody was. Marie linked arms with Peri, and they trotted over to the tent and waited inside, four more girls were also in there. "We wait here for Fabian, soon it will be time," said Marie. Max and Robin both found trees and they could just about make out the camp through the fog.

"Right, we're in position, we just wait now. Peri isn't going anywhere until after this event, whatever it is." Robin began to climb his tree and then pointed to the trees opposite. "Go over there and climb up high, we will have a strategic position to strike anything coming towards us or in our scope. Here take this walkie-talkie and call me when you're in place." Max quickly ran around to the opposing trees hoping he wasn't seen and climbed up a sturdy trunk. He was lying on a strong branch facing the camp and then once comfortable, he radioed Robin.

"I'm in place!" Now they waited patiently.

Floyd, Freda and John split from Seren and Poppy. They moved cautiously towards the campsite and crept to strategic positions so that they could see everything. Floyd and Freda heard a twig snap, and they twisted round to see two strong men. Floyd moved to intercept, but the men were too strong. One man on the left struck Floyd hard on the temple and he quickly fell to the floor; the man grabbed Floyd's arms and pulled him back up again. He held Floyd in a head lock and choked him until he fell unconscious. The other man quickly took care of Freda too, but John was able to run away without being struck. He was eager to find Seren and Poppy to warn them. The two men ignored the holy man and concentrated on Floyd and Freda. They carried them both over their shoulders and headed towards the bonfire. They fastened each person to the tall stakes right in full view of Max and Robin.

"He's got Floyd and Freda, but I can't see to get a clean shot. What can you see?" Max whispered into the walkie-talkie.

"The same Max, they're covering themselves well," came Robin's reply. They had to be patient, wait for an opportunity to hit each man or Fabian if necessary.

"Stay calm Robin, we'll nail them don't worry," promised Max.

"Check!" Robin said in response.

Max checked his tracker, and the red glow stayed constant, meaning Peri was no longer moving; this concerned him a little. The girls in the tent now waited for Fabian to appear, as it was a couple of minutes to eleven. Each of the six girls had the same feeling as the other. They knew something magical was coming and they were glowing with excitement. The hospital had a clock tower, and the seconds counted up to eleven o'clock. Fabian wouldn't appear until the eleventh strike of the bell. John caught up with Poppy and Seren, he told them about Floyd and Freda being captured by the two bodyguards. They hid behind trees waiting for action; they could see Floyd and Freda from their position.

"I need to leave and acquire some holy water. The men know there's at least three of us here so far; they don't know about you two yet," John said.

"Oh, the hospital chapel should have some holy water Father," reminded Poppy.

John separated and headed for the hospital chapel. The chimes began for the eleventh hour, and the girls began to file out of the tent.

Peri was behind the five girls and then the other six joined them which made up the assembly of twelve. They walked towards the campfire and entered the circle, then stood in front of the twelve stones lying on the ground, one girl in front of each stone with Peri at the top. The bell rang the eleventh time, and the fog lifted, and Fabian just appeared out of thin air. He was wearing that coat again. As the fog went away the fire grew in intensity. This made their uninvited guests Floyd and Freda squint and turn their eyes away. The twelve girls kept staring straight into the fire as Fabian stood in front of a large piece of stone. Two of the other burly men carried over another goat, picked especially for this evening. It was tied to a long pole and over the large piece of stone were two upright struts, on to, which the men placed the pole. Then they walked away. Fabian raised his arms up to the sky and began the ritual ceremony.

"Disciples of Lucifer, our Lady of the Darkness! Hear us, we are your servants, come forth for we have your vessel. She stands and waits for you to enter her, so you can begin your revenge on God Almighty, our supposed guiding light, ha!" Fabian laughed at that last part and all the twelve girls began to chant again.

"Lucifer, Lucifer, Lucifer!" Even Peri was saying it. She was looking at Fabian, and he beckoned her over. She stepped forward as the others kept on chanting. "Vessel, Vessel, Vessel!" Fabian held her shoulders and turned Peri around, so she was facing the other girls. Fabian slipped off the goatskin coat and placed it over Peri's shoulders, once again. Fabian then invited Peri to sacrifice the goat. She had done this before, so she wasn't fazed this time. While Peri was holding the knife and preparing to kill the goat, Fabian turned and laced the thirteen goblets with the same powder as before.

"He's putting some powder into the goblets Max," informed Robin, who was looking through binoculars.

"I knew she had been drugged without her consent, the Bastard!" Max said in response, they quietened down and waited for positive action, before striking.

Peri turned to begin the sacrifice and placed the knife with confidence against the goat's throat this time. She made the same L shaped incision up and across; Fabian then quickly moved each goblet to catch the blood from the flow.

"I can't believe it; Peri killed that goat!" Robin added with surprise that she'd done so with such ease.

"What?" Was Max's response, just as surprised. They went quiet again, Max had his scope trained on Fabian, but Robin kept his focus on Peri, Fabian stood behind her, obscuring Max and Robin's view. Floyd and Freda looked on in disgust at the way Peri just calmly killed that animal, and now they were going to drink it's blood, like a group of savages.

Seren and Poppy watched from their places but were disturbed by two of Fabian's henchmen. Two big hands from each man went across their mouths and they were firmly held, to prevent them from screaming. They were then dragged away to the centre of the camp and tied up like the others. This was done in full view of Max and Robin, but neither man could see John.

"Blasted bully boys!" Max whispered down his walkie-talkie.

"Hey! Hang on in their pal, John's still out there. He's our last hope for a distraction," Robin tried calming Max down again. Fabian was still in Max's eye line and Peri was shielding him from a clean shot. "Christ! Why don't you realize what's happening Peri?" He asked himself, feeling that if she were anything like him at all, she would have found this all too strange.

The ceremony continued, by this time the girls had all encircled Peri with Fabian still behind her. They each held the goblet of blood, and at once drank every last drop. With the coat draped over her shoulders, Peri slipped her arms inside the sleeves and again it accommodated her form. It appeared to shrink to her size, but when Fabian wore it; it looked twice as big.

"Daughters of Lucifer! Welcome to the Sabbath Moon, in just two minutes it will be midnight, and it will be all our birthdays," incited Fabian. He turned to Peri and asked her what she would like before they summoned their great Mistress. "Peri Keeble, you have the opportunity to deliver a message to our audience, the ones outside the circle, what would you like to become of them?" No sooner had he asked her that, Peri began to levitate again, this time higher off the ground and turning horizontal. Both hands this time changed into claws, and she began to make a request.

'Who are they, where are they hiding? Show me, I'll see to it that they can't harm us here."

"Out there, in the trees, they have guns," replied Fabian, pointing to the circle of trees around them.

"No! You can't kill him, I won't let you, by the power entrusted in me. Oh, Lady of the Darkness, make it so they can't shoot Fabian." Peri shouted.

Suddenly a flash of lightning struck the trees that Max and Robin were hiding in; it ran down the branches and each man convulsed in agony as the electricity charged through them. Robin fell out of the tree, dropping his rifle down, it landed butt first, and stuck up vertically, as Robin slammed straight onto it. This added more pain to his electrocution. He made a hideous gurgling sound below, Max was helpless to assist, because he too was in great pain, but he didn't fall; he held fast in his position. Robin was dying on the grass, and all Max could do was watch. The lightning strikes had destroyed the walkie-talkies. For the moment Max was alone, so he focused on the centre of the camp, where Fabian was still smothering himself with Peri's position.

"What about these interlopers? What have you got planned for these?" Fabian pointed at Floyd, Freda, Seren and Poppy.

"They can burn in the fires of Hell!" replied Peri coldly.

Did they hear her right? This was good little Peri Keeble, who wouldn't hurt a fly, going around and maiming people. The fire in the centre arced out to each of the captured Watch members. They looked like fiery arms reaching out for them and trying to grab at their heads. These arms began lurching ever closer to them.

"Stop there, right this instant!" Interrupted John Sobers, the last of members. "This is holy water, and I will use it on you. Now stem your flames and hear me Satan! You will not take these souls tonight." The fire crept back and left the four alone, returning to the centre and looked completely normal.

'Too late puppet of God, the Sabbath Moon is now here, the twelve have been collected, she will now come forth and reign on earth once more." Fabian chuckled and held Peri, still floating in the air, and still blocking Fabian's head from Max's viewfinder.

"If I have to shoot him, just to get him out of the way, then that's what I'll have to do," Max said to himself,

Peri wasn't her true self right now. She had been drugged, and Fabian was controlling her. Max aimed low at the legs, but just as he was going to pull the trigger, Fabian's four henchmen were running over towards his tree. He instantly turned and fired at each one who caught a bullet to the chest. They lay sprawled out on the grass before him, they weren't moving. Max had managed four clean kills; importantly, he was still in the game. Fabian heard the gun fire and straightaway grabbed Peri down from her levitation, He pulled out a stiletto dagger and held it to her.

"You fool, Old Man Keeble! She's ours now; can't you see? She will give herself fully to the all-powerful Lady of the Darkness. She will be sacrificed to allow our mistress a channel into Peri, where she will become her." Fabian raised his left hand up and the eleven girls began chanting again.

"Vessel, Vessel, Vessel!"

"No! Stop him, John!" Max yelled from his vantage point; he knew that this would give him the shot he needed to take out Fabian. John uncorked the silver bottle containing the holy water and dowsed Peri in it; Fabian just pushed the dagger into Peri and held her while he chanted.

"Take her Lucifer she's yours, take her!" Then he whispered to Peri. "Happy birthday Peri Keeble." Just then the fire shot out and surrounded Fabian and Peri, the image of the Devil clearly showed through the flames and the markings on the coat began to glow. John splashed more holy water over them both and the force of the fire threw John to the ground, he rolled around putting himself out of the flames and then he began the cleansing ritual.

"By the power of God, I command you to return to your realm, leaving this girl to me. Take the man, but leave me this girl, get back Satan, with all my strength, I will thee away!"

The fire shrank enough for Max to get a shot off, it hit Fabian squarely in the forehead. He fell backwards into the fire and began to burn on it. Max climbed clumsily out of the tree, still smarting from that lightning strike. He scurried over to Robin, and found that he was definitely dead, no pulse, no breathing. He would have to tell Freda. John jumped away to free Seren, who then freed the rest. Fabián continued to burn rapidly, the smell of him turned their stomachs. Max bounded over to help Peri and cradled her softly in his arms. She was still wearing the coat; all the power was now hers. Fabian had passed it on to her. The fiery markings had stopped glowing, and it was just a normal brown coat again.

"It's okay Peri, I'm here it's all over now, shh!" soothed Max. Her stab wound was deep, but not life threatening.

Seren, Floyd and Poppy helped the other girls to safety, and they were put in the van. Poppy drove them to the nearest police station to explain what happened. The police were delighted to learn it was the eleven missing girls, from six counties. Freda had gone to find Robin. She sat silently with him and remembered their life together. She was on the one hand happy he died helping his friend, trying to set them free from this nightmare, but on the other, sad she'd never see him again. She didn't blame Peri or Max, the man responsible was dead and that was the end of it.

Several hours later, the fire was put out. Fabian's body was recovered from the middle of it and the four henchmen were cleared up too, all declared dead at the scene, Robin had a separate wagon for his journey to the mortuary. Peri was taken by ambulance to hospital, with Max accompanying her. The police had contacted Teresa, and she went to see her daughter at the hospital. John and Floyd shook each other's hands and then made their way home, but not before they were both asked to give statements by the police as they scoured the place for evidence and began an investigation. Max had killed five people, so he was arrested upon arrival at the hospital, leaving Teresa really confused. Seren spent the night at the hospital telling Leon about what happened to Peri, but he didn't seem to care anymore. He now had Andrea in his life, and she was the only person he was interested in.

After Peri's ordeal at the hands of Fabian Le Vor, she was put in the same psychiatric hospital for analysis, to evaluate her sanity. All everybody kept on repeating was what they had witnessed, the shape of the Devil surrounding her like that. . Placing her here was for her own safety as well as for others.

Boffin the cockatiel found Peri again. He located her at the hospital, so he flew back and forth from the trees to the window she was sitting in, just to be close to her.

The cult was dismissed as a mild nuisance by the town, they preferred the story that the girls were kidnapped, then rescued by Poppy Jeffries, who got a hero's welcome when she returned to school. The goatskin coat was taken from Peri, laundered and placed in the hospital's charity shop. Nobody knew the true power of this garment, except for Peri of course and from now on, whoever the wearer may be, they will be granted power beyond their wildest imagination.

This concludes story one; **'Seduced by a Cult.'**

The End.

Story Two
Soul Searcher.

Foreword

Fifteen years later, Ben Grantham, a down on his luck man, finds the Goatskin coat at a hospital charity shop. From the moment he puts it on, his life would never be the same. This is a story of prayer versus desire. Trying to resist temptation or to avoid it altogether, will only end one way.

Chapter One

Ben and that Jacket.

It was October 2008, a cold, rainy Thursday afternoon. The hospital called Ben Grantham on his mobile phone, with urgent news. His biological mother had been found, and she was in her final stage of terminal cancer. One more piece of bad luck. So much bad luck that has chased Ben around for all his thirty-three years. Abandoned by her when he was just one, he had searched for her all these years. And now to be told, she'd been found dying in hospital, right around the corner from where he was squatting. He headed for the hospital, asked politely for Margaret Grantham at the desk, thinking that was her real name. Ben was tall and slim, a very typical man of his age, charming enough to those who don't know him, but to the few that do, they have worked out all his angles.

"I'm sorry Sir, there isn't a Margaret Grantham staying here, actually," said the receptionist. She continued typing as if Ben wasn't there. He was used to this.

"No really, you must have, they called me to say she was staying here, she's got cancer, I must see her!" Ben insisted.

"You come here all the time Ben, asking to see someone. The last time you conned your way in, you were caught trying to steal drugs from the pharmacy," she remembered.

"But I'm not lying now, please! Just ask the consultant to let me see Margaret." He begged.

"The only Margaret staying here; goes by the name of Maggie Bracewell. That doesn't even remotely sound like Grantham, does it? Plus, I shouldn't be telling you that anyway!" She was very obstinate. Ben was getting agitated. He had a short temper and was about to explode on the young lady, if he didn't get his way.

"Look Miss, Kelly! Maggie is my Mum, my biological mother. She has cancer, she's dying, and I must ask her why she abandoned me!" He yelled at her and the whole reception area stopped there and stared at the stand -off.

"I can see why she abandoned you; you lie, you cheat, and you steal. Who would want a child like that?" Miss Kelly said rudely.

"I didn't steal, cheat or lie when I was one did I? Now one last time please, let me speak to Maggie Bracewell!"

"That's enough you two," said a consultant - one of the outpatients had gone to fetch him. "Miss Kelly, it was me who tried to reach Mr Grantham, so if you wouldn't mind booking him in, please?" The Consultant asked quietly. Miss Kelly did that and the Consultant walked with Ben to the ward. "I am Doctor Echo, yeah, please don't repeat the joke, okay? Your mother isn't very well. She only has moments to live. We have given her morphine for the pain, and she is stable, so that she can speak with you." The Consultant explained.

"Thanks, I appreciate it." Ben then entered the ward and saw that it was a bed, two beds over. The curtains had been drawn all around it; the other patients were lying in their own pain and self-pity, or optimism, whichever bed he looked at as he walked by.

"Mr Grantham, please be careful, she is very frail, so please don't excite her." Dr Echo added. He pulled the curtain around slightly and Ben saw his mother, for the first and last time. She was propped up in a sitting position. The nurse was taking out the feeding tube. Maggie had been given a bit more morphine for the pain, and she had a smile on her face. She looked thin, yellow in complexion. Not how Ben had imagined her on the way there.

"I- needed- to- see- you- before- I- went, - to- explain- things," Maggie wheezed after every word.

"To explain what? Why you left me at that house thirty-two years ago?" Ben sounded bitter, but he kept his voice down. He took his hat off and scrunched it between his fists. He felt uncomfortable, but he was determined to find out the answers, he'd been asking all his life.

"I-suppose-I-deserve-that-,I-don't-want-to-fight-with-you-. For-my-last-moments-I-would-like-them- to- be- happy- thoughts," Maggie struggled to finish the sentence, and she looked decidedly weaker. Ben leaned forward on his chair and held her hand, then asked her three questions.

"Who is my father? Is he still alive? Why did you abandon me?"

"I- wanted- a- girl-, Ben-, desperately- wanted- a- girl-, your- father- was- called- Ben- too-, you- took- his- name-, he- couldn't- cope- with- your- adoption-, we- felt- you- deserved- a- better- start- in- life-, he- killed- himself- twelve- months- after- you- were- gone-. I- couldn't- love- you- Ben- I- am- so- sorry- I'm- sorry- but- I- was- just- a- kid-, who- was- only- thirteen- when- I- had- you-. Your- father- was- fifteen-." She eventually explained.

"I tried to find you, when I turned sixteen. Nobody wanted me for more than a month at a time, it was horrible. One of my foster parents broke my leg and my ribs. How could somebody do that to a six-year-old kid, tell me mother? Because I just don't get it." He had tears in his eyes; he'd forgotten how to cry.

"You- shouldn't- call- me- Mother- Ben. Now- I- want- to- tell- you- that- you- have- an- Aunt-, who- is- still- alive-, she- is- my- younger- sister- Jessica- Fielding-, find- her- and- tell- her- I'm- sorry-, she- never- forgave- me- for- giving- up- her- Nephew," Maggie revealed, the last words she would speak to Ben. She let her head move back to the pillow and softly drifted away. Ben was still holding her hand as he felt her get colder. Dr Echo and the nurse had to move Ben out so that they could record the death of Maggie Bracewell at 16:45, on Thursday, October 16th, 2008.

"Mr Grantham, the hospital will be finished with your mother's details by Friday, upon which you can arrange her funeral." Dr Echo led Ben away again and out of the ward. "Go and get yourself a cup of coffee, I will join you in a minute," Dr Echo suggested kindly.

"Yeah sure, a coffee. I think I'll get a coffee," replied Ben.

This wasn't the first person he'd seen die, several of his junkie friends had passed away on their crack or heroin, through overdose. Over the years, it was a sight he was very used to. Most of his friends were dead, but at least he still had a living relative, whoopee! He thought about it as he sat there. The canteen assistant brought over his coffee. Behind her in the shop he saw a rack of clothes. He took a little sip of coffee, then rose to go and have a closer look. He browsed for a bit and then saw a couple of coats mingled in with shirts, trousers, blazers and dresses. One garment stood out more among the rest; an animal skin jacket, tan in colour, but it had faint markings on it. He slipped it off the hanger and tried it on. When he held it up, it looked small, like it belonged to a slender female, but as he slipped his long arms in, the coat seemed to wrap around him and fit him snugly. It was light and comfortable.

"I am definitely buying this, when I get my benefits," he said. Ben loved the coat and hung it back on the hanger. "Tomorrow, I'm coming back and I'm buying you." Ben often spoke to himself, "Promise me you will be here tomorrow?" He asked the jacket and placed it back on the rack. The price of the jacket was fourteen pounds, affordable and it was for charity. Maybe if he gave a little to this charity, he would get some back and a small amount of luck too. He returned to his table and just stared at the jacket. As the jacket swung there, a letter B appeared on the right sleeve. Another one appeared lying on its back facing the other at ninety degrees. Sounds familiar, doesn't it?

Ben finished his coffee and went home for the rest of the afternoon. He paid the jacket no more attention until his benefits reached his bank in the morning, He got home and as usual reached in for the string and pulled the key out through the letterbox and opened the front door; it smelt of stale farts and Marijuana smoke, a heavy hint of heroin wafted around and the distinct smell of patchouli oil, which doesn't really disguise the smell, when there's drugs being consumed on this level. Ben abstained from drugs, except for nicotine. He had enough on his plate as a grown man, without an addiction to cope with. He entered a room, green in colour with the words CHILL OUT! painted above the door. There were two people sitting inside, supping smoke through a homemade bong, a device for smoking weed with. The man was red-faced as he sucked the smoke in and then blew a funnel of smoke out in one continuous stream.

"Fucking hell! What a rush!" said the man as the girl giggled at him, waiting for her turn. She loaded the bong again and sucked it up herself.

These were the only two friends that Ben had left. The man was called 'Minge' because he can be so obnoxious and this is the polite version of what they usually call him, plus it rhymes with Ginge. The girl is called 'Doorbell' just based on the fact that everyone knows that you use the key-on-a-string to get into the flat. She just rings the doorbell, making somebody answer every time. The smoke fogged the room and made Ben cough.

"Peasant!" They both said to Ben and then laughed out loud. These two were always getting stoned on weed, nothing else they would rather be doing than sitting in their own breath and laughing at each other. Ben waved a channel of clean air and headed for the sofa.

"Found my Mum today and now she's dead, talk about bad luck!" He eventually said to them.

"Really? Oh bummer, sorry Ben, have some of this and bloody cheer up man!" Minge offered, in his usually untactful way. Ben shook his head and declined the offer; he did sneak one of Doorbell's cigarettes to smoke though.

"Hey! We need those for my next mix, so don't smoke too many!" Doorbell objected, she had a selfish disposition, and everything has to be me, me, me, with her.

"Alright, I'll only smoke half of it, okay Doorbell?" Ben conceded and lit it up, puffed five or six times and put it out again.

He left the room to be by himself. The only person able to willingly listen to Ben was Father Peter Flaws, who had known Ben, since he was a child. After a few minutes reflecting on things, Ben decided to go and visit Father Peter. It was a long stretch to get to Peter's place; he lived across the town, just down the road from the church which he served. Ben reached Peter's and rang his bell.

"Ben! How are you? Do come through." Peter invited him in and led him to the garden.

The Priest liked to sit in the rain; he calls it a charge of Holy Water from the Lord Almighty himself. "Why so late and what's on your mind?" Peter asked as they reached the table.

"I found my mother today."

"That's good news, isn't it?" Replied Peter.

"She died Father, died of cancer, today of all days, right in front of me."

"Oh! Then that isn't good news, I'll get the brandy." Peter went to find some.

"She did explain to me why she gave me up, I finally got closure on that. Then she tells me that I have an aunt. Seeing as you know near enough everyone in this town, you might be able to tell me where I can find her." Ben explained, just as Peter returned with the brandy.

"Drink this, Ben. It'll warm you, then tell me this woman's name." Peter sat and waited for Ben to reveal the name.

"Aah! Thank you! Yes, mother had a sister, younger than her and she's called Jessica Fielding."

"I do know the woman. She works at the psychiatric hospital in Boundford, our neighbouring town." Peter then wrote the address down on a piece of paper. "Here take this and go see for yourself." Peter insisted.

"I will Father thanks, thank you for the drink." Ben was always kind to Peter, as Peter was the same with Ben.

"Now get home and have some sleep. Tomorrow is a new day!" Peter said in his cheery optimistic way. Ben waved and then went home as instructed. Ben would have his benefits and that jacket he was looking at earlier today. When Ben got home and got in the door, he just flopped down inside it, curled up to get some sleep. Once asleep nothing could wake him.

It was Friday morning; the rain had stopped at least, the daylight shone at Ben through the door, waking him up. He looked down towards the other people, still lying down, waiting for the post. Just hanging out of the girl's pocket was a ten pack of cigarettes. Ben slid along and took the pack without disturbing her. He took one cigarette and tried putting the pack back again. This did disturb her though and she slapped her boyfriend awake to defend her. Ben's hand was in her breast pocket, and the boyfriend went to launch a punch in Ben's direction. Ben was quick to move, and the boyfriend punched the wall instead, yelping as his knuckles thumped hard against it. Ben got up and apologized to the man and the whole fracas was over in minutes. The boyfriend just scowled at Ben and the girl sat with her arms folded, ignoring Ben's apologetic stares. The awkwardness was broken by the postman's hand pushing a fist full of letters through the door. There was a massive scrabble getting to them. Ben finally got past and quickly escaped the melee. Ben was keen to get his cash and head to the hospital to buy that jacket, hoping it was still there for him. He paced towards the Post Office and waited in the queue. Minutes later he was holding his fifty-four pounds, and with a smile on his face he walked to the hospital. As Ben reached the hospital, he looked through a window, where the shop was. There it was , hanging on the rail waiting for him, the goatskin coat. Just like yesterday tempting him over. He quickly moved to the shop and browsed again quietly, before going over to select the jacket. He took it to the counter and the lady behind it made a comment about the coat.

"Thank you for buying this, it suits you. Do you know that it's been at the shop for fifteen years?" Ben laid his fourteen pounds down and quickly put it on. He looked at the mirror just to check the look. "Yes, that jacket definitely suits you," the lady added, and Ben walked back out to the foyer of the hospital. Dr Echo was walking toward him and Ben stopped to speak with him.

"Mr Grantham, you may begin the funeral arrangements for your mother today. Her GP has signed off the death certificate, she's ready for you." Dr Echo informed him.

"Thank you, Dr Echo, I must find my Aunt and she can help with all that. I'm too busy today, soon as I've seen her, we'll be in touch," replied Ben, as he sidestepped Dr Echo and walked away from him.

"But Mr Grantham, it must be today!" Dr Echo called back at him.

Ben continued out of the hospital and out to the main street. Here he waited to catch a bus to Boundford and to find his long-lost Aunt Jessica. He stood counting his money, forty pounds left; he needed to be wise; the money should last a fortnight. He slid the money into his new jacket pocket and checked the timetable for the bus. At this point he was by himself at the bus stop, just minding his own business. He began to wonder what Aunt Jessica looked like. Only ever seeing his mother in a frail state just that once, didn't give him much scope to imagine Aunt Jessica as he would like to. If she was younger and Ben's own mother was thirteen when she had him. He estimated Aunt Jessica was about forty. He stopped guessing and decided to be surprised when he saw her.

❈

Chapter Two

Too much power for one man.

While Ben stood at the stop, a few more people began to gather. A large limping lady came beside him, waiting for the same bus. Ben checked his watch and saw that the bus would be due soon, ten minutes away. A further few minutes passed and there was quite a crowd building for just one bus. All the while he stood beside this large lady, just minding his business, nothing seemed to be brewing until he moved a little to his left but didn't see the large lady's foot. His twelve stones squashed her foot, and she gave out a yelp. Then flew into a rage.

"Why don't' you look where you're going? Of all the spaces to occupy in this bus queue, you have to stand on my bad foot? You're a clumsy little bastard is what you are." The lady scowled hard at Ben, never one to back down; Ben was quick to defend himself, with dire consequences.

"You know what would really please me? Is if the next bus that comes this way, ploughs straight into you and kills you stone dead. I can't believe how rude you are, it was an accident, that's all Madam."

"Unbelievable!" came her remark.

She moved about two metres down to the other side of the bus stop out of Ben's way. Ben kept glancing over at her, until the bus came into the turn of the road and headed towards the bus stop. At first everything seemed normal, until the driver suddenly started sneezing at the wheel. He lost control of his bus briefly, as he swerved after his first sneeze. Now he was in the wrong lane, had to swerve back again narrowly missing cars. He sneezed for a second time, and he looked back at the passengers. He could see anguish and panic all over their faces. The angle was too steep to park parallel to the stop, instead the bus mounted the kerb and headed towards the large lady, ran straight into her. She screamed as the whole bus knocked her over head on, and she fell under the front wheels. There was a horrible crunching and scraping sound which some of the waiting passengers gasped at once. The bus had stopped, the lady rolled a bit and then the back wheels hopped up and finished up on her head and remained pinned there. Shouts of "oh my God!" were heard and one lady had to mention it.

"You said that could happen!"

She looked at Ben and he looked away, he felt the rude lady deserved it. The other passengers quickly got off the bus; the Driver was apologetic to them all and was frantically dialling for an ambulance. The waiting passengers were in shock from the incident, but once again someone dying in front of Ben was something he was used to. He looked at the right sleeve of the jacket he was wearing, he saw the letter B and the other one facing. It showed clearly now and then one singular notch appeared on the cuff, right before his eyes. This disturbed him more than the bus driving over that rude lady. He stared at the sleeve and quickly slunk away from the mayhem. Going to see Aunt Jessica would have to wait. The wail of the ambulance coming made the passengers move away from the bus stop and the fire rescue team came to jack the bus up, so that they could reach the large lady jammed underneath. She was in a bad state; her scalp had been peeled off as the bus had scraped over her and the right-hand side of her body had been crushed by the weight of the bus. Soon the police arrived to tidy and take statements. The large lady was dead of course just as Ben had wanted. But at this point he didn't realize what sort of power he possessed. One or two witnesses reported that they saw Ben and the lady arguing and then after he said what he said, the bus did run over her. The police looked about for Ben to ask him to verify these facts. But he was nowhere to be seen. A couple of ladies gave a description of Ben, and the police knew instantly who he was. Ben was a bit of a thief, but he wouldn't wish anyone misfortune, such as what happened to this large lady.

Ben marched quickly away from what he just caused and continued to walk to the squat As he rounded the street, three builders on a scaffold platform were repairing a supporting wall between number 3 and 5 of Drinkwater Avenue. They paused to amuse themselves with Ben, as he tried to walk past unnoticed.

"Hey Grantham, I knew you at school, you were a proper wimp back then!" The first tall builder shouted over.

"Oh yeah! I remember him," joined in the second shorter builder. "Grantham, the kid who nobody wanted, you loser!" He laughed. This rubbed Ben up the wrong way. His upbringing was his own business and not one for people to pour scorn over.

"Ha ha! The kid with no folks." The third builder decided to have a pop, and that was all Ben needed. Ben just coolly turned on his heels and faced the three of them.

"Hey! Harry Prince, I'm not a wimp anymore, you skinny fucker! As for you turncoat Burman, some mate you are, you should just keep your mouth shut, or someday I'll shut it for you. And you, I don't know you, but I'd be careful, that platform doesn't look very stable, it could fall and kill you at any moment." Ben turned and sauntered off towards the flat and the builders just catcalled after him.

"Hey man; put your handbag away, we're only joking." Ben just did a 'wanker' sign at them and continued to walk.

Just as Ben said, the platform they were standing on began to wobble and some poles from above started to loosen and crashed to the road underneath. The sound reverberated up and down the avenue. The three builders clung onto the rig, but it was futile. The rumbling got worse and the whole platform collapsed and the weight of it all fell on top of them all. First Harry fell on his back and one pole fell length-ways through his chest. "Ulunha!" was the sound he made as all his air gushed out and he just lay still. The second builder; Burman, landed flat on his front but two poles crashed against the back of his head, and killed him outright. The third builder was still desperately hanging on to the shaking platform, but the rest of it just fell and he landed on the road and broke his back as he landed. Ben turned to look back before he disappeared into the flat and saw the aftermath. Once again what he'd hoped for had happened. He stared at the sleeve of his new coat and the Roman numeral IV appeared, replacing the single notch he'd seen earlier. Now he knew what his fourteen pounds had bought him - a coat that fulfils his heart's desire, and he could do anything to anyone, so long as he was wearing it. Four people had caused him trouble and those four people were now dead. He was going to test this again. He didn't look for long at the builders; soon there was a crowd in the street trying to help with the carnage caused by the collapsed platform. Another siren wailed in the distance to come and examine the dead builders. Ben smiled and found his friends Minge and Doorbell, once again in the chill out room, still sucking up their bong smoke.

"Hey! Nice coat, can I wear it sometime?" Doorbell asked.

"I'd like to wear you Doorbell, around my cock!" Ben replied, jokingly of course.

"You couldn't afford me sweetheart," Doorbell rebuked, Ben just shrugged and sat on the sofa again.

She suddenly got up and sat next to Ben on the sofa. She'd never done that before. Minge was too busy, cooking the next batch of mix to go into the bong, to notice. Doorbell leaned over and unzipped Ben's trousers and took out his dick. She knelt up on the sofa and slid down her shorts and Ben could see her pussy. He stiffened as she positioned herself on top of his dick and rode him well. Just like before, what Ben wanted, Ben got. He hadn't had sex for years, so soon came up inside her. After a couple of thrusts, he climaxed and Doorbell straightened up again, she'd never done that before either. She fixed her shorts and rejoined Minge on the floor again. She didn't really know why she did that, just the impulse to do so overpowered her, but she wasn't ashamed. Ben cleaned up and left the two bong-heads to themselves. Doorbell looked at Ben sheepishly as he left. The coat definitely has an unlimited power. Ben found an upstairs room to sit in. It was empty except for a small homemade hammock hanging there. He stole it for a couple of hours, just to get some shut eye.

When Ben awoke, he realized it was the following day, he had slept right through, probably because of the excitement of yesterday. Today he was going to see his Aunt Jessica. He left the squat to catch a taxi; he asked the driver to take him to Boundford Psychiatric Hospital. This took several minutes to reach. He paid the driver and wandered over to the hospital reception. He had never been to Boundford before; it was a stuffy place, somewhere for all the snobs and posh people to live. That was the concept he'd thought of anyway, but he was about to get a reality check. He rang the bell at the inquiries office, and a small woman came through.

"How can I help you Sir?" She said.

"I would like to see Jessica Fielding please." Ben replied.

"You mean Doctor Fielding, for what reason?" The lady then asked.

"She's my aunt, I wish to see her please?" The lady went from the office to find his aunt. She knocked on the door of Jessica's office.

"Come on in"

"Sorry Doctor, your nephew is here to see you."

"Nephew? I don't have a nephew. Wait, you mean Maggie's kid? He's been out of our lives for thirty-two years, tell him I'm not interested," she said with a certain coldness. The receptionist returned to see Ben; he had leaned against the inquiries desk with his elbows on the counter.

"I am afraid that Doctor Fielding does not acknowledge the fact that she has a nephew; sorry, you should go," relayed the receptionist. Ben was about to respond to this rejection but was disturbed by a couple of porters escorting a patient through to the wards from the dining room. It was thirty-one-year-old Peri Keeble. Remember her? She was calm until she saw Ben standing there in that magical coat again. She broke free of the porters and lunged at Ben, holding on to the coat with clenched fists.

"Take that off, right now. Don't keep wearing it, it's dangerous. See? I told you didn't I, it's the Devil in there, it's the Devil!" The porters tried dragging her away, but she held on to the coat and she was defiant. Jessica could hear the shouting and came through to see what the commotion was. Ben saw his aunt for the first time. She was lovely looking; her permed brunette hair made her look very sexy in Ben's eyes. He'd guessed right about her age, she was forty. Ben was holding Peri's wrists, trying to free himself from her grasp.

"This woman is mad, get her off me, will you?" Ben said in frustration.

"Peri, I know, it's the Devil, please let the man go, he's hasn't done anything wrong," Jessica tried to convince Peri. Peri grabbed the cuff of the coat and pointed out her letter on the left- hand sleeve.

"See this, it's a P. My name is Peri, it took me in too, the jacket it fits you right? But it looks too big for me, but it shrinks or swells to fit you snugly, yes? You must get rid of it; your soul is in danger. Satan, she has you now, take it off please, she'll kill you!" Peri warned. Ben looked at the sleeve and saw the P and the other one, just like his on the right- hand sleeve, but there were eleven other letters circling the left sleeve. Peri saw the Roman numeral IV. "When that reaches twelve, she will take you." She added. Ben didn't believe this. All the bad luck he's had over the years, made him think that the Devil used him as a plaything anyway - now this was his reward.

"Okay lady, you are clearly mad, please let go, okay?" As soon as Ben said that she released him and bowed her head.

"Oh, lady of the Darkness, please forgive me." She said, and then the porters took her away.

"I'm so sorry about that. Are you alright?" Jessica asked as she looked at Ben properly. "You are Maggie's boy? You look like her, worst luck for you, I detest that woman." She declared.

"She's dead, Aunt Jessica, she died two days ago of cancer." Revealed Ben.

"That woman is cancer," Jessica responded cruelly. Ben changed the subject.

"Why was that woman yelling at me like that? Is she crazy?"

"Come through to my office and we'll discuss it privately in there," invited Jessica.

Ben followed her through and gazed at the back of her. She had a very sensual walk. Ben was getting that feeling again, one of lust. He kept his thoughts to himself about what he would like to do with her, because she was his aunt.

"Is your name still Ben?" She asked as they sat at her desk, Ben nodded and kept staring at Jessica. He now knew that as long as he wore that jacket, everything he asked for, he will get it. He just has to express it audibly.

"Aunt Jessica, why was she saying all that?"

Jessica frowned.

"Please don't call me Aunt, it makes me feel old? I shouldn't be telling you anything about patients but seeing as she so vehemently insisted you get rid of that coat; I'll explain a few things. That girl is Peri Keeble; she's been through a terrible ordeal, thanks to a cult, which swept the towns and counties fifteen years ago. It and they took her in, practiced Satanic rituals, believing they were Disciples of Lucifer, as she explained it. Her family and friends tried to rescue her, but she succumbed to terrible things, she was sixteen at the time. She explained to me that she was required to sacrifice goats and drink its blood to release the soul of Satan. She also believes that Satan is a woman. A man staying here before her had the same theories as her, but he escaped and hasn't been seen since. Peri's father killed the supposed cult leader and five others; we think that Peri had a psychic event brought on by stress, because we couldn't find any links to a cult known by 'The Disciples of Lucifer' whatsoever." Jessica halted her explanation.

"So, it was all in her head?" Ben suggested.

"We've tried all sorts to cure her, she just doesn't respond to anything. She's been at the hospital for fifteen years, but soon she'll have to be released, the government has earmarked closure of this hospital. This is very sad for us all, this stupid 'Care in the Community' scheme." She cursed.

"Thanks for clearing that up for me; may I come and see you again then Jessica? I would like that very much."

"Of course you can, I'll just jot down my address," she wasn't so stern now. Or was it because Ben wanted to see her that made her agree? Nevertheless, she handed the address over and showed Ben out of the hospital. "See you again then, Ben"

Jessica winked at her nephew and his heart flipped and flopped. He was falling for his own aunt - surely that wasn't allowed. He thought. Ben waved and left Boundford, calling the same cab to collect him. His encounter with Peri had a lasting effect on him. It was as if every word clung like glue to his mind as he walked to the side of the road. The cabbie returned and took Ben home. On his journey he practiced his wishes in the back of his cab. He asked audibly for every traffic light to remain green while he was in the cab, but if he wore the coat they happened, however if he took it off, they didn't. He audibly asked the driver to waiver his fare for his final wish.

"Don't worry about it mate, I like you, it's on the house," said the Cabbie. Ben smiled to himself as the cab left without payment.

"Come and get me tomorrow then." Ben suggested.

"No problem!" The Cabbie tooted his horn and left the side of the road, to collect another client. By then though Ben's command would wear off and he wouldn't remember.

Chapter Three

Three more souls for Lucifer.

The longer Ben wore the goatskin coat, more power he gained. He practiced on innocent animals, but he checked his sleeve and not one animal soul was invited on -the figure still remained at IV. He quickly realized that the jacket wanted human souls. So, Ben only insisted on taking those who deserved to go and not the honest 'Joe Public' that passed him by every day, oblivious to his misdeeds.

"Yeah, I'll do it like a vigilante." Ben said to himself, the standing letter B on the sleeve glowed red in agreement, sealing his deal.

Now all he had to do was find these individuals. He thought about this while he was on his way over to Aunt Jessica's house. He was wary of the numeral XII, some sort of reserved thought that his encounter with Peri Keeble had lodged in there. Ben had given the address to the Cabbie, who was now his traveling slave for any chore Ben deemed necessary. He was soon outside the house of Aunt Jessica. He marvelled at the double-garaged property with safety gates and hi-tech CCTV system. He thanked the driver and paid him a pound for his trouble.

"I've already paid you for this, remember? That was the pound I owe you." convinced Ben.

"Of course it was Mr Grantham, just call and I'll come get you," the Cabbie offered.

"Not today thanks Drive, I'll be here a while catching up with my Relos." Ben concluded the conversation, and the Cabbie drove away again. He pressed the buzzer on the gates expecting a friendly answer.

"Who's this?" came a gruff reply.

"Err, Hi! I'm Ben Grantham, I've come to visit Jessica. I am her nephew."

"She doesn't have a nephew; her sister gave him away. So, that privilege is now void for you. Now fuck off before I call the cops, we want nothing to do with Maggie Bracewell and her bastard offspring." This man was like a mountain that wouldn't budge. "You still fucking here?"

"Listen mate, you will let me in, she will know who I am when she sees me." Ben tried the jacket trick, but he didn't realize that he needed to be face to face with the character, to have its desired effect.

"She isn't here, now piss off before I come out there," the man challenged from behind his fortress.

"Why don't you do that, because I'm not going anywhere, until I see Jessica Fielding." Ben was the equal to the man's defiance.

"Okay, I'm coming out there, but I've got a fucking shotgun. Don't make me use it" The man threatened.

Ben quickly realized that the man was very paranoid about something or someone and decided not to take the guy's soul just yet, despite his slur and insults to him and his mother's good name. "I'm coming out!" said the man as a shotgun slowly appeared through the front door, followed by a skinny man, balding and in his late forties. Ben knew that this man had been through a rough time and quickly sympathized with him. As the man came close to the gate, he checked up and down the street but kept the gun trained on Ben.

"Listen Mister, that gun really isn't necessary, is it?" Now that Ben was facing him, the coat's magic seemed to be working. The man put the safety back on and lowered the gun by his side. "Tell me your name"

"I'm Stuart Shaw, your Uncle Stuart of sorts I suppose."

Ben then asked: "Why do you live like this?" He was curious to know.

"I put a rotten gangster away, he is Lucas Paramore, I suppose you know him? He and his criminal contacts tried laundering money through my company. I did a deal with the police to nail him and now he has his cronies after me. Please don't ask who, 'cause I don't know, you could be one of them, God only knows." Stuart explained. This was the reason for his paranoia. A funny thought went through Ben's mind, about Stuart Shaw, paranoid about Paramore.

"Listen, I'm not a gangster, I've come to see my Aunt Jessica. Could you let me come in and stay until she comes home, please? She's cool about me coming over really!"

"Fine, this way then!" Stuart pointed to the small gate to his right, Ben's left, and opened it by the press of another buzzer. The gate slid across and Ben stepped through. No sooner had he crossed, the gate slid quickly back again. Stuart checked Ben over and satisfied that he didn't have a weapon of any kind, he took Ben inside.

"Yeah, a beer would be lovely, thanks!" Ben suggested to Stuart.

"I'll get you a beer," copied Stuart, and he went to get a can for Ben. Stuart returned, handed the beer over, sat by the window looking out.

"So! Tell me about my Aunt then. Uncle Stuart, why aren't you married?" Ben became nosy.

"We don't like the word marriage; it is a bind to which we're not inclined to be held to." Replied Stuart, he took the safety back off the gun as a car slowly drove up the street; it was a car that Stuart didn't recognize. "Shh! Shut the fuck up for a bit" The car came back down the street and stopped opposite the gates of the house; Stuart stood away from the window for a few moments as the occupants surveyed whether anyone was in. Ben could see the passenger screwing on what looked like a silencer and the driver already held his gun. This looked like it could be gangsters to Ben.

"Wait Stuart! I've got a plan." Ben left the safety of the house and walked towards the gate. "Can I help you, Sirs?" Ben asked in his usual mischievous way.

"Where's Shaw? Tell him to come out of hiding," the driver asked.

"He ain't here! I'm doing some work for him, but I could leave him a message."

"No offense there, mate, but you don't look like a worker, you have a lazy demeanour. Now tell him Lucas has found him, and he is coming for his money!" Added the passenger.

"Oh, I'm not offended, but it looks like Lucas is too much of a coward, to come and face Stuart himself. Reckon I'm right in saying that; no offence meant." gambled Ben.

"Shaw has a restraining order against Lucas, that's the only reason he doesn't come himself, now tell him that from us!" Ordered the driver.

"I'll do the telling, thanks mate!" Ben saw the driver's expression change to a more menacing stare as his patience was wearing thin, but he had the jacket, didn't he? "Now I reckon you should shoot your pal here in the head, plop him in the trunk of your car and take me to see this Lucas, maybe we can do a deal?"

The driver instantly shot the passenger through the side of his head, and he fell to the ground; the grass caught the spray of blood and his grey matter. When Ben was gone, Stuart would have to clean it off. Just like Ben suggested, the driver picked his friend up and rolled the body into the trunk and Ben pressed the buzzer to get out and headed for the parked car. "Now fucking get me to Lucas?" Ben commanded.

As Ben climbed into the car, he saw his sleeve instantly change to the numeral V, meaning five souls were taken. As they drove to Lucas's, Ben kept looking at the driver, he needed to plan what to do with this guy. Very soon he would need to put this into action. He gave it some thought. They were pulling up in the drive of Lucas' house. "Cool now that you've brought me here, after I've got out you can just shoot yourself, because you can't take killing your pal back there!" Ben then got out and walked to the door of Lucas's. "LUCAS! I HAVE STUART'S MONEY, MAY I COME IN?" yelled Ben as the silenced gun went off behind him. He looked back to see the driver's head slumped out of the window dripping blood on to the lavish paving slabs of Lucas' driveway. His sleeve then changed to VI, now he was halfway to twelve. "WELL?" Ben shouted, one more time.

"Alright, alright! Stop shouting, the neighbourhood will hear." said Lucas with consideration. Not the tough guy his buddies had claimed. "Come on then; let's see this money" he invited. Lucas saw his driver dead in the driveway. "Charlie, get rid of that out there, will you?" He asked as he approached the man inside. "And find me another driver?" He added. Charlie obeyed and then Ben and Lucas were alone. "Forgive me for saying, but you don't look like a rich bloke. Shaw was taken to the cleaners by my men, while I was inside, so how have you got his money?" Lucas was very astute and didn't suffer fools gladly. He was a large man; Ben noted a difficulty in Lucas, wheezing and walking slowly, to his desk.

"I've brought your original stake back, which is fuck all mate!" Ben explained. Lucas admired Ben's tenacity, but like most gangsters there was a limit to which he was going to be pushed.

"I invested seven hundred and fifty thousand pounds into his company, then he cut me off and got the cops involved." corrected Lucas.

"Yeah, he said you used him to launder your drug money," Ben did some correcting of his own.

"Don't judge me, it wasn't drug money. I run a protection business." Lucas straightened Ben out on that fact.

"That's low, you're a fucking loan shark, and you should be put down, you parasite!" Ben remembered what one of his foster mothers had been put through, because of those sleazeballs.

"Again, you judge me, but you don't know me. I've worked hard to get where I am." Lucas was beginning to tire of this conversation.

"The only place you're going is to hell, and with my help, I'll take you there. Oops! Nothing like a fatal heart attack to end your fabulous career."

Ben closed his eyes and listened, he could hear a heart beating faster and faster, which took Lucas into a seizure at his desk, Lucas suddenly grabbed his left arm, turned and fell to the floor, gasping and red-faced, trying to stay alive. A couple more seconds it was over. Lucas breathed his last breath, and Ben opened his eyes again. He stared at his sleeve to now see the numeral read VII. Ben scooped up a large pile of money from the desk and slid it into the goatskin coat. Ben had freed his Uncle Stuart from years of paranoia. Now he owed him a favour, a small amount of time with Aunt Jessica. Ben called for his usual taxi to collect him from Lucas. After he had been brought back to Stuart's house, Ben told the driver to ring for an ambulance and give the address of Lucas's place. Ben pressed the buzzer at Stuart's gate. Again. the same paranoid voice answered.

"What now?"

"Don't worry Uncle Stuart, your problems are over. Lucas is dead, he won't be bothering you again." The gate buzzed without an answer, and it slid open, allowing Ben to come through to the house.

"Dead? How? What happened?" Stuart asked as Ben entered the house.

"Heart attack apparently. I went there to ask him to cool it with you and he just keeled over in front of me, died right there, nothing anybody could've done about it. Here he left you this!" Ben tossed the large batch of money at Stuart who clumsily dropped it by surprise.

"Thanks Ben, it's taken a load off my mind. Now excuse me I must sort out the lawn, there are brains and tissue on it. You can wait inside for your Aunt if you want," Stuart was a more amicable person now.

Ben had achieved more in one afternoon, than the whole legal system had in seventeen years. Stuart now thought of Ben as a member of his family regardless of Jessica's opinion of him. Ben sat in the chair that Stuart used to watch from and watched his uncle tidy the lawn Then Aunt Jessica came home in the middle of his tidying. She drove in and parked, then went back to Stuart and kissed him rather fully for a few minutes; they were clearly in love. They broke off their kissing and it was clear that Stuart was telling her that Ben was in the house and what had happened that afternoon. She glared at the house, forgetting she had invited him over. Stuart had finished and came back to the house holding hands with Jessica as they walked. Ben was slightly jealous of this. Seeing Jessica kissing Stuart like that, made him want her even more. Again, peculiar feelings to have about his maternal aunt, but these were his feelings. Jessica came first into the house, and smiled at Ben, but it was a false smile; whatever Ben was feeling about her, she wasn't feeling the same about him.

"I'll spare you two hours today, okay Ben? Then I think it would be best if you leave us alone for a while. We still need to adjust to you being in our lives, you have no cousins, we decided not to have kids. So, you see, there isn't much to keep you around." Jessica's words hurt him.

"Two hours is all I need, just tell me more about my mother, what was she like and why did you fall out? Then I'll go, Stuart can put the kettle on whilst you explain," again manipulating him with the coat's magic. Stuart did this and Jessica sat opposite Ben to talk about families.

"Your Mum was a selfish bitch; she didn't care about anyone else. She stole both my parent's love. Then she became pregnant at thirteen with you, thanks to Ben Grantham Snr, who couldn't keep his dick in his pants. They argued about what she should do, Mum thought you should have been aborted, Dad wanted you to be born, and they would raise you as our brother, but of course Maggie wanted a girl. I was going to be an aunt at eight, think about that for a minute, how exciting that would be for me at that age. You were born a boy, originally called Gareth, after my father's middle name. Your mother couldn't bond with you and a year later she signed adoption papers to have you fostered out. Your name was changed to Ben when your father killed himself, not a pretty story, but that is how it happened. I wasn't allowed to keep in touch with you and our hatred for one another grew over the years, then it became irreparable. So, you see, I don't have anything in common with you. She's dead and you are a reminder of a mistake she made, that I detested her for. Oh good, here's the tea!" Jessica had zoned out and had forgotten about Stuart for a moment. Ben just stared at her, he still fancied her. Now he was on the verge of wanting her physically as well, though she was so cruel about his mother, but he couldn't help himself. Jessica was Ben's ideal woman, the right height, the right shape, the right looks, to him, everything ticked the boxes.

"You should ask Stuart to go out for a while; he's been cooped up in here for years. I'd have thought you'd be more grateful to me for helping him."

"Yes, you are right I should. Stuart, we need some groceries, please go out and get us some?" obeyed Jessica. Stuart did exactly that, leaving Ben on his own to work some magic with her. As soon as he'd gone Ben stood and drew the curtains... "Why are you doing that?" Jessica asked.

"Because you are going to stand up, strip off and show me everything, then you're going to come over her and shag your nephew." Ben insisted. Jessica did stand up, she did start stripping, right down to her bare skin, and the impulse to do so was too great. Jessica stood in her magnificence and walked sensually over towards Ben's seat. She writhed in front of him, which excited him even more, she slipped down on to the floor and pulled eagerly at Ben's trousers, they came off, his shorts came off, the coat came off and his sweater, but that is when it all changed.

"What the hell am I doing? You pervert!" Jessica was appalled to see her naked body tantalizing her nephew. "Get the fuck out of here! Go on, take your clothes and never come back!" She was furious with Ben. She realized quickly the jacket was a tool to get whatever Ben wanted.

Chapter Four

Jessica knows about Ben.

Ben was frantically dressing before being seen naked in public. On the other side of the door, Jessica was doing the same, Stuart wouldn't be too long with the groceries, and he would think she was having an affair, given his recent paranoia. He would be difficult to convince otherwise.

"You violated my trust Ben, don't ever come back here, I know what you're capable of now. If you continue to pursue a relationship with us, I'll tell everyone who knows you how evil you can be. You're every bit Maggie Bracewell's son!" She was yelling through the intercom at him.

"Don't worry, I'm going!" Ben hurried down the drive and Jessica buzzed the gate open. Ben sprinted at top speed past a befuddled Stuart, who was returning from the superstore. Jessica was just about able to fasten her bra and pull her sweater on before Stuart strode through the door. She had an exasperated look on her face.

"What the hell! Did he do something to you?" Stuart noticed the closed curtain, moved to calm her and kissed her forehead, before hearing her answer.

"Ben, he made a pass at me, my own nephew! I couldn't stop him, he overpowered me, and I was defenceless," she explained.

"There is something funny about him. He'd say something, and you'd end up doing it, reluctantly as well. I'm sure he did those gangsters in. How do you think he does it?" Stuart saw reason for once; the paranoia was gone, no more doubting her. Jessica didn't tell him Ben had her naked though, that was her secret.

"It is odd, let's watch the CCTV footage of earlier, we can see how he does it," suggested Jessica, and Stuart went upstairs to get it.

"Here we go!" He said and loaded the disc into the player.

He fast-forwarded to the Ben incident; they watched every second of it. "Look! He asked me to lower my gun, but I didn't want to. When I was in the house, he couldn't manipulate me, until I stood there." Stuart revealed. "I'll wind it on until - you see what happens next" he added. They watched the driver, and his passenger swagger out of the car towards Ben. Stuart changed the footage to a side view so they could see them all talking. "These are tough guys, they wouldn't back off that easily, watch what he says next?" Stuart offered, they saw Ben speak to the driver and then witnessed him shoot his friend at point-blank range in the head.

"Urrgh! Disgusting!" Jessica remarked, looking green from all the blood.

"Shall I stop? Because Ben says something else, and the driver dumps his buddy into the trunk, then they all leave together. One hour later he returns to tell me they're all dead. What do you think about all that then Jessie?" Stuart was eager for her opinion.

"Well, he's got them off your back, but if the cops come sniffing, you are their main suspect," Jessica warned him. "We've got enough here, to get Ben going to the Chief Constable, to clear things up, which will keep you out of the picture. I'm so glad you're not a fish out of water anymore. I've got my old Stu back." Jessica leaned over and kissed him again. Stuart paused the footage and kissed her in return. They kept at it, until they whipped themselves into a frenzy and couldn't resist each other any longer and they disappeared for sex upstairs.

Ben scurried to the safety of his place. Jessica had rumbled him, and he was worried about how it would turn out. He had overstepped the mark by a massive margin with her. He scampered up the path to the front door of the squat and got himself in, breathing a sigh of relief to close the world outside for a few hours. The benefit of all this was Jessica and Stuart didn't know where he lived or how to get in touch with him; this was an advantage. He found his familiars in the chill out room; Minge and Doorbell were tickling each other and laughing raucously. Ben skipped past them rolling around and sat on the sofa. He stared at the jacket in the mirror by the door, the goatskin coat was getting him into trouble, but the urge to wear it every day was too hard to resist. He had disposed of seven people so far, which at first, he innocently didn't realize he'd been doing, but now it was apparent that the power to wield such evil, was within him. This nuisance of Jessica knowing and by now she'd have told Stuart, he needed to do something about it. What if they call the police? Stuart knows he helped get rid of those thugs today, what if he told Jessica that titbit of information? They'd have him over a barrel, wouldn't they? If he had to do it, then they must go, he thought. Doorbell broke away from Minge to smoke some more weed. This time she kept her distance from Ben, but he knew he had to watch what he said, he took off the coat and sat watching them, not even daring to say anything to them, in case the jacket wanted their souls. He studied the jacket a bit more closely and noticed that some of the symbols were actually moving about. This startled him, and he left the room again to find a more private space.

"I'm not wearing you tomorrow, you'll have to stay in here until things die down," he told the jacket as he opened the wardrobe which swarmed with woodlice and other critters looking for a dusky damp space. On the shelf was a box, he folded the coat up inside and closed the lid. He turned the wardrobe round to hide the doors from any jerks that might like to take other people's property. "You will stay here until I need you again!" He told the wardrobe. He left the squat to visit with his dear friend Peter Flaws. Maybe a few hallowed words from the Holy Father would help soothe his tormented soul. He'd blown any chance of claiming some family after his stunt with Jessica; he cursed himself as he walked to Peter's place. The rain came again. Ben noticed that it hadn't rained for the whole time he wore that damned jacket, the moment he took it off he was soaked through. Dripping like a drowned rat at Peter's door he knocked three times. Peter came through to answer.

"My man, I would have turned around and gone home again, the heavens have been open since eight o'clock my friend!" Not that he cared; Peter was as drenched as Ben was. "Come on in Ben. Something's obviously troubling you, that's the only time you come over here" he added. With his arm across Ben's shoulder, he took him through to the conservatory, sat him down and fetched the brandy again. "Come on then, what's the trouble with you this time? You know I won't tell anybody." Peter promised.

Ben sat and told Peter what had happened so far, ever since he bought the coat, telling Peter it was as if the coat had beckoned him over and began to twist his mind and body into a dangerous hitman for Lucifer herself. Of course he recited Peri Keeble's encounter with him too, and now Ben sought Peter's wisdom about how to solve this issue. Peter recounted what Ben had told him and then he would give him some advice.

"Let's see? You bought a leather coat for fourteen pounds, put it on and ever since you have been bothered by people who have been rude to you, or threatened you in some way. They are dead because you told them that would happen to them, so Lucifer has claimed seven souls out of a possible twelve he or she wants to consume. To top that you molested your aunt and killed some terrible gangsters who ruined your uncle's life. This Peri Keeble woman is obviously off her rocker - pardon the expression. If there were bodies' littering this town, they'd have been on the news, wouldn't they? I'm sure it's your imagination running away with you. You were like this as a boy, that's why nobody wanted to keep you for more than five minutes." Peter wasn't having any nonsense.

"It's bloody true Father, these things have happened to me, I swear!" Peter frowned at Ben for cursing in his presence. Swearing was for the weak-minded, were his thoughts on it.

"Where's this jacket now? Why haven't you got it with you, or is it invisible?" asked Peter, making a sideways mockery of all this and then apologized after Ben's troubled expression returned.

"I have locked it away. I suppose the only way to convince you is to show you, then you'll believe me," Ben challenged the Priest, who believed actions always speak louder than words.

"You bring the coat and give me a demonstration, and then I'll consider what you've told me, but right now I don't care for long stories, it's getting late, you should go home." Peter looked tired and wearily saw Ben out. As soon as Ben stepped outside again the rained tipped down once more.

"I'll put the coat back on and then it won't rain any more, you'll see!" Ben said as he left Peter's haven for his squalid conditions back at the squat.

Peter shook his head and waved, then closed the front door on his friend. Ben got absolutely sodden getting home; he thought it must be some penance for telling on the jacket to somebody else. He had white trousers on and a white t-shirt that was practically see-through when he'd finally got home. He found the hammock in the old room at the back of the house and occupied it for the remainder of the night. If somebody wanted it back, they'd have to tip him out of it, he thought. Ben stayed inside the squat for three days after this.

Jessica and Stuart snuggled with each in the bed, Stuart had his arm around the back of Jessica's shoulders and his right hand was softly stroking the top part of her right breast, the rest of her was secluded under the blanket. Jessica just pandered to Stuart's caressing; it had been years since he was this caring. She was thinking about one of her patients Peri Keeble, after finding out what Ben was capable of. Was Peri as delusional as everyone had claimed? Jessica had only spent the last five years at the hospital; she was keen to find out the backstory of how Peri came to be there in the first place. Jessica started a conversation with Stuart about it.

"You know, I'm not normally allowed to discuss things to do with patients outside of the hospital, but there's this woman you see, I've been treating her for paranoid delusions for five years, but with little success." She began. Stuart moved his arm from behind Jessica and turned on his side to face her. His interest enthused her to tell him more. "She came to the hospital as a sixteen-year-old girl. The people of Boundford had witnessed some peculiar goings on leading up to the night she was brought to us. Peri Keeble is a disturbed young lady they told me when I joined, so I studied her before taking over her treatments."

"What happened to her then, people don't just go mad do they? There's always a catalyst, right?" Stuart was eager to hear more.

"Peri always maintained, with a degree of normalcy I might add, that she had been seconded by a Satanic cult called 'The Disciples of Lucifer.' Where upon she was asked to perform sacrifices and drank blood of goats in order for them to release the soul of the Devil, who – now get this Is a woman" Jessica made quotation marks with her fingers at the woman part. Stuart was gazing at Jessica intently, waiting for this discussion to reach somewhere. "She says she wore a coat, made of goatskin, that let her imagine things and they would literally happen. A young boy for whom she had no plans or desires for was driven blind because she wished it." Stuart gasped and then thought of what Ben was doing. He knew it was happening the same way; Ben made that crook shoot his friend because Ben wanted him to. "That must be the same goatskin coat that Ben has got his hands on, and if you don't mind me saying so? Looks very real to me!" Jessica concluded her revelation, and they remained quiet, absorbing all the similarities between Ben and Peri. Jessica was going to talk with Peri as planned in the morning.

The following morning was grey, dismal and windy, the howling gale woke Ben with a start, it was as if the wind had called his name, but realizing through the fuzziness of his half-awake state, he must have synchronized a dream he was having, with the blowing sound from outside. Ben rubbed his eyes, and swung his legs over the side of the hammock so that he could gather more momentum and strength to get up. He went to the room with the wardrobe in it and met two semi-naked people, lovemaking on the floor.

"Fuck off!" The couple screeched out in unison, Ben just sidled around them and in mid stroke the couple stopped to sigh at the audacity of Ben, just coasting around them whilst they were locked together.

Ben turned the wardrobe around and grabbed the box and then quickly left the room again. He hurried to the bathroom and took out the jacket and slid it back on, this time it seemed tighter, as if somebody else had worn it. What the coat did in fact was revert to Peri's shape, before Ben had bought it. But soon a warm comfortable feeling; rose within him as the jacket swelled to accommodate Ben again.

"For a moment there, I thought you were mad at me!" Ben remarked.

"I am fucking mad at you Ben!" replied the coat. The sudden shock of this garment talking to him sent him reeling backwards and he landed on the toilet. "Don't be alarmed, I've been with you all the time, you've just ignored me that's all!" The voice added. It was a woman's voice, but it sounded metallic in tone, almost robotic, kind of what a Sat-Nav device would sound like. "You haven't spoken to me since the day you bought me at the hospital, how rude! Now I'll do all the talking, and you do all the listening!" The voice commanded him.

"And what if I don't?" Ben challenged. The coat began to shrink, it wrapped tightly around him, constricting the air out of him, until he could no longer breathe. "Okay! Okay!" Ben huffed and the coat released its vice-like hold on him again. "Why are you doing this? I just want to be left alone."

"Because you're an easy target Ben, get me the five remaining souls and I will release you. You have until the end of the month to solve this problem, if you don't bring them to me, I will take you instead and my next conquest will help me further." It's the Devil, thought Ben and realized Peri was telling the truth, but now the coat was clinging to Ben until the deed was done. Ben shivered and tried to remove the coat again, it constricted once more and refused to budge. He felt a burning sensation; quickly he checked where it was coming from. The jacket had welded itself to Ben's skin; one tug felt like acid being poured on him, Now the Jacket was in control of him, instead of him being in control of it. "No more flirting with women Ben, you've a job to do, five more souls and be quick about it!" The voice had gone again, Ben sat in the bathroom thinking for a few moments. To gather such people in a short amount of time would take some doing. Ben resorted to his vigilante stance. He decided to hit the streets again and strike the people who deserve it. Ben checked on his friends downstairs. Minge and Doorbell were sleeping top-tail on the sofa; Ben crept over and took a cigarette from Doorbell's box.

"Put it back Ben, I know that sound!" said Doorbell. Ben gave in and put the cigarette back. "Surprise me and buy your own, then maybe I'll willingly give you some of mine," she added.

Ben felt ashamed and left her alone. He did buy his own cigarettes and headed for town. He wanted to find that cabbie, then he could drive further afield. Hearing Peter's lecture ringing in his ears about bodies littering the streets, made him feel this way. He wanted to chat with Peri again and find out more about what happened to her; now he could understand why the coat drove her so crazy.

Jessica had a busy morning ahead of her. She was keen to get her meeting with Peri done too, and then she could be released after the assessment; if the Doctor deems Peri capable to cope on her own, the woman could leave the hospital today. Jessica quickly dressed before Stuart awoke and she went out to the car. The ignition stubbornly refused to fire the engine and now she hadn't much choice but to wake Stuart to get it started. Jessica returned to their room, she shook Stuart awake who threw on a white towel and followed her down to the car. Stuart climbed in, pulled the choke out slightly, waited ten seconds and twisted the key. This time the car decided to yield, and he gave it a few revs to show it who's the boss. Jessica swapped places and he kissed her goodbye. Now Jessica was on her way to work. She planned her morning at the hospital. Coffee, Peri, assessment, lunch and then find Peri somewhere to live and home thereafter. The other part of her plan was to locate Ben, get him to see the Chief Constable and have Ben keep the cops from suspecting Stuart, just in case bodies started to appear. A busy day, but one Jessica Fielding was determined to enjoy.

Chapter Five

Jessica's plan.

Jessica headed straight for the coffee machine, her anticipation of speaking to Peri made her nervous. She'd spoken to her over a thousand times during the past five years, but nothing quite like the experience of this morning could compare to any other time. The Doctor poured two cups of coffee and headed for her office; she angled the casting couch so that it looked comfortable and then summoned the receptionist to gather the porters with Peri Keeble. Jessica clutched her coffee with both hands and stood by the window, with her backside slightly supported by the sill and warm radiator. The knock from the receptionist told her Peri was here.

"Please enter" Jessica called out after a five second countdown. The porters brought Peri in, and they moved her to the couch, they swung her legs up and laid her back, then released the restraining belts tied around her arms. "Good morning, Peri, make yourself comfortable please. Gentlemen, you can leave us now." The porters left and closed the door, Jessica stared down her half-moon glasses at Peri, she began to unravel her inner thoughts just one more time.

"This is our last meeting, Peri; what do you think about that?"

"I'll miss you, Doctor. Having you here has made all the difference, I've never felt so comfortable around a person before, except for perhaps Fabian, my inspiration."

"Your inspiration? He tried to kill you Peri, didn't he? I for one would have felt extremely uncomfortable about that!" Jessica sipped her coffee, then moved to the stool by Peri's side, placing the cup on its saucer at the desk.

"He was trying to summon her, one small cut for her to enter me and then she would consume me, I wasn't afraid, I was ready. Then my dad killed him and told me Fabian was bad."

"You say she, but you mean Lucifer, don't you? Fabian believed her to be a woman, didn't he?"

"We all called her the Lady of the Darkness, only Fabian shone the light for her to be free, for the Devil to rise in me." Peri sounded the same, just like the first day Jessica saw her, rational, believable and most importantly not mad at all.

"But you wore that coat, didn't you? When you wore it, you felt powerful, yes?" Jessica reminded her.

"Yeah! It's made of goatskin, with ancient symbols dating back to before the birth of Jesus himself. It feels like velvet when you wear it, it can shrink or stretch to any size. When the coat decided to pick me, it granted me power beyond my wildest dreams."

"Can you remember what it let you do; do you want to remember, I mean?" Jessica prompted.

"Leon Wilkes, he followed me everywhere, staring, taking pictures, stalking me at school and at home. He was creepy and menacing. He used to watch me getting undressed in my room, that boy saw everything and knew everything about me. That night with the fog, I said out loud for Leon to go blind, so that he couldn't see me anymore, I just wished it that's all. When I got to him his eyes were bleeding, and he was blind. I didn't know I could do that." The same stoicism came with Peri's words, not a hint of remorse.

"Very good, we'll break there for a few moments, here have some coffee?" Jessica passed the cup to Peri, and she drank it fully without a gulp. The Doctor refreshed her cup with another and returned to her office. Jessica set off with a different tract this time, bringing Ben into the conversation. "Last week, when you met that man with the Jacket on, is it the same one you wore?" Peri checked first then remembered.

"Yes, it is, on the left cuff, my initial was still there. The man's name began with a B and he had already claimed four souls. It's the work of the Devil; she took Fabian and now she wants this man." Peri was still displaying the same restful pattern as if she had started the session.

"His name is Ben, and he is using the coat to bring bad things to people. Can you help me track him down and persuade him to destroy it?" The Doctor insisted.

"You can't beat the Devil herself, you need a person of higher standing with God, only they can protect him now. That's how John was able to save me last time. If Ben has killed more than once, then he will have a taste for it, the temptation to do more will be too strong for him to deny." warned Peri, who had mentioned John Sobers in one of their earlier chats.

"We have to persuade Ben to give up the jacket. We can find you some place to stay and bring Ben over to you, Peri. You don't need to be here at the hospital anymore; we've got to try something!" Jessica pleaded.

"Find me a place to stay and then call John Sobers, he's the only one who can save Ben now." Peri was quietly waiting for Jessica to agree. The Doctor called the receptionist and ordered her to arrange accommodation for Peri outside of the hospital, and to locate a Mr John Sobers, then have him meet Jessica and Peri. The receptionist followed Jessica's orders and for now asked for Peri to be taken away to the ward one final time. It had turned lunchtime, and Jessica was keen to find Ben, she needed him to go to the police. Once this was done, she could coax him to Peri's safe-house and have the jacket destroyed. She thought. The porters took Peri away and Jessica set her plan in motion.

Ben had asked the Cabbie to take him to the hospital, he really needed to speak to Peri again, plus he had the coat on, so nobody could stop him anyway. He waved the Cabbie away once more and strolled towards the hospital entrance. The same lady he had spoken to before was standing at the counter. Ben reached her and she held her hands up to stop his advance.

"I'm sorry Mr Grantham, but Dr Fielding will not be seeing anybody today, she's out for the remainder of the day."

"I haven't come to speak to her, it's one of your patients I wish to see, Miss Peri Keeble, so if you wouldn't mind taking me?" Ben pressed. The lady just walked in front of Ben and led him through to the wards. Peri was in her dorm and had drawn a circle with chalk on the floor. She had candles circling her and in the centre. She was sitting cross legged and meditating. The candles weren't alight, but she was waiting for the visit. The lady peeped into the dorm and spotted Peri sitting there.

"There's a man to see you Miss Keeble," she said. Peri looked up and Ben cut in front of the lady and Peri immediately lit the candles.

"Thanks Miss that will be all!" Ben said and the lady left them. By the time she reached reception, she'd forgotten what she was doing. "Why have you got those lit?" Ben asked as he approached Peri.

"Come any closer and you'll burn!" Peri warned him; this made Ben stop in his tracks. "That's quite close enough!" She insisted.

"Why do you want to burn me, Peri? I don't understand."

"Because I've already told you, the Devil is in you, and she wants you to gather souls. How many have you taken this time?" Ben showed Peri the sleeve of the coat, it read VII. Peri continued. "This protects me from her, John Sobers instructed me to make it when he visited last time."

"Oh, really Peri, please blow out these candles and let me speak with you" pleaded Ben

"Bad luck Ben, your charm with the coat won't work on me here. I'm protected by a holy circle you see. I think the candles will stay lit, say what you've got to say then leave!" Peri wasn't budging.

"What will happen to me if it reaches twelve, I have to know?" Ben asked.

"You will become the vessel, just like I was in line to be. She will enter your body and take you over, unless you take your own life and spare the fate of five others. Your life for the safety of mankind." Peri offered Ben an alternative.

"No, I will not take my own life, she has me already and I must do as she commands, then she will release me," Ben replied. Peri shook her head and just gave Ben this stern warning.

"You have made a deal with the Devil, you can't break that deal, unless she breaks it first. You are damned one way or the other." Peri returned to her meditating and Ben shuffled on the spot waiting to hear more from her, but she didn't speak at all. Ben didn't have much of a choice and left the hospital with very little change from his visit. As soon as Ben had left the hospital, Peri blew out the candles, she rose onto the bed and waited for her release. She hoped that they had located John Sobers and found a place for her to live, but she didn't fancy staying in Boundford. It held too many bad memories.

Jessica was on the phone at her favourite café, speaking to a person who was last in contact with John Sobers, a man called Wilbur Vance. He had taken over John's parish, whilst John was on a sabbatical and his mission took him to India. He wouldn't be back from there until January, which pretty much ruled out the man helping her against Ben. Wilbur Vance knew of Peri's situation because John had often talked about her, but told Jessica, Peri would only trust John and decided to steer clear of anything that could tarnish his good reputation. Jessica understood of course, which now meant she would have to find another way of tearing that jacket away from Ben. Jessica had one more chore to do, before returning to the hospital. Find Ben and take him to the police, just to steer them away from Stuart. She finished her lunch and headed for her car. Right then as if by luck, there was Ben across the street getting off the bus from Boundford.

"Ben, over here!" She called. Ben looked very nervous as Jessica headed his way. Ben put his hands in his pockets as she stood by him. "I'm angry about what you did Ben, taking advantage of me like that, I felt violated, but if we can see past that and maybe you can do something good for me, I could forgive you."

"I am really very sorry Jessica. It was immoral of me to think you could feel the same way towards me as I feel about you. I will do whatever it takes to earn your forgiveness." replied Ben.

"Then come with me to the police and tell the Chief Constable to look elsewhere, in case those two bodies from Lucas turn up unexpectedly." She asked.

"There's a third person, he's called Charlie, he looked like Lucas' right-hand man, he saw me. I could pin the whole lot on him for you, that should throw them off the scent." offered Ben.

"Come on then, let's do it!" Jessica agreed. Jessica crossed the road and Ben walked with her to the car. She drove to the police station and waited in the car park for Ben to go in. He met with the Sergeant at the desk and the big man looked back at him.

"What's wrong my man?" The Sergeant asked.

"I'm Ben Grantham, a man called Lucas Paramore was found dead from a heart attack three days ago and the man responsible is Charlie, his accomplice." Ben told him.

"Charlie is his brother. Are you sure he did what you say he did? Where's the evidence?" The Sergeant replied.

"You don't need evidence, you know it's Charlie, so you must tell the Chief Constable, that if any bodies show up, it's him who did it, I heard Lucas saying it to Charlie, honest." Ben added.

"I'll call the CC over here now for you Sir." The Sergeant beckoned the Chief Constable and Ben repeated his information. The magic of the coat forged an unflinching resolution from the Chief Constable.

"Thank you, Ben. We will go to see Charlie and bring him in. Thank you. You are a credit to your family Sir!" Ben left the station and found Jessica again.

"It's done, Stuart won't be bothered by the police, okay?" Ben reassured her.

"Good, here's my mobile phone number Ben, call me and we can meet up, but because Stuart mistrusts you, I'll find us a different place, just leave it to me. In a few days I'll be in touch." Jessica closed the window on Ben after she gave him the card and then calmly drove away. She now needed to find a place for Peri to live.

Ben watched Jessica drive away and then walked home to his squat. His mind had been scrambled over the last ten days, he had got sidetracked which meant one less day to gather the five remaining souls, but of course they needed to be worthy souls, where would he find these? What would happen if he didn't do it in time? These thoughts burned his mind, and the coat felt very tight around him, not comfortable at all. The first day he tried it on, he hardly felt it. Now it was heavy and constricting. His face was pale as if the life force was being drained out of him. His conversation with Peri scared him and the evil inside him, the woman was convinced it was the Devil. He remembered how Peri had protected herself and thought about copying her. As he reached the squat, he looked at himself in the reflection of the window. He couldn't recognize himself; in his place was a thin narrow face with horns sticking out and curling back behind his ears. "My God is that what I look like now?" he said.

"Ben, this is what you're gonna look like if you fail me. At the moment you and I are the only ones who can see this, but come the 31st, everybody else will." The jacket warned him.

———◄❯———

Chapter Six

Idle hands.

Jessica had returned to the hospital; she had good news for Peri; she went to find her on the wards. Peri was looking out of the window realizing she would be free from here this afternoon. She had been crammed in this place since her late teens and hadn't really experienced any adult life outside of here. Although her mother and brother visited her each month, they could only take Peri out to the gardens to talk things over. Max Keeble was still serving a jail term for killing five people in an unprovoked attack, so Peri knew he couldn't visit, but she was determined to visit him when she got out of here and away from the Doctor. Peri moved to her dorm and began packing some things into a case that the hospital provided for her; she kept the candles and chalk. Wherever she was headed, she needed to use these to guard herself. Even though Fabian was dead, the agent of all that was still around, eager to possess her or worse destroy her for the betrayal. Her loving cockatiel Boffin died six years ago, so the first thing Peri wanted to do was visit a pet shop to buy Boffin Mark II. Jessica saw Peri busy packing and made her way over.

"Good news Peri, we've found a lovely flat for you in Maythorne, the town over from this one, I know you said that you didn't want to live in Boundford anymore, so I hope you don't mind. Ben lives there and so do I, so for our purpose of getting that evil jacket away from him, it would be somewhat easier." The Doctor had worked very hard for Peri.

"Thank you, Doctor, did you manage to get in touch with John?" Peri inquired.

"I rang the number you gave, but it seems John is in India until January, so he won't be available to help us. His locum said he didn't wish to get involved with his affairs, and seeing as you will be staying in a different parish, he was reluctant to travel across, sorry Peri."

Jessica felt sad for a few moments; she knew that Peri's help rested on her being able to reach John Sobers.

"Doesn't matter Doctor, we've tried. Ben didn't seem to want to volunteer and give over the jacket anyway. There is only one way Ben will be free from that coat and that is if he dies, sorry to sound like this, but he has five souls to gather, until she rises again. Ben told me he couldn't take his own life, but that doesn't mean someone couldn't take it for him." Peri was putting dark thoughts into Jessica's head.

"But I couldn't kill anybody, and I don't know anybody who could." said Jessica. She didn't like where this was going, but if she didn't stop Ben, then she would have five more deaths on her conscience. "Come on let's get you away from here, then we can talk about this later." Jessica took Peri's arm and held the case out for a porter to carry. "To my car please Henry" she told the porter. Jessica and Peri left the hospital for a short drive to Maythorne.

Thirty minutes later they turned the car into the street containing Peri's new flat. About halfway along Jessica stopped the car and reversed it into a double driveway. The whole street was brand new, part of the Government's new Care in the Community program. One hundred outpatients from the Boundford Psychiatric Hospital, needed to be housed and this was the grant the Government had given to contain them. Peri stared at the new buildings and Jessica spoke whilst she looked.

"Peri your apartment is on the ground floor and facing the front, okay? I'll come with you, and you can tell me what you need to furnish the place. Once you've settled in you may have your independence."

"I've never had a place of my own, I'm kind of scared, thank you for doing this." Peri replied gratefully.

"Just remember we need to find Ben, get him to come here and then we can grab that coat of his," Jessica added as they went in through the common door of the apartment block. A sixty-year-old man with white hair, tall and thin met them at the hall, just in front of the door to the apartment. It was he who had registered the place for Peri. He opened the door using a big set of keys and gave a spare one to Peri.

"I hope you like it Miss Keeble, we've provided you with a three-piece suite, a bed, a cooker, washing machine and microwave. The rest you can buy yourself, and then you can put in a more personal touch, okay?" Said the man.

"Thanks, are we allowed pets here?" Peri asked; she was desperate for another cockatiel as company.

"Only ones that won't foul the carpets, so no cats or dogs. I'm a fan of lizards myself, what about you Miss Keeble?" questioned the man.

"I like birds, I want a new cockatiel, but I'll decide on the name when I see him," Peri replied.

"Very well Miss Keeble, good luck with this place. It's been nice to meet you." The kind man went away.

Peri moved through the flat and Jessica gave her a few moments to feel comfortable and settle in. Peri put her case on to the bedroom floor, then immediately drew a circle with the chalk around the case. She took a bottle of water out of her cardigan, some holy water given to her by John, she sprinkled some on the floor within the circle. Peri took out the candles and placed them on the line drawn on the floor. She was ready for any confrontation with Ben and his shadow. She quickly closed the bedroom door and returned to Jessica.

"I would like to do some shopping then please Doctor Fielding." Jessica opened her bag and handed her a cheque for two thousand pounds, the start- up grant issued by the government. Enough to get bedding and living essentials, and of course, her true purpose of finding a new pet. Every fortnight she would get a standard fifty-four pounds to live off, until she can find work. Jessica explained all this to Peri and then they were ready to add substance to this place.

"Okay Peri, let's shop." Peri linked Jessica's arm, and they left the apartment to do their shopping. Jessica needed to locate Ben next and have him come to Peri's place, so while they shopped, she kept a keen eye out for him. Although he was back at the squat safe and sound, Jessica wasn't to know this. She didn't want any more people dead because of Ben and she was determined to stop him.

Back at the squat though, Ben managed to squeeze himself into the chill out room, where there was a party being celebrated. Judging by the amount of smoke in there, the party had been going on all day. A huge circle in the middle of the floor had formed and a large amount of mix had been cooked up.

"What's the cause for celebration then Minge?" Ben asked his friend, who was busy twirling the mix with a half- bent teaspoon.

"Oh, the new guy, he's brought all this gear and wishes to stay with us. He has nowhere else to go, because the police are after him for something. Anyway, you should say hello, I'll take you to him. You'll like him he's something special this one."

Minge stood up and led Ben to their new housemate. At the back of the squat was a large conservatory, and this is where the new squatter had chosen to live, a whole room all to himself, with no questions asked, as much drugs as you could handle, but just keep your nose out of my business was the contract.

"Here he is, come and meet Charlie" Minge added.

Ben's heart leaped up into his throat at the very mention of the name; of course it was Charlie Paramore. Just Ben's luck, he'd shopped him earlier, now he's sharing the squat with him. Minge had met Charlie whilst out and about and then brought him back to the squat. Judging by the number of drugs here, he'd raided Lucas' secret stash, then chosen to latch himself on to the nearest Hobo for cover. At the very least, Ben had the coat, so any trouble out of him and he'd take Charlie's soul there and then, but that meant he'd be showing Minge his power. Ben decided to wing it for now, take whatever abuse Charlie threw at him and deal with it later when it was quieter.

"Charlie, meet Ben" Minge introduced.

"You were the last person to see my brother alive, tell me what happened to him? Please, I have to know" Charlie did recognize Ben, but didn't know it was he who had shopped him. Ben's nervousness showed and the gangster knew he'd done something.

"I went to speak to him about laying off Stuart Shaw. He got angry with me and was shouting. Then he went red in the face and clutched his arm, then after a couple of seconds he was still on the carpet, I did call the ambulance." Ben lied, offering this as an icebreaker. Charlie knew that Lucas never lost his temper, he'd have Charlie do that for him, 'just had to ask'. What else are brothers for?

"The ambulance came about thirty minutes later, I was already at the house you see, and I spotted a stack of money missing too, so you really didn't try hard enough to save my brother, did you?" Charlie pointed out. Ben gulped and knew that Charlie was the real muscle in Lucas' group. "I don't care about the money, but you had something to do about my friends ending their lives, didn't you?" Charlie added. Minge just frowned at Ben; he couldn't believe they knew each other already.

"Hey, I'm gonna head back to the party, okay?" He interjected and sloped off again.

"Where did you hide their bodies?" Ben asked, knowing that with the coat on, Charlie would tell him.

"I wrapped them in tarp and dropped their bodies into a deep lagoon, under the creek." Everyone knew about the creek, it is one hundred feet deep in the middle. It could easily hide two goons from the police, that's if they were reported missing. Nobody had done and Ben knew he was in the clear so far. Later he would decide on a way to get rid of this inconvenience.

"Listen, I'm sorry about your brother really, but I didn't have anything to do with him dying like that, I swear," Ben charmed his adversary, and Charlie relaxed again.

"Okay then, you can leave me alone now. I'll only be here a couple of days. Here's some fags okay, now mind your own business alright?" Charlie tossed a twenty pack of cigarettes at Ben who caught them enthusiastically.

He smiled wryly at Charlie and left him alone as requested, Ben then returned to the chill out room and sat on the sofa once more. He opened the packet of cigarettes and smoked one, seeing as they were free, it tasted sweet and mellowed his thoughts instantly. The last one he smoked was days ago. One thing sailed through his mind though, he hadn't caused any ill deeds towards anyone else; he had foiled the Devil for once. It was close to midnight and three days away from the end of the month. But Charlie being under the same roof chafed at Ben's conscience a little bit. The circle of lightweights began to dwindle as the levels of their incapacitated states rose within them; they sauntered off to bed, leaving as per usual, Minge and Doorbell to mop up the remains of the mix. Ben laid his head on the arm of the sofa and decided to sleep the day off. His mind was still whirring around thinking about Minge bringing Charlie too close for comfort. Ben began to drift off to sleep. He usually talked to himself whilst sleeping, nearly everybody does this, but if you are wearing a goatskin coat, this could have a detrimental effect on things. At first Ben was muttering inaudibly, but then bright as a button he said this.

"Minge, go and strangle that Bastard Charlie. Seeing as you brought him here, you must get rid of him now!" Ben was quiet again.

Minge puffed out his last gulp of bong smoke and did as Ben had asked. Doorbell hurriedly scooped up her turn and ignored everything else going on. Minge rose and went down to the end of the corridor, out to the conservatory and over to Charlie who was sleeping deeply. Minge placed both hands around Charlie's throat and pressed his thumbs against his windpipe. The pressure woke Charlie, who slept with a blade in his pocket and summoned the energy to fish it out and slapped it into Minge's stomach twice. This made Minge squeeze even tighter around Charlie's throat. Minge tightened his grip further and being as wasted as he was, didn't even feel the blade repeatedly stab him, six, seven, eight times as he was choking the life out of Charlie who was frantically trying to struggle free. Charlie managed one more stab to the body of Minge before dying and dropping the blade down to the floor. Minge lay there bleeding to death on the conservatory floor, with Ben just a few metres away, sleeping soundly on the sofa, oblivious to what just happened. On Ben's coat sleeve the numeral changed once more, this time from VII to IX. Even in his sleep, Ben had caused utter devastation. This he wouldn't realize until morning. Ben had inadvertently killed a good friend; someone he'd known for years, was dead. A subliminal message from his subconscious had sent his buddy to his death.

By morning there was one hell of a kafuffle, a huge scream rang out through the squat, waking everyone including Ben. Doorbell had slept where she was last night. She felt a slight sickness and rushed away to the toilet. She stumbled in and sat there for a few moments. She'd had heavy sessions before but never felt quite like this. She was feeling extremely rough around the edges. She leaned her head against the basin as the bile began to rise in her throat. Then she was thoroughly sick. The screaming woman had stopped for now and Ben went to see where all the noise was coming from, and then he saw them. Minge had several stab wounds to his body; he looked grey and stiff. All his blood had oozed away from him across the floor. The screaming girl was standing in it too. Just a few feet from Minge's body lay Charlie. He was also grey and his throat was red raw where Minge had throttled him. Ben took one look at his sleeve and knew whilst sleeping he'd managed to kill two more people. It seemed whatever he did or didn't do, he couldn't break the deal he had made. All this was way out of control now. A crowd had formed to see what the commotion was, and then one responsible person stated the obvious.

"They are both dead. We need to get out of here, call the cops and don't bloody touch anything." Then he saw the girl standing in Minge's blood. He took out his mobile and called the police as everyone vacated the squat. Ben found Doorbell standing outside and she didn't even know Minge was dead. Ben thought it was best if he didn't tell her about him. Instead, he told her about a person they could call upon so long as she played along, but then he had the coat on didn't he, so naturally she'd obey his every command. Ben knew that they couldn't come back to this place again; the squat was gone forever, now it was a crime scene. He found a payphone around the corner and decided to call Jessica and to ask her for advice. He gave Doorbell a cigarette to smoke whilst he was inside the phone booth.

"Jessica Fielding!" She answered.

"It's Ben, something terrible has happened, I need your help, just for a couple of days, please?" He sounded lost and confused.

"What's so terrible Ben? What have you done?" She pressed him urgently, knowing it would be something awful.

"I'm not sure exactly how it happened, but my friend was killed last night and so too was Charlie Paramore, that gangster." Ben still had that same vagueness as his first sentence.

"Did you cause it? Do you know what happened?" Jessica said.

"Maybe, I don't know. All I remember is that I went to sleep after meeting Charlie at the place I stay. My mate had brought him back to hide from the police, but now one has been strangled and the other stabbed to death. I hadn't said anything to anyone as far as I can remember. Sorry to impose on you like this." Ben explained and Jessica offered him a way out and a place to hide for a while.

"I have an address you can meet me at. Do you know where Cortez Street is Ben? Flats fifty to fifty-five. Meet me there?" Ben hung up the phone and headed there. This was Peri's new place.

Chapter Seven

The Devil to Pay.

Jessica wasn't too sure what to do about Ben once she got there; she hadn't planned anything solid, or how to get that jacket off him. Secondly Peri was also none the wiser for his visit. Jessica would have to juggle everything once she'd got there. Ben reached the taxi rank where his good old reliable Cabbie worked, with Doorbell in tow, trying to keep her from knowing about their friend Minge. She kept on asking Ben questions.

"So, what happened at the squat? Why can't we go back there? Where's Minge? Why didn't you bring him too?"

"Cos there's only room for us two at my aunt's place okay, Minge is a big boy; he can take care of himself alright?" Ben fired back at her. He held her hand tightly and called inside the radio office.

"Hey! Haven't heard from you in days!" The Cabbie piped up as they entered.

"Well, we've been kicked out of our house. Somebody went and died, didn't they?" He double-checked with Doorbell. She just nodded to his charming influence. "Take us to Cortez Street, could you?" Ben asked. The Cabbie took up his keys and binned his new coffee straight away. He then escorted his fare to where Jessica was waiting.

Peri saw her pulling the car around into the driveway, she smiled and waved at her. Jessica responded with a casual nod then she parked. Peri had bought her new pet the day before, not a cockatiel, it was a Myna bird and now he was settled, singing along to the CD player, already picking up Peri's favourite song with a few shrill whistles at the chorus. Because of his sleek looks, she had called him Fabian of course. He was out on the stand she also bought, but with a guest coming, Peri put Fabian inside his enclosure in the other room. To keep him quiet she turned off the music and pulled the black sheet over to make him think it was night. Jessica buzzed the intercom, and

Peri went to let her in. The Doctor stepped into the apartment, but she had a strange look on her face.

"What's the matter with you?" Peri asked.

"Peri, it's Ben he's killed two more and now he's on his way over here. Sorry but he needs to be stopped before he does any more damage." explained Jessica, she was almost out of breath saying this.

"No! He can't come here. You deal with him, I'm going to my safe place", There is no way you can get that coat off him just by talking to him! Peri thought she should remind Jessica of that point, just one more time. She hurried to her room and lit the candles once inside the circle; she sat again lotus style to meditate.

Jessica moved toward the window; she was anxious now that she had to deal with Ben alone. When Jessica saw the taxicab pulling into the drive, she was a relieved woman to find Ben had brought a female companion with him and relaxed a little.

"Stay here Drive? I want to make sure this place is okay," Ben said as he took Doorbell by the hand and headed to the block of flats. The Cabbie turned off his engine and stayed where he was.

Jessica moved out of the apartment and into the hall. When Ben buzzed the main intercom Jessica pressed the open button for Ben and his friend to enter. Ben wasn't covered in blood and didn't look like he'd been in a struggle either. But when she looked at the sleeve of his coat, it was clear he had done something to harm those two people. She became wary again as he approached her. "Jessica this is Doorbell, she's a friend of mine from the squat. Say hello to my Aunt, Doorbell"

"My real name, if you like is Julie Hart, Doorbell is just a nickname they've given me," she said and shook Jessica's hand.

"You look tired Ben; you look starving too. Come inside and explain everything to me?" Jessica wanted to know all the facts. Meanwhile she was thinking of ways to prise that coat off him.

Ben just nodded and followed her in. He didn't want to say anything to force Jessica to do things. Jessica also knew this. In the bedroom Peri could hear Jessica come in with Ben and her eyes snapped open. The presence of whoever Ben was carrying was now in her new apartment, but unable to reach out to her, thanks to the circle of fire. Peri stayed still and listened to what was going on.

"This is not your apartment Jessica, who owns it?" Ben asked, but he didn't really ask, it was whoever had possession of him.

"The Government owns it, and Peri stays here. She's been discharged." Jessica looked over her shoulder at the bedroom door.

"Is she here now?" Ben strode towards the door and opened it to see Peri sitting in her circle, the candles glowed intensely around her in a protective hue of orange and yellow. So long as she stayed within this circle, she was safe, and Ben couldn't touch her.

"You shouldn't be here Ben. I warned you that if you don't take off the jacket, she will destroy you. Three more souls and you are hers, just do the right thing and end it all now?" Peri pleaded to him, but he was deaf to it. "You cannot hurt me, you must go somewhere hallowed, like a church and she can't hurt you there either." She added. Jessica and Doorbell were standing just behind Ben. Jessica quietly raised her arm up. She was holding a table leg, taken out of a flat packed box on the floor. She brought the table leg down diagonally and hit Ben across the head with it. He fell to the floor, reeling from the pain, his neck rung from the blow, but he wasn't unconscious. Ben rolled onto his back to face Jessica and shouted at Doorbell to help him.

"Doorbell, you're my friend. Take that leg off her and beat her to death with it?" Doorbell lunged at Jessica, grasped hold of the leg and they tussled with it for a few moments. Doorbell wrenched the leg away from Jessica and proceeded to bash her head in with it. She raised her hands up to protect herself against it, but Doorbell clouted Jessica hard enough, that it forced her back through the door. Ben and Peri could hear thuds and screams as Doorbell finished Jessica off with a flurry of hits to her face and head. As Ben came out of the room Doorbell was still standing there hitting Jessica over and over again. "Okay Doorbell, you can stop now!" And she did stop, the mahogany ooze from Jessica's head wounds were staining the carpet as it flowed away from her.

"Two more souls Ben Grantham! Two more souls!" Peri called after him from her safety zone.

Ben's sleeve changed again this time from IX to X. Ben grabbed Doorbell by the hand and ran away from the apartment; the Cabbie started his car immediately as they climbed back in. "Take me to the Rectory" Ben shouted. As Ben and Doorbell left, the candles surrounding Peri dimmed, letting her know that she was safe again. Peri caught the taxicab leaving and knew the company where he worked. She wrote down the car number and went to help Jessica. Knowing that she had already gone didn't faze Peri at all. She'd seen dead people before. Peri looked through Jessica's handbag and found her mobile phone, Stuart's number was the first on the list of missed calls, and Peri called it back.

"Jess, where are you? I've been trying to call you!" Stuart answered and Peri delivered the bad news.

"This is Peri Keeble. Sorry but Jessica is here at my apartment. Ben was here too. He made somebody kill her. Please come over I'm scared?"

"I'm coming over now. Where do you live?" Stuart felt the fury wash over him and went straight for his shotgun.

"Cortez Street, fifty to fifty-five." Peri replied.

"I will be there soon!" Stuart made for his car and slung the gun onto the back seat, stuffed a handful of cartridges into his jacket pocket, then started up the engine and careered the car with all his driving skills over to Peri's place.

Ben, Doorbell and the Cabbie were calmly driving towards Peter Flaws' Rectory, the only hallowed place that Ben could think of. It seems that Ben was now leaving a trail of bodies behind and witnesses. This had him worried; Peri was still back there with Jessica. Who knows what she would be doing now. They turned into the road on which the Rectory stood, and Ben knew that it was situated at the end about three quarters of a mile along. Meanwhile inside the Rectory, Peter was watching the evening news, he was seeing the report unfold about the two bodies from the squat recovered by the police. He knew that Ben used to stay there and wondered if he was responsible because of that coat, he was told about. Ben was screaming for help and he just laughed at him, his conscience pricked at him, and he became alert. If he can't stay there anymore, where was the first place besides his newfound Aunt's would Ben head to, mine of course? Peter thought. He quickly wrote a note and left it on the front door and instantly left the rectory. He then hurried towards the church, further down the lane; he stood inside and waited. "God protect me now" He whispered and then crossed himself. The Devil was coming, and he needed back up. Peter turned for inspiration from the Madonna and Christ icon hanging over the altar. "Of course! Holy water," he quickly searched for something to contain it. Just outside in the churchyard was an old glass cider bottle; Peter scooped it up and took it to the font. "Forgive me, a vessel for the Devil, but I need to contain some of your offering!" Peter prayed again, then crossed himself once more, after filling up the cider bottle, he knew how to protect himself from the forces of evil and began to prepare for Ben's arrival.

Stuart reached Peri's flat. He knew that Ben wouldn't be there, so he left the gun in the car; he buzzed the intercom for Peri to answer. She didn't even look outside and just buzzed Stuart into the apartment.

"Where is Jess?" was his only greeting as he rushed by her.

"Come on in, she's just over there!" Peri replied, staring at the back of him. All these people, treating her place like it was theirs. She followed Stuart in and knelt opposite him beside Jessica.

"Ben did this? So, he's still wearing that fucking coat of his then?" Stuart began his personal inquest.

"Well sort of, she hit Ben first, but he was able to ask his girlfriend to do it for him and yes, he is wearing that coat, but nobody can take it off him now, unless they destroy her first. Together, they are too powerful." explained Peri.

"Let's go and find out where they went to and do exactly that." Stuart ordered. Peri took Jessica's phone with her and followed him to his car. "Call the Cops and get them to come here and sort out Jessica. Then we can concentrate on the real task."

Stuart was like Fabian in most ways, so Peri just went along with him on this. Peri called the ambulance and the police to collect Jessica's body. She also called the taxi rank to inquire about a passenger called Ben Grantham and where he'd been taken. The controller told her that it was to the Rectory. She then told this to Stuart.

"They've done what I said and are heading for hallowed ground. Let's get ourselves to the Rectory and fast before there are two more deaths. By then we definitely won't be able to stop her!" Peri's insistence didn't need questioning and Stuart drove straight there.

Ben had reached the Rectory first and then told the Cabbie to go away and leave him there, a last command to his dear friend. He was still holding Doorbell and pulling her along to the front door. Ben found the note and read it: **Dear Ben, just saw the news about what happened at the squat. I believe you now, about your coat and what it can do. I can't face you and your Demon alone, so I have gone in search of divine wisdom. If you need me, I'll be at the church. I am sorry that I didn't believe you before. Have faith, your friend in kindness, Fr P S Flaws.**

"What does he mean by that?" Doorbell asked, she was reading the letter over Ben's shoulder.

"You needn't worry about that. Come on he's at the church, this way." Ben really couldn't explain about Minge; Doorbell would hate Ben for doing that to him. He took her hand again and walked briskly towards the church, down the old winding lane.

Thanks to Stuart's fast driving, he'd caught up with Ben and just saw the familiar tan coat disappear down the lane. He parked the car and reached behind the seats for his shotgun. Peri got out and waited for Stuart. Something about him felt safe, so being with Stuart was a wise option. She saw the gun, but she wasn't worried. Her own father Max was holding a rifle the last time she saw him. They huddled behind bushes first to see how far down the lane, Doorbell and Ben were. Upon seeing them halfway along, Stuart then followed in, down the lane with Peri slightly behind. Luckily, she still had the bottle of holy water in her cardigan. Stuart loaded cartridges into his shotgun and cocked the pump, ready for action. The noise could be heard by Ben's favourite voice, the metallic one from the coat.

"Someone's behind you Ben!" He stopped dead and made sure Doorbell didn't hear it either. Just behind him, Stuart was getting ready to take aim and fired a round, but Ben eluded him with a quick sprint. The shot sprayed into the trees just beside Doorbell. She was very startled and ran to the left until, finally she was far enough away from Ben. She ran fast into the graveyard. Stuart carried on walking to the church. He cocked the pump again but added caution, for now he knew Ben would be ready for him. Ben was more concerned about where Doorbell was. Doorbell ran right into the front garden. Peter then came from inside towards her.

"Listen, if you're with Ben, you are in mortal danger. Come with me please." He implored.

He took her by the hand and led her inside again to safety. Ben's primary concern was Doorbell finding out about Minge, who really was her only best friend. Ben was just somebody she liked to talk to every now and then, but without his influence to charm her, she resorted back to her own state of mind. The enchantment doesn't last long once you are more than one hundred yards away. He reached the front yard but crouched down behind the fence. He couldn't go inside, so he waited for Stuart to reach the same place. He would take him by surprise and grab for that gun he so loves. Then he could make him go and get Doorbell for him, just to explain things. Peter sat Doorbell down in the vestry and closed the door.

"What's your name girl?" He asked.

"Julie, friends call me Doorbell though," she replied.

"They aren't really friends then, are they? I'll just call you Julie." Peter felt useful here.

"Thank you, please tell me what is wrong with Ben. Why is he acting so crazy, running away and not telling me straight what's happening?" She pressed him.

"The coat he's wearing, he says it is possessed by Lucifer, who now owns his soul, with which he agreed to begin with. But I think now that friends are getting hurt, he's seeking shelter, but I can't help, you see I am on the side of our lord God and Ben is beyond help I'm afraid. With each soul the Devil captures, she becomes stronger, and Ben becomes weaker. The boy has had such tragic luck all his life, an easy target for an evil force to dominate." Peter explained.

"She? But I thought that Lucifer was..."

"...The Devil can manifest itself into many forms, man, woman or animal, whatever it is you believe that to be. Ben believes Lucifer is a woman." Peter felt it necessary to say this before Doorbell could complete her observations.

He then prepared her for the rest. "Ben has been involved in some bizarre things recently. He has caused the deaths of at least nine people, as far as I know. He's told me about seven of them, but I didn't believe him, because he wasn't wearing the coat you see. The last thing he said to me was that he was going home to get the coat and prove it to me. He doesn't have to do that anymore. The squat was on the news you see, a man called Charlie Paramore and another called Patrick Boaz, were killed at the squat," Peter paused to let Doorbell absorb the news. Patrick was Minge's real name; she remembered him telling her once. Her best friend had been killed by Ben!

"Ben killed them?" Doorbell quizzed, her expression was one of anguish and she crossed her arms over her chest and grabbed her shoulders for comfort.

"I think so Julie, I don't really know that, but if he's coming here. Maybe he wants to give some sort of confession, you know, get it off his chest? We'll just have to wait and see what he says," Peter replied. They sat quietly and waited for events to unfold.

Outside, Ben was still waiting for Stuart to emerge, and as he stepped into the gate Ben reached for the gun. Stuart squeezed the trigger, and it exploded loudly, echoing around the churchyard. Ben tore the gun away from Stuart and cocked another round into the chamber before pointing it at him. Peri stayed hidden, anticipating what Ben had planned. Peter and Doorbell had heard the gunfire from inside the vestry. Peter rose out of his chair and went to see what was going on.

"Stay in here Julie" he ordered Peter rushed over to the tall window nearest the altar and saw Ben pointing the gun at another man, whom he didn't know.

"So, Stuart, you found Jessica. Do you know she tried to kill me?" Ben pressed the shotgun into Stuart's chest.

"She's been going on about killing you for ages, ever since you tried seducing her," Stuart replied.

"I won't kill you if you go inside the church and get Doorbell out here for me." Ben gave the order. and Stuart went and did just that.

Ben walked behind him to keep the enchantment alive. Peter called to Doorbell soon as he could see Stuart coming into the church.

"Julie, to the bell tower, do it now, you'll be safe there!"

Doorbell ran two steps at a time, heading for the bell tower as Stuart entered the church. Peter stood and approached him, and he could see Ben standing outside holding the shotgun.

"You are now inside holy ground. She cannot harm you in here. Go that way and wait. I'll deal with Ben."

Peter pointed at the altar and Stuart headed there. Peter knew that Ben couldn't enter, and now he'd rescued two people's souls where Ben couldn't reach them. So long as they stayed inside, they were safe. Peri stayed hidden, but she had her holy water and took four sips from it. That was enough to hide her essence from the Devil. She continued to watch this stand-off. Peter stood inside, he was on one side of the door, as Ben stood outside, pointing the shotgun at Peter. He called from inside the church.

"You've got the note then my friend. What can I do to help you, Ben?"

"I wanted to show you what this coat was capable of. You did say that the proof is in the pudding, right?" Ben challenged him.

"I already know about Patrick and Charlie, and by the look on that man's face, you killed Jessica too."

"I didn't do it personally, I ordered Doorbell to kill Jessica, after she tried to stop me! As for Charlie and Patrick, they took each other out, I have no recollection of asking them to do that."

Peter could see the numeral X on Ben's coat sleeve and remembered him saying that last time the numeral was VII. "But look at your sleeve Ben, now it says X. That means three more souls have been added since I saw you last. How do you explain that then if you didn't have an influence over their deaths?"

"You killed Patrick, you liar!" called Doorbell. She had climbed to the top of the bell tower and through the hatch to the turreted roof, so she could see Ben.

"Stay inside Julie!" shouted Peter from inside the church. She ignored his advice and stayed there waiting for an answer.

"Tell me Grantham? Did you kill Patrick and Charlie?"

"Doorbell, I didn't mean to kill him. I swear. I was sleeping then," explained Ben. She could see his sleeve as explained to her by Peter and knew he was behind it fully or at least planned for it.

"I really hate you, Ben! You took my only true friend from me, how could you? I'm calling the police to tell them." She went to go back inside.

"Wait! Doorbell don't go back yet. Please let me explain?" Ben was testing whether the coat still worked on her or not and it did. Doorbell stopped and turned back around to face Ben. "I can't let you call the police Doorbell." Ben had a threatening stare in his eyes. Doorbell saw it finally. His eyes changed to a ruby red colour and his pupils changed to narrow slits. These, in her mind, were the Devil's eyes.

"YOU ARE THE DEVIL!" She screamed out loudly and went to move away from the roof.

"If you believe that then you should jump!" A voice called out from within him. Not a thought Ben was thinking of at the time. Doorbell climbed up on to the keystone. Peter rushed out and stood next to Ben so he could see.

"Don't do this Julie! All you have to do is go back inside and you will be safe!" Peter tried his best to stop her.

"Jump!" said a powerful voice and Doorbell stepped off the roof and plummeted to the ground. The concrete path below collected her body with a heavy thud. She groaned a little and then sighed her last breath.

"What evil is this? She was an innocent!" Peter exclaimed in full astonishment. He shook Ben by the shoulders. "You have the strength to stop her. Please Ben? I implore you to stop this now!"

"TOO LATE!" A thunderous voice came from everywhere.

"No, it's not! That's only eleven souls; there's one more to collect and I won't do this anymore!" Ben wouldn't have killed Doorbell; he just wanted to stop her from calling the police.

"Check your arm, Ben Grantham. The deal is complete, twelve souls for your freedom," came the same booming voice.

Ben looked at the sleeve and it had changed from X to XII. Then the penny dropped, they had sex recently, didn't they? Doorbell was unknowingly carrying Ben's child. Ben began to lift off the ground and turned around to face Peri. She was crouched behind the trees all this time. She saw Doorbell fall to her death and then the voice controlling Ben called out to her. "Are you still my disciple child?"

"No! I have seen what you can do. Fabian was my master, and you took him from me." Peri replied and through Ben the voice returned this chilling message.

"Then you leave me very little choice, I must take a disciple; Ben here will do!" The voice laughed.

"Ben! That'll make you Judas in my eyes. If you go to her this way, you will be little more than that to me from now on. I cannot be your friend." Peter warned him.

Ben needed friends and family to make him feel wanted and he'd just lost the one real family member he would have cherished all of his life, his unborn child, that was being carried around by Doorbell. This was too much to take and an overwhelming surge of reality came flooding forward. He had been weak, a foolish man who fell for the charms of something he didn't understand, but now he had the chance to correct those mistakes. He remembered that ugly look of his reflection in that window.

"I will not let you take me. Stuart come out here!" Ben called and Stuart came out of the church and faced Ben, hovering above the ground. He was a little bit surprised by Ben's next request. "Take that weapon and use it on me, please. It's the only way to stop all this. I made a mistake and I'm sorry. You are the only one who came, who can correct that mistake. Besides, you owe me one, remember?" Stuart knew what he did for him concerning Lucas and his heavies. He retrieved the gun from the grass, it was already primed to fire, and he held it closely at Ben's chest. "Do not hesitate, pull the trigger, do it now!" Ben commanded, with his one final enchantment. Stuart fired the gun at Ben. The shot sent Ben spinning backwards against the cedar tree, which stood just behind Ben, where Peri was hiding. She gasped as Ben landed on the floor, his head bent backwards facing her and he spoke for the final time. "Thank you, Peri Keeble!" Peter, Stuart and Peri knelt by Ben's side; just to make sure he was indeed dead and not some trick played by the Devil herself. He wasn't moving and neither was Doorbell. There was a nice even spray of shot in the middle of Ben's chest. As Peter lifted him forward, the coat was now loose. He dragged it from Ben's body and folded it up into a neat square. He then took it inside the church and hid it in one of the prayer pews for safe keeping. This jacket would not claim another victim of circumstance like Peri Keeble and Ben Grantham.

Stuart and Peri helped to tidy up. They decided to report Ben and Doorbell's demise to the police. The summary would be that this was a crime of passion, once they found out that Doorbell was pregnant. The remaining three all swore to keep these events secret. They had halted the Devil's progress for now.

This concludes story two 'Soul Searcher.'

The End.

Story Three
The Priest.

Foreword

With nobody to pay for Ben Grantham's funeral that responsibility falls to a Priest called Father Peter Flaws, he was the only man who knew Ben well enough to care about him. He has been left with all of Ben's belongings including the Goatskin coat of course. This mysterious garment immediately takes possession of Peter's soul. He may well regret the day he let Ben Grantham, into his life.

Chapter One

The undeniable truth.

Sixty-year-old Father Peter Flaws would be required to preside over four funerals in the coming few weeks. With a heavy heart he also had to conduct the cremation ceremony of Ben Grantham. He simply couldn't allow the Devil to have Ben's body after what he'd witnessed. The first funeral was for Jessica Fielding. There weren't many people at the service. She was out of favour with her family, but Stuart and Peri came to send her off. If she were alive, that would be all she would have wanted here. Her will was simple; everything she had went to Stuart, including her house. Peter was reading the funeral rites by the graveside.

"Our Lord God, we commend this body to the ground, so that her soul may ascend. Let Jessica lie in peace and guide her to eternal sleep." Then he began with 'The Lord is my Shepherd' prayer. After which the chief mourner signalled to lower the coffin down. There weren't many pallbearers, only two on either side. Stuart stood, with tears strewn over his cheeks, gripping the earth with his fist, and then he sprinkled it on to the coffin lid beneath him. Peri stood close by, watching intently, she didn't feel any emotions about the occasion, and she certainly wouldn't be coming back for Ben's service. She linked Stuart's arm with hers and they stood quietly offering prayers for Jessica. Peter shook Stuart's hand now that his part was done.

"I hope you find peace Stuart. God be with you at this time." Peter left following a quiet nod from Stuart. He went back to the vestry for some peace and quiet.

The other three ceremonies were conducted in similar fashion, again with a scant audience and subdued send offs. Back at home, Peter had time to reflect on recent events, but dwelt on his regret that he didn't believe Ben's story when he needed his help. He also weighed up the difference between good deeds and evil actions. Why when you pray for something positive, it seldom delivers, and then you wish for something bad to happen, it does so instantaneously. Peter drank some brandy and sat thinking about the coat he had taken from Ben. Did it really influence the man through the will of the Devil, or was he just plain crazy? Peter measured this carefully, before lifting himself up from his easy chair and stared in the mirror.

"Well, there's only one way to find out." He finished his brandy and headed back out to the church.

As he got there, Peter slowly walked over to the Madonna and Christ icon hanging over the pulpit. He stared at their faces, looking down on him. Sadly, Peter moved away and knelt by the altar to pray, dipped his two fingers into the font and made the sign of the cross before offering his prayer.

"Lord, forgive me, I should have helped Ben, instead I poured scorn on him and turned my back to it all. Before I realized, it was too late to do anything."

Just as he finished with an Amen, the pew with the goatskin coat behind him started shaking and drew Peter's attention. He turned on his knees and stared at the seat. Hesitantly, he stood and walked toward it. The pew was still shaking violently until he reached it. Peter flipped the lid of the pew open, stared at the goatskin coat lying inside. He lifted it out and looked at the markings on it. He caressed the sleeve with the letter B on it, and just over that was the numeral XIII, which meant the Devil had claimed Ben's soul after all, even though he had decided to end his own life. Peter was a large man and the coat held a slightly smaller frame, from the first time Peri Keeble had worn it. She was the only person so far to have escaped its influence, but that also inflicted mental torture on her. Even so. Such a brave person thought Peter.

"If I try it on in here, nothing can harm me, I'm in the house of God after all." He muttered to himself.

Peter slipped his hand into the left-hand sleeve and to his astonishment, the sleeve grew to match his arm's length. He slid his other arm in and pulled the cuffs forward so that the coat could wrap around his portly frame, and it did so with room to spare. The shoulders were a bit tight, but they soon adjusted when he widened them. A perfect fit, it was surprisingly comfortable, like another layer of skin. But when he held it out in front of him moments after taking it off, it felt very heavy.

"I think you should come home with me; it will be safer. If somebody should find you here, you might rise again."

He folded the coat over his arm and walked back home with it. On the left-hand elbow another letter P appeared and the same letter again lying on its side facing the standing one. The coat had recharged itself and Peter Flaws was now the target. A conflicted man would be easy to control; all it had to do was gently push all the right buttons.

Peter hung the coat on the back of his easy chair and stood looking at it against the glow of his warm log fire. He thought to himself; that if he could resist wearing this sheath of evil, no harm could be caused. But he had already tried it on, and the coat could only get stronger if the correct numbers of souls are gathered. Maybe he should have buried it at the church; however, he wanted to test his theory.

"So how do you work then?" Peter asked it.

"I work in different ways. For Peri Keeble who was a strong young lady, I was a lure, so that she would become the vessel for me to travel on earth." A hollow voice answered back, to his amazement, a female voice but unfamiliar to him.

"Why did you choose my friend Ben?"

"Oh no, he chose me. We needed each other, but halfway through he discarded me but by then my strength had tripled. With each dastardly deed, I simply became stronger. Too strong for Ben."

"You tempt your victims in with their heart's desires, then take control of them, possessing their souls? That's the very definition of evil to me." Peter offered that just to appease his conscience.

"Those views are outdated these days, you shouldn't call them victims anyway, they chose the path they walked, good and evil will always tread the same plane. Just like dark and light, right and wrong. It's written and cannot be changed." The voice seemed wise and every bit the equal to Peter's questions.

"Enough questions, I must sleep now."

Peter turned away from the coat and headed to his bedroom. Just before he reached his door. the voice called out loudly, filling the room.

"Don't forget to say your prayers"

"I'll never forget." Peter replied and went inside.

He knelt beside his bed and looked up at his statue of Mary, clasped his hands together with rosaries and prayed. "Oh God Almighty! My father in heaven, please protect me in my hour of weakness. I confess to have spoken to your former general and fear she may be trying to claim me. With all your wisdom I plead for your forgiveness. May you watch down on me from high and protect me from evil, your servant and subject, Peter. Amen!" He stood and nervously climbed into bed, pulled the eider- down up to his throat and nestled his chin. He relished the warmth it offered him, and he instantly went to sleep…

…As the dawn chorus outside woke Peter, he turned his waking head towards the window and to his astonishment, a chair with the goatskin coat was there before his eyes. Peter sat up and pulled the covers with him, cowering behind them.

"I said a prayer to God to protect me. What are you doing in here?" he asked from beneath them.

"Let us see how long it takes for that request to actually happen, shall we?" replied the coat.

Peter was confused; he had left the coat at a considerable distance away in the sitting room. "How did you get in here?" He asked it.

"You sleepwalk Peter, but of course you wouldn't know that though. Being asleep at the time, you carried me in here." lied the coat. Peter conceded that it could have been possible. "Looks like you were hankering for my protection, I can provide that solace, if you'd let me." offered the coat.

"No, not ever!" Peter was defiant; he wasn't going to be tricked into wearing it. Then as Peter began dressing, he heard three sharp knocks on the door.

"Quick, it's the police, they want to question you about all the recent deaths. Put me on and I'll protect you. I promise." The coat was too tempting this time, as a wave of panic came across Peter.

"But I haven't done anything." Peter said innocently.

"Father Flaws? It's Detective Constable Bill Klein; we need a few words with you please." came the bellowing voice from the other side of the door.

"Hurry put me on. Together he'll believe anything we say to him." a final offer from the coat.

Peter grabbed the coat, slung it around his barrelled frame. The coat swathed him in confidence, and he marched towards the front door.

"Gentlemen! Please forgive me, I was dressing, what could I do to help you?" Peter smiled and the two officers at the door relaxed.

The first police detective to Peter's left was tall and thin, in his early thirties. He wore a blue two-piece suit without a tie. The second to his right was shorter, and forty to forty-five years of age. He had red hair, and he wore an olive green jacket and dark brown trousers, which reminded Peter of a tree in his garden at the church. He noticed the coat on Peter, but didn't comment.

"We are making routine inquiries into the deaths of Ben Grantham and Julie Hart. You were a witness to the incident, weren't you?" said the second detective.

"I'm sorry, but I didn't get your name there, Sir." Peter was looking at the man expectantly.

"DS John, Father," he flashed up his identity card.

"Please come in and take a seat. Do you want some tea?" Peter offered.

"That would be good of you, thank you Father," replied DS John. Peter went away to the kitchen and made the tea. Whilst there he consulted the coat on his next move.

"What should I say? They seem very determined." observed Peter through the hatch of his kitchen.

"Just say what you like, they'll believe you, remember I'm protecting you. See how quickly your prayers are answered." The coat was whispering back at Peter. DC Klein was looking back through the hatch at him.

"Sugar?" Peter asked as he noticed the man staring.

"None for me please, one and a half for the Sarge, both white. Cheers!" Bill answered. Peter spooned in the sugar as requested and brought the teas through.

"Now then, what is it you need from me?" Peter began as he placed the teas down between the two detectives.

"How exactly did Julie Hart die? We already know how Ben got killed." DS John inquired.

"Apparently, she jumped to her death, when she learned Ben had caused the death of her best friend Patrick Boaz, but I wasn't there to see it. I was inside trying to calm down another man, Stuart Shaw. He was distraught over the death of his partner, Jessica Fielding." Peter replied with such speed and conviction; DS John had trouble writing down his explanation.

"Right. I see, can we also ask you, did Ben have anything to do with the death of Dr Fielding?" DC Klein asked.

"No, that was Julie Hart, Ben didn't do anything to her," defended Peter.

"Thank you, that ties in with the evidence taken from the scene of the crime, but we shouldn't have told you that," explained DS John.

"That's okay. I'm a Priest, you can confess all to me and it will stay with me. You needn't worry about it," replied Peter.

"Thank you for your time. We have all we need," the DS left the last of his tea and ushered his colleague out again.

"Goodbye gentlemen, hope to see you again under better circumstances," Peter closed the door as they reached the car. "Yes, they believed everything I said, that's amazing." Peter was enjoying the power of the coat a little bit too much here.

"See what I told you, I can offer you protection a lot quicker than God can, don't you think?" The coat had delivered on its promise to protect him.

"Maybe so, but I am not about to get carried away with this. You won't turn me like you did with my young friend Ben," Peter kept his defiant head once again.

Then he tried taking the coat off, but it just wouldn't budge. He tried ripping the sleeves downwards, but he stumbled forward and struck his head against the mantelpiece. As he moved back away from it holding his forehead in pain, the coat became tight. He sat on the sofa feeling very constricted.

"You cannot remove me right now; you made a pact with me. Now that I have sworn to protect you against all adversities you face, I must honour this. You have twelve days under my protection and not a day later," the coat had a vice-like grip on Peter and wouldn't let go until the job was complete.

"I will find a way to get you off me, before the twelve days are up," Peter warned the coat. Soon as he said it, the coat loosened, and Peter felt comfortable again.

"Give it your best shot, Mr Flaws." challenged the coat.

The name of the man spoke volumes. Never before had the coat encountered such a worthy recipient, a servant of God, with a conflict of faith; nobody could be more suitable. The coat was going to enjoy this challenge.

Peter sat miserably on the sofa. He had been harangued into wearing the coat and now he regretted doing so, because he either must die before, or allow the coat to do as it wished with him for the twelve days contract and probably die also. This was his dilemma. He decided not to discuss anything else with the coat whilst it was on him. Peter's thoughts were his own and he wasn't going to share them. Now that the edgy atmosphere had gone, Peter was able to go about his daily routines, preparing his sermon for evensong and practising playing his favourite instrument, the oboe. He played at a very high standard, and anyone walking outside, would hear that haunting sound of his playing and stop to listen. Today it was a more sorrowful tune, the Ducks' theme from 'Peter and the Wolf.'

Chapter Two

Let the games begin.

With the evening quickly drawing upon him, Peter wondered how he could disguise the coat and still go about his business, attending his evening sermon; he had a good turnout on Wednesdays for a reason he couldn't fathom. In the church where he served, there were at least half a dozen busybodies that would gossip about the coat and it would be all around the parish by midnight. To top it all, his vestments were kept at the church. Then he remembered that he kept a great coat in his wardrobe, for heavy rain. He moved to the bedroom and checked. Peter grabbed it out and swung it around him, then fastened up the buttons. Hmm it still fits, he thought to himself, gazing in the mirror at it and making doubly sure the goatskin coat could not be seen underneath.

Five o'clock arrived and Peter stepped out for his little walk to the church. By a small miracle it started to rain, which saved him hunting for excuses if he met anyone along the way. It took his usual ten minutes to reach the church, and a small group of his congregation were milling around outside, eager to go in. Mrs Anthea Dredge and her younger sister Gail were the first to notice Peter. He had a small crush on Gail, but his vow of celibacy prevented him from pursuing the matter. They were always there to hear his sermon, loved hearing him speaking and interpreting the gospels. Both were aged between forty and forty-five. They also had dark red hair. Anthea was a little broader in shape than Gail, which made her look stern. Gail was single, didn't have children and her hips told that story, as they were narrower, compared to the other four women standing together, who all had given birth. Anthea, Mrs Edith Walker, and her Husband Lee, Ms Ellen Bracken and her two sons Charlie and Bernard, finally Ms Stella Coleman and her new beau Trevor. Ellen always dragged her reluctant sons to church, to learn morals and standards. She was in her sixties, tall and thin as a stick. Her sons who were sixteen and seventeen respectively, only came to the Wednesday sermon, because Lionel Bracken, Ellen's husband was home at the weekends and deemed that a time for the family only. Edith and Lee Walker are the same age as Peter, went to the same school as him and they married a year after leaving school. They have two children who are in the armed forces and actively serving in conflict right now. Stella Coleman has been widowed and for years kept men at arm's length until she met Trevor, who whisked her off her feet. Stella has two children, Ailsa and Kilo, an unusual name for a boy, but she always wanted originality with the names she chose for her children. These were the people standing, waiting to go in. The others were beginning to come in behind Peter, a short walk up the road.

Peter swung the small gate open and walked with confidence towards the entrance of the church. Just then a huge force compelled him to freeze in his tracks. He tried to step further along the path, but he couldn't muster the power to move. It was as if someone had attached a bungee cord to his back and it was pulling him back away from the church. The goatskin coat prevented him from going into the church and the others realized he was having difficulties. Peter remembered that the wearer of the coat could not enter a holy place of worship. So, this meant he wouldn't be able to deliver his sermon or even enter the church for at least another twelve days. Peter needed to think of a good reason why he couldn't go inside, but instead he spontaneously vomited, stumbled over and lay on his back by the grass. Anthea and Gail rushed to his aid and the others just watched. They had never seen Peter ill before.

"Father, are you okay?" Anthea asked and she moved to the left side of Peter. Gail followed her and flanked him in support. By this time at least thirty people of his congregation were standing and looking on.

"No, I can't move. I'm sorry everyone, but I cannot open up today. I don't feel very well at all." He fell to the floor again.

"Come on we'll take you home then." Gail offered. "Ladies and gentlemen, the sermon is cancelled tonight due to the sudden illness of Father Flaws, sorry please go home until you hear more news." Gail announced this and helped Peter up and over towards her car. "It's okay Anthea, I'll take him home by myself, thank you everybody." Gail said as she loaded Peter into the passenger side of her Mini Cooper. The congregation just stared as she drove away and out of sight. Gail kept gazing over at Peter; she was worried. He'd never been violently ill like this before. She drove to the end of the lane and turned into Peter's driveway.

"Thank you, Gail, thank you very much." Peter started feeling better the moment he reached his home, but just to be sure, Gail followed him to the front door of the house.

"I just wanted to see you in safely. Maybe I can make you something while you settle in?" Gail again offered out of kindness.

Peter felt something nudge him hard in the back and forcibly move him closer to Gail; she held out her arms to stop him lurching over. Then his hands plunged accidentally, straight onto her breasts. He felt another nudge and he squashed Gail against the wall of his small porch. Gail pushed her arms out to brace herself against his bulk and she eased him away a little.

"I am so sorry Gail," Peter said, still shocked that he'd done that to her.

"It doesn't matter. I'm sure it was an accident, you aren't well and quite clearly not yourself," replied Gail with understanding.

They were still in an awkward embrace, but Peter managed to get the key from his coat pocket and opened the door. Whatever was forcing them together had stopped just for now and they were able to get into the house.

"You relax and I'll get you that drink" ordered Gail and plonked him down on his chair. "What can I get you?"

"Tea would be absolutely fine, thanks," Peter replied, panting a little.

Gail went to the kitchen and made the tea; she'd been here before and knew her way around. While she was gone Peter scolded the coat for its untimely intervention.

"What the blazes was that? I didn't want Gail knowing how I felt about her. I took a vow."

"Oh relax, she feels the same. Why else would she send her sister packing and bring you home by herself? She's lonely, and her stifling sister is preventing her from enjoying herself." The voice of the coat replied.

"Nothing could ever happen. Please don't interfere." Peter begged.

"You'll regret this for the rest of your life. Who's going to tell? They certainly won't believe me. Anyway, I've done my bit; the rest is up to you."

The voice of the coat ended their brief conversation, as Gail returned with the teas. Peter sat and watched Gail pour the tea and studied her while she did this. Gail removed her coat and gloves, revealing her clothes under it. A knee length beige skirt, a pale blue open-necked cardigan, and this had a loose button at the top. If Gail leaned too far now, she'd be revealing to Peter exactly what she was wearing underneath. Peter privately wished this to happen. Soon as he had done, Gail bent forward, the button came open and her breasts could be seen instantly, encased in a heavily strapped bodice. Peter couldn't help staring at her. When she looked back and noticed him staring, she clutched her cardigan together, blushed and moved away with her tea and sat down, completely embarrassed.

"My apologies Father, that was most indecent of me." Gail remarked, admonishing herself at the same time.

"Don't worry Gail, I won't say a thing," Peter spread his palms out wide and accepted her apology. Gail drank her tea down and sat awkwardly clutching her cardigan.

"Thank you for bringing me back tonight, Gail. I just don't know what happened. I was fine until I got to the church. Luckily you were there though." Peter broke the awkward silence and Gail responded.

"Are you cold? You're still wearing that big coat. Why don't you take it off?"

"Uh! Oh, yes. I am, sorry but I can't just now. Why don't you finish your tea, I shouldn't keep you here too long. Your sister will worry." Peter was keen to hide the nasty coat underneath.

"I'm sorry, I must be a burden. Of course I'll go now," replied Gail.

She rose to leave, and Peter did likewise, but the great coat snagged on the sharp corner of the coffee table and tore it open. This made Peter lunge forward again. Gail could clearly see the goatskin coat underneath it. Peter just looked at her knowing she would recognize all the ancient symbols on it.

"Evil! That's just evil! Father why would you wear such a despicable thing?" She went to leave immediately. Clearly, she had seen this kind of thing before. How else would she have reacted this way, thought Peter.

"Gail please, I can explain!" He went to stop her from leaving.

"No, you can't tell her about me, I won't let you," the voice of the coat again spoke out of turn. A poker from the fireplace shot past Peter's cheek, making him flinch as the poker plunged straight through Gail's chest. She shrieked loudly as she was thrown forward and landed a metre away from the front door.

"WHY DID YOU DO THAT?" Peter roared. He stood completely shocked at the sight of Gail's still body, oozing blood across the ground.

"It was necessary, she would have told everyone, and you know it," the voice of the coat replied coldly.

"Everybody knows she brought me here and will certainly know I had something to do with this," added Peter, panicking at this stage.

"Don't worry Peter, I'll protect you. Now grab the rug she's lying on and pull her outside to the car," ordered the coat.

Peter did as he was told. He wrapped the rug tightly around Gail's legs, twisted both ends and pulled her toward the door and outside to the car.

"Now place her in the passenger seat and drive her halfway down the lane." The coat commanded again.

Peter did this and strapped the seatbelt around Gail's shoulders to keep her up whilst he drove the short way down the lane. "Stop here and move her over to the driver's side. Once you've done that get out and start walking away. You don't want to see what happens next."

The coat was very forceful, but he obeyed the instructions and pulled Gail across to the driver's side from outside the car. He started to walk away from the car and after fifty metres or so it caught fire and started to burn fiercely. Peter turned to look and saw the poor Mini drenched in hot flames and the woman he secretly loved burning inside of it.

"How on earth am I going to keep it together enough, so as not to seem suspicious?" Peter asked.

"Don't worry Peter, this looks like a harmless accident; nothing to do with you," the coat tried soothing the issue, but it wasn't working.

"Damned right this has nothing to do with me. You can't keep killing people to supplement your existence. This must stop."

Peter tore his great coat right off and stared at the left arm of the goatskin coat. There, one singular notch under the capital Ps and Peter knew the coat was using him to gather souls again.

He stumbled back to the house and cleaned up all evidence of Gail's visit. After this he wrote a letter to Bishop Andrews of Maythorne and Boundford, explaining his sudden illness and the need to find a locum, so he can recover. Finally, he raked the gravel on the driveway to remove the Mini's tyre marks. Peter tried to get some rest, but he couldn't. The guilt of what happened with Gail prevented this and the worry of what might happen if Anthea became suspicious. The following morning came by quickly; he didn't speak once to the evil garment that had attached itself leech-like to him for the past two days. Knowing he only had eleven days left pleased him somewhat. Peter felt the need to get out of the house for a few hours, get some fresh air and contemplate on what transpired last night.

Before doing this, Peter visited Ben Grantham's unmarked grave, using the public footpath and passing the burning remains of Gail's car. He arrived and knelt by the headstone. He stared at it and then began cursing loudly.

"Damn it, Ben, why did you bring this into our lives. You've caused nothing but hurt and heartache ever since. You're a total fool, but now it has me. Well let me tell you old friend, it isn't going to beat me!" Peter spat those last poisonous words out like venom and threw his crucifix down and walked away. He kept on walking away from the grave, the church and his home until he had walked the whole three miles to town.

The wreck of Gail's car had been discovered. Two dog walkers had found it and called it in. A Fire Rescue Team was busy trying to cut what was left of Gail from the car. A police car and a Coroners' wagon stood waiting to collect the body to begin the arduous task of identifying her. Only part of the number plate was left untouched. PC Myles Gibbons, one of the officers at the scene, radioed this in to find out the car's owner. After finishing with this task, he returned to another police officer present, PC Callum Byford.

"This one is strange. Nobody heard this car crash, and there are no impact marks on the bloody thing," said Callum, as he scribbled into his notebook.

"What are you saying then? It just landed here and caught fire," mocked Gibbons.

"No mate. To cause this amount of damage to a car, the impact would be huge, and the car is too new to have had any engine problems. That's what I mean, no crash, no fire, very weird." explained Callum.

"So, someone started the fire, is that what you're saying? Have you tried asking the fire crew their opinion?" quizzed Myles.

Gibbons walked across to ask them that question, Callum returned to the squad car and waited; he would do what it takes to find out what happened here. The whole thing felt very iffy to him, and asking firemen stupid questions wouldn't solve this. The body was cut free and taken to the wagon. Now the responsibility of telling a loved one that this person had died fell to these two officers, as soon as they knew this person's name.

Anthea rang her hands with worry; Gail was never away from her side for more than a couple of hours, until now though. She had taken the stricken Father Flaws home and surely would have returned immediately, but being out all night was absurd to think about. Anthea called the police, to report her sibling missing.

"Hello! Maythorne Police." A woman answered.

"Oh hello! I'm Anthea Dredge and I wish to report that my younger sister has disappeared. I'm very worried that something has happened to her. If you'd like I can come by and give you a photo of her."

"Yes, please do that Mrs Dredge, then we'll conduct a search for her, okay? Please don't worry too much, will you?" said the woman in response.

"I will try, thank you, I'll be along shortly," Anthea finished the call and went outside.

Chapter Three

Extenuating circumstances.

Gail's body had been at the mortuary for three hours. The coroner had been away at another examination, but now he'd arrived and was being briefed by the two policemen who were at the scene of Gail's accident.

"We've checked the partial on the registration plate against the DVLA database. Only ten new electric blue Mini Coopers have been bought this year, and only one belonging to a Miss Gail Eldridge in the Maythorne area. We can assume the lady on the table is this woman. The accident was very strange, no impact, nor was there tampering of any kind," explained Callum Byford.

"Yeah, and the fire rescue team inspector says there wasn't a combustible compound that caused the fire either, she just caught fire," added Myles Gibbons.

"That is very odd, very well I'll examine the body and deliver my results later today. You should concentrate on finding her next of kin then; if you think it is indeed Gail Eldridge," opined the coroner. The two policemen left the morgue to do this.

The coroner was the esteemed Dr Emile Jordan ME, aged fifty-six. He had studied bodies such as Gail's since he graduated. He was a driven individual, very succinct and methodical. He looked a little like George Clooney. His colleagues commented on the resemblance, and he was very flattered by it.

He called for two of his lab assistants and then scrubbed in to look at Gail's injuries. The flesh smelled of burning, but it was only a slight aroma, as if covering something else up, enough fire to take two or three layers of skin off at any rate. Emile laid his surgical instruments down in a row, all in order of what was needed first, scalpel, rib separator, chest clamp, sample dish, weighing scales and bone saw. His two assistants - a male called Hugh Daniel, and a female called Kerry Staines, arrived in similar attire to help collect data from the victim. They were the same age, twenty-five and started at the mortuary at the same time. By now they were used to the look and smell of the place. Emile set the ball rolling.

"Right, now you're here I can begin with the examination of Jane Doe, cut from the car at the scene of a suspicious accident." He said.

"Burned alive was she, Doctor?" asked Hugh.

"Too early for that analysis, give me half an hour and I'll tell you," Corrected Emile. Kerry stayed quiet, she always observed, and didn't have the confidence of Hugh to question Emile about things. She was good at taking notes and samples though.

Emile began the cutting then paused after he saw the hole the size and shape of a twenty pence piece a centimetre from the middle of her left breast. He checked the police notes handed to him, not a mention. So, he quickly knew they were looking for a sharp instrument that was not present at the scene, and probably the cause of death, before the body was placed in the car. Whatever the weapon, it had been thrown with such force that it had sailed clean through her body and out the other side, piercing her heart on the way out. That was almost certainly the cause of death, but he continued the study for further findings. He beckoned to Hugh as he tried to turn Gail onto her side, just to look at the wound from the back.

"I would say we're looking for a fire poker or something of that kind, which is what has killed her," Emile looked over at Kerry and she neatly wrote everything down. "She was driven to the spot where the fire took place, this is the puzzling thing. There's not a smell of anything combustible and this my fellows is a very clumsy attempt at a cover up." Emile concluded his preliminary report. Then he needed his assistants to sign off and agree with his verdict.

Anthea arrived at the station to see the police about her missing sister. She parked the car and went inside. The policewoman at the desk spotted her coming and pulled the window open.

"Hello there! How can I help?"

"I'm Anthea Dredge. I called earlier about Gail, my sister. She's missing you see, and I was told to come across and give a description to you, so we can find her. I'm very worried."

"And what is the surname of your sister please Mrs Dredge?"

"Eldridge, Gail Eldridge," Anthea was speaking loud enough for Callum to hear, and he looked over at the reception window. He had already heard of that name this morning, so he came to the window and took over the inquiry.

"Hello, I'm Callum Byford. I heard you mention a name; would you mind coming this way with me? I would like a few words."

"Why? Have you found her?"

"Just follow me this way Mrs Dredge. I'll explain it all in there." Callum opened the door to a small room with a desk, two chairs and a computer in it. Anthea followed in and sat down clutching her bag, fearing the worst. "Can you describe your sister for me please Mrs Dredge?"

"Forty-three, hair the same colour as mine. She is taller, but thinner than me and she drives a blue Mini, almost new. She's been missing since yesterday evening. She doesn't do that, she knows not to." Anthea explained.

"I see, well this morning I was called to a scene because a car that you described was found on fire and a person inside, who I'm afraid was dead when we got there. We are treating it as suspicious right now. Unfortunately, we cannot tell if it is your sister yet, tests are going on."

"Found where? Please I must know"

"Quarter Mile Lane, halfway down, sorry." Callum stopped when he noticed Anthea was weeping.

"She had taken Father Flaws home. He'd been taken quite ill you see. She drove him home, then she was going to come back home." Anthea revealed.

Callum now had something to investigate, but he hadn't been told yet about the hole in Gail's chest. He wrote down what Anthea had said. He would check this out later and showed her to reception again.

"We will check out what you've said to us, then we'll contact you. If in the meantime your sister does come home, please tell us, okay?"

Callum tried to swerve Anthea away from thinking it was Gail, but with what she had just said, there couldn't be much doubt. He walked out with Anthea to her car. He looked to his right to see Gibbons, arms folded, impatiently waiting for him. He nodded gently at Anthea, left her and went over to Gibbons.

"Let's go and see Father Flaws. See if he saw anything last night." He slapped Gibbons on the shoulder and climbed into the squad car.

Peter just wandered through Maythorne High Street, oblivious to everything around him and ignoring anything coming from the goatskin coat. People were staring at the coat but not making any comments about it. Walking the opposite way was Stuart Shaw. He noticed Peter and saw he was wearing the very damned thing that killed his beloved Jessica. Peter walked past ignoring him and Stuart grabbed him by the shoulders, which forced him to stop. Stuart fired three quick questions at him.

"Why are you wearing that? It killed Jessica. How could you be so callous and why are you wandering around at eleven in the morning?"

"Get off me Stuart, don't pry or you'll get yourself killed. One person has already died because of me. I don't want more on my conscience." Stuart let go of Peter's shoulders and he began to stride away from him.

"I'll help you Peter, I promise. I'll get you free from that abomination, so help me I will!" Stuart yelled after Peter.

No sooner had he said that; a large piece of brick came from a shop roof and hit him on the head, blood began trickling from the wound and he collapsed. It had wiped him out completely. A gathering of people stopped to help him.

"We can't have him telling anyone. When he wakes up, he'll have forgotten this," explained the coat.

"Well, let's hope so anyway," Peter mumbled this and continued to walk further away from the Town Centre and populated areas.

After visiting the police station, Anthea was driving home when she spotted Peter walking aimlessly. She pulled over to the side of the road and wound down her window.

"Oh Father, can we speak please?" She called after him.

Peter halted and the coat spoke up but quietly. "Speak to her and don't worry, I've got your back."

With that assurance he turned to face Anthea, who stepped out of her car and stood under him as she always did when speaking to him. At first, she didn't notice the coat Peter had on. All the symbols had become faded and inconspicuous.

"Anthea, how are you this morning?"

"Not well I'm afraid. I'm sick with worry, because Gail didn't come home last night, and the police think she may have been killed in an accident."

"I am sorry to hear that. I'm very fond of Gail, but I can assure you, when she left me, she was fine."

"She died two hundred yards from your house Father. I'd think you would notice something like that, because you would have to walk past it." A tinge of panic set in for Peter. Anthea was becoming a busybody.

"I don't like your tone Anthea. Are you accusing me of doing something?"

The symbols on the coat began to light up and this is when Anthea saw them. She gave out a loud gasp. Peter reached out and pressed a hand to her mouth, before she could even yell out how evil he was.

"Quick, get her into the car now!" The coat instructed.

Peter checked to see if anyone was watching, then dragged Anthea around to the back seats and rolled her in. She was so shocked to see Peter acting like this but couldn't speak. He took a rag from the floor and pushed it into Anthea's mouth. There was a skipping rope in the storage compartment and Peter took this to tie her arms with. He didn't quite know why he was doing all this, but he was doing it all the same. He swung her legs out so that she was flat on the back seat. He closed one door and moved around to the other door, opened it and leaned over Anthea, still not sure what he was really doing. He suddenly rolled Anthea's skirt up and slid down her tights, slipped the shoes off and took the tights off completely. A very helpless Anthea looked terrified at this stage. She thought Peter was going to assault her, but instead he took the tights and wrapped them tightly around her ankles, securing her completely.

It was now that the coat spoke again. "Take the car away from here and we'll dispose of this nosy pest."

Anthea heard it this time, and knew Peter was being controlled. Peter got into the driver's seat, started the car and drove. He remembered that Maythorne has an old quarry, so he headed for it.

After arriving at the quarry, Peter steered the car to a rock face and parked. He reached into the glove compartment, saw an envelope and red lipstick; he took these out. On the envelope he scribbled down a note. "Without my sister, I feel alone in the world." He placed the note on the passenger seat of the car and climbed out. Moving to the back of the car, he stared at Anthea. She took a glimpse and as she did, his face changed from the familiar, friendly Priest to a horrible, twisted, evil monster. In disgust she turned her head away. Peter opened the door and untied Anthea's hands and ankles, then closed the door again. Anthea's back doors had childproof locks, so now she was stuck inside her own car, not really knowing what was to happen next. Peter checked over the edge of the rock face, a clear one-hundred-foot drop. Nobody was working on the quarry anymore. He returned to the car and opened the driver's door. He reached in and released the hand brake, stepped away again and pressed the door lock down and slammed the door. Moving round to the back of the car, he placed both hands on the trunk and pushed with all his might, sending Anthea's car forward and over the rock face. She shrieked all the way down to the impact at the bottom, a huge noisy clatter reverberated and echoed around the quarry. Peter took one last look at the wreck down below. Anthea was surely dead, the back window had shattered, sending her out through it. Half of her was lying out, she was definitely lifeless, but her eyes were wide open, still accusing and her face speckled in dark red blood.

"You had better return home Peter; at least she's out of the way now." reasoned the coat.

Peter screamed at the top of his voice, and it echoed around the quarry. Now realizing what he'd just done, he stood staring sadly at Anthea's limp, dead body.

"It's perfectly reasonable to assume she took her own life, the police will see this." The coat was just relentless. It seemed to be the more he wore this garment, the worse Peter became. He'd just murdered a woman, now he was supposed to just go home and act as if nothing happened. He trudged away and found the nearest bus stop.

Stuart had been taken to the hospital. The ambulance announced this to A&E. A team of nurses and triage staff assembled to receive Stuart and tend to him immediately. The gurney was wheeled straight into surgery. It took a few hours to stop the bleed, remove the clot, and tidy Stuart's head back up. Now he was resting in a recovery ward. Peri Keeble had been told about Stuart's mishap; she'd just arrived and was waiting for the anaesthetic to wear off. Although she wasn't family, she still managed to squeeze in and see him. Peri sipped her coffee twice and placed the cup down. Next, she took out her flask of holy water and tipped some onto her fingers and wiped it across Stuart's forehead. That seemed to rouse him, and his eyes opened slowly, his hazy vision only just made out Peri's silhouette. A few more minutes and he woke up fully, he sat bolt upright and spoke.

"Peter is now wearing that damned evil coat." Peri crossed herself and stroked Stuart's shoulder.

"Then we will stop him, the same as we did with Ben, right?' Peri soothed him and pushed Stuart back down and he lay there peacefully, secretly pleased he had her in his life.

Chapter Four

The smell of evil.

The noise from the quarry had been reported to The Maythorne's Environmental Health Department, that an explosion went off there, but their noise abatement team insisted that nobody works at the quarry to create such a noise anymore, but the complaints were followed up, nonetheless. Vernon Stephenson, a fifty-year-old handsome, extreme sports lover and Marilyn Gill, a thirty-year-old Goth looking lady with a stark difference between the two, drove out to investigate and found the wreck of Anthea Dredge's car. They had called Maythorne CID who sent Scenes of Crime Officers Davy 'Wavy' Holderness a forty-four-year-old, wise looking man and Penny 'Forum' Durant, a fresh faced twenty-four-year-old assistant. DI Nathan Joyce, thirty-nine years of age, with ambitions of finishing his career as DCI. DS John and DC Klein, whom you've already met, also attended. They all converged on the quarry more or less at the same time. Now they were talking strategies.

"We need a few ropes and a whole lot of mountain equipment to get down there, Guv," said Wavy; the Chief Investigating Officer, to Vernon and he called a number to arrange this.

"So, tell me Wavy, who's down there and why are they down there?" Nathan pressed for specific answers every time.

"I've called in the plates to the Crimes INC Database. It doesn't appear to belong to any crooks Guv," DS John intervened briefly.

"First glance, I would suggest a suicide attempt, but we'll know more once we get down there." estimated Wavy.

"But these footprints here, either side of the tyre marks and those ones at the back here, suggest differently," offered Forum.

"Good, not suicide but foul play, not a criminal but an anonymous member of the public." Nathan sighed and gazed over the edge of the drop, his vertigo kicked in and he stepped away. "Yes, I think it's best if you go down there and take a look," delegating to Wavy.

"Guv! I've patched the plates to DVLA; they've come back with a positive match of a vehicle registered to a Mrs Anthea Dredge. She's the elder sister of the victim from yesterday morning's accident. Gail Eldridge." At last DC Klein had connected the dots.

"Good man, we'll make a DS of you yet Mr Klein," Nathan then turned to see another vehicle coming into the quarry, a Jeep with a surfboard on top and the Beach Boys playing loudly from it.

"Not from noise abatement then, is he Vern?" He just shook his head and felt embarrassed. The Jeep roared up to the waiting party, swept to a stop in one huge arc and kicked up dust everywhere. The music stopped playing to the relief of the DI. A small man appeared from the driver's seat.

"Anybody ask for some climbing equipment?" It was the best friend of Vernon Stephenson's and surf bum Eugene Calhoun. He just waved and went to help Eugene with the equipment.

"DC Klein, go to the drop with the SOCO's. I'll call the Coroner and DS John can acquire some lifting equipment and then comb the area up here for some more evidence." Nathan gave his instructions then called the coroner's office.

With the harnesses in place and the ropes primed at the rock face Wavy, Forum and DC Klein were ready to descend into the hundred-foot pit. Slowly they abseiled down to the bottom. Forum got there first, followed by Wavy and DC Klein having got stuck halfway, was the last to join them. They circled the car, and DC Klein took out a notebook and recorded all the findings of Wavy and Forum.

"The front driver's door is open. The aftermath of the impact indicates that the victim was in the back of the vehicle, as it hit the bottom," relayed Wavy and DC Klein wrote this down.

"Here's a note and it's written in red lipstick," added Forum. She then slipped it into a clear envelope for handwriting analysis later. DC Klein scribbled furiously as he tried to catch up with them. "There should also be prints to come off this." She had found the lipstick, it had rolled under the passenger seat, and Forum took this and slipped it into a small evidence bag. Wavy moved to the back of the car and studied the large handprints on the trunk; he quickly collected them with a large adhesive patch, a perfect print of each hand.

"Let's hope they match the lipstick." He then slid this into a clear envelope; they were getting a lot of evidence, suggesting it wasn't a suicide. They hadn't even studied the body yet. "Are you keeping up Bill?" Wavy was staring over at the DC. He looked back and nodded; pen poised for more info. Wavy and Forum both opened a door each at the rear of the car and leaned in over the bottom half of Anthea. "She had a ligature on her ankles, she has abrasions where they were tight on her," Wavy commented stiffly.

"The same on her wrists," added Forum who was pointing it out to DC Klein. He quickly jotted down 'tied up' to save time. "Poor cow was alive when the car was pushed over the edge." Wavy nodded, moved away and closed his car door gently.

"Okay this was murder. By whom? We will find out from the nice prints the killer carelessly left behind for us." concluded Wavy. DC Klein folded his notebook away to prepare for the climb up. "Okay let's tell Nathan what we're dealing with here." Wavy gestured an order to climb back up.

The three of them had spent fifteen minutes down there, plus a further fifteen climbing back up again. Nathan, with his eyes firmly shut, leaned over to pull DC Klein back up. DS John helped Forum and Eugene strained to pull up Wavy, but he made it eventually. He quickly retrieved his equipment and packed it all away. A convoy had entered the quarry whilst they were down there, a crane carrier, a flat-backed lorry and the coroner's wagon.

"Well, anything interesting?" Nathan asked impatiently.

"Bog standard murder Guv, with a crumby scribble of a suicide note, made from lipstick. Bloody tied her arms and legs, then drove here and pushed her over; gravity did the rest. Now all we have to do is get this lot back to the crime labs and sort it all out for you. Then you can haul the son-of-a-bitch in." Wavy showed Nathan his little horde of evidence and then got into the van he'd brought.

"Thanks, Wavy, I'll call you later to conclude my report, cheers Penny," Nathan was leaning in the driver's window. He tacked this on the end, before she could speak up for herself. They both smirked and drove away. "I wonder what she knew?" Nathan asked himself, before his guys could reach him. "Okay men, we'll let this lot do their jobs, while we do ours back at the office so we can find Mrs Dredge's killer." Eugene sped off first, followed by CID, leaving the rest to collect the wreck.

At the Rectory, Peter had returned home off the bus. He turned into his drive to see Bishop Andrews, a creaking old man in his late sixties, standing at his door holding his letter. Another panic attack and this time, no response from the jacket, dull and absolutely no visibly ancient, evil symbols. Peter was left on his own here.

"Your Grace, I wasn't expecting you. How is it you are here?"

"Peter, I'm curious about this letter. It's addressed to me, but there isn't any writing inside, see?" Bishop Andrews showed the blank letter to Peter.

"But I wrote on it, telling you I wasn't well and needed time to recover." He stared hard at the empty page.

"Well, you look okay to me Peter, just a little tense. Why is that?"

"I can't explain, because if I do, you'll think I'm crazy, or worse harm may become of you."

"Ha..ha..rm?" Bishop Andrews laughed, he was thinking; maybe Peter was having a breakdown, following the news of Gail.

"Please, your Grace, you must allow me space at this moment in time. The locum is already in place; he can deliver my sermons."

"I came here to offer you counsel, following the death of one of your parishioners, Gail Eldridge, but you appear oblivious to all the news and gossip. It's all over Maythorne." The Bishop explained. He now became wary that Peter was not as upset as he perhaps should have been, by this revelation.

It was now that Peter needed the coat to help him, but it remained dull, perhaps the Bishop wasn't very threatening or was it because he was a staunch holy man. The Bishop moved closer to Peter and then he could smell an array of different aromas coming from his clothes. Sweet perfume, the fragrance of a woman perhaps, another smell of sulphur; volcanic and acrid. Also, a stale body odour emanating and mixing with the three. Combined they gave the Bishop a clue as to what happened here yesterday. Peter breathed it himself, then realized it was the stench of evil, an evil that he had taken part in.

"Peter! What has happened to you, what have you done?" Peter was shaking his head and began to explain.

"No, not me, the coat, can't you see, it takes you over and makes you do things. It talks to you and twists things around. You don't know what you are doing, and it hurts!" He blurted out all this and sounded like a madman.

"Then take it off. All you have to do is take it off!" Bishop Andrews was trying to be rational, because Peter was clearly delusional.

"It killed her. Gail, she knew and ran. It picked up the fire poker and threw it at her. There was nothing that I could do. She died in there, in the house. It made me move her and then it burnt her, oh no... no! What have I done, why am I telling you all this?" He was ranting now and being hysterical, at least in the Bishop's eyes anyway.

"You killed Gail Eldridge?" The shock in the Bishop's voice rocked Peter.

"No not me, It. The coat, this fucking thing, it won't let me go and I cannot take it off!"

"Of course you can, look, I'll help you?"

Bishop Andrews reached for the coat, but Peter moved back, as he did so the Bishop caught hold of the sleeve and dragged it down Peter's arm, as easy as that. Peter pulled his arm back again. The sleeve came right off, making the Bishop lose his footing and still gripping the sleeve, he fell backwards and over onto the gravel driveway, hitting his head very hard. He was still and quiet. Not another one, thought Peter in total disarray. What was he going to do now? With both palms pressed to his forehead and clearly in shock, he just stared at the Bishop. He wasn't breathing and he definitely wasn't moving. Peter thought he had killed again. Peter pulled the sleeve of the coat back up and it quickly tightened on him again.

"You should listen to yourself? You sounded like a lunatic. I killed her, I did that, and I did this." The voice of the coat mocked him and then snapped Peter back out of his transfixed gaze on the Bishop. "You did those things, and you killed this charming old holy man." Peter nodded and finally accepting his fate, decided to just ride the storm, until the coat had no further need of him.

"I need help with his body; will you help me?" Peter asked the coat.

"Of course, Peter. Remember I've always got your back!" The coat laughed thunderously around the driveway. "But I can't claim his soul. You will have to bury him somewhere nearby."

Peter went to his garden for a wheelbarrow and collected the Bishop's body into it. He quickly moved the frail man to a set of trees while he cleaned a small pool of blood away and brought out a shovel. After this he moved the wheelbarrow to the church yard, here he quickly dug down into Ben Grantham's unmarked grave, six feet by two feet, and three feet down. Finally, after digging, Peter heaved the wheelbarrow's contents into the hole and sealed the Bishop inside. "You need to clean yourself up, the smell will give you away to any good policeman." Collecting all his tools up and reclaiming his crucifix, Peter returned to the Rectory. His final act of the day, so he thought, was to clean and rake his driveway. Cleaning himself up would be difficult; he made a promise to the coat, that if he could remove it to shower, he would wear it for as long as it needed him.

"Well, that my old friend is when we've reaped ten more souls, the poor old Bishop doesn't count."

The coat loosened and Peter finally relieved of this burden, felt one hundred times lighter. He floated to the bathroom and took a couple of hours solace from that terrible thing back there. Then as if by fate, the shower cut out and spurted freezing water at him. Shivering he made shrill gasps and climbed out for the towel. As Peter dressed again and slipped the coat on, he had questions for it again. He clutched his oboe; it had been two days since he last played.

"When we first got acquainted, your plan was to guide me for twelve days. Why didn't you intervene with the Bishop, when he questioned me?" Peter played the oboe softly and listened to the coat's reply.

"He had crossed himself with holy water before meeting you, probably because of the news of Gail. You priests do that in times of sorrow and in your search for divine inspiration. Therefore, I couldn't show myself to him, as hard as you tried to convince him otherwise. That's the only reason." Peter stopped playing as a knock at the door interrupted them.

"Who is that at this hour?"

"Two policemen, different ones in uniform. They'll question you about Gail. Stay calm and they won't suspect anything."

"I didn't kill Gail, you did. I'm not getting into trouble because of you!"

"Quieten down, will you? All they can hear is you talking to yourself, I'm not here."

"Really? You're so certain of this?"

"Yes, you sound like a crazy ranting fool right now. You should answer the door, before they knock again." Then there it was; another three knocks, Peter hesitantly opened the front door to Callum and Myles, the two police officers.

"Good evening, gentlemen!"

"Father Peter Flaws?" asked Callum.

"Not by nature though," he replied half-heartedly and opened the door wide.

"We would like to question you about your interaction with Miss Gail Eldridge, two nights ago." He led the two officers in, and they sat in two separate chairs at Peter's invitation.

"You are most welcome to ask, but it is a straightforward answer. I took a turn for the worst at the church. Gail and her sister came to my aid. It was then that Gail offered to drive me to the door of my house, then she left." This tallied with what the locals had said.

"You were ill, by your own admission. Why didn't she help you inside then Father?" pressed Myles. Peter fidgeted then he gave a reply.

"Gossips around the parish have already noted a bond had built between us. She didn't want to add fuel to their fire." Something else that tallied from witnesses earlier.

"You fancied her, is that what you're saying Father?" Myles stabbed out the question so quickly.

"I was fond of her, but I have taken a vow of celibacy, nothing could come of this bond except friendship.'

"But it's still okay to fancy her surely, or did you reach out and touch her for helping you, she didn't like it, screamed for help and you killed her." Myles was now driving home his suspicions of Peter.

"No! I didn't kill her; not sure how can you prove this anyway?"

"But we heard you say that, from behind that door, Sir."

"Enough of this nonsense. , I want you two to leave. You can't pin this on me, how dare you!" Peter was now glowing orange and red, showing all the evil symbols on the coat, making Callum and Myles cringe in fear, they couldn't believe what they were seeing. "Now leave, before you two get hurt!" warned Peter.

Callum grabbed for his baton, extended it but a force from nowhere wrapped the baton around his throat and choked him. Myles was a picture of fear witnessing all this, but he still summoned the will to reach for his taser.

"Father, release my colleague or I will fire this taser, you have been warned."

Peter flipped his hand up and the taser followed in the same direction and discharged itself at Callum's chest, both bolts making him convulse and Myles was sent straight through the window behind him. The baton around Callum's throat tightened even more, sapping all the energy out of him even as he was still shaking from the taser hit. Peter looked through the smashed pane and saw Myles sprawled out on the bonnet of their squad car. He wasn't doing much. Callum stopped shaking and now he was foaming at the mouth. He wasn't breathing either.

"Excellent! Two more souls, we should move the bodies elsewhere." Both officers were lying dead; the coat had stopped glowing and had become normal again.

"Thank you, yes. Okay I'll take care of it."

He dragged Callum out to the car and placed him in it and then Myles followed after a bit of a struggle. Peter drove the squad car to the outskirts of Maythorne, parked it next to a bus stop on the border of Boundford. It was dark, he had a long walk back home and a cool air soothed his already fraying nerves.

Peter couldn't believe what he was doing. His actions and that of the coat's were becoming blurred together as one.

Chapter Five

Loss of two fine officers.

It was six o'clock the next morning when the call came to Maythorne Police. A report from a bus driver saying two police officers were parked at the bus stop 'sleeping on the job' was his observation. He gave the squad car number 4237, and the desk soon knew by the log, it was Myles and Callum's, two of the most dedicated uniformed officers at the station. Control radioed them for a response.

"This is Tango Echo One, are you receiving this transmission; Sierra 4237? Over!" The controller repeated the call three more times, but there wasn't a response. He relayed his concerns to Inspector Garden, the duty officer and the highest ranking one nearest to him. He took Sergeant Cole with him to where the car was reported. On the way over, they had passed Peter; stumbling back home towards the Rectory but didn't make that connection just yet. Sergeant Cole parked in front of the bus stop. He knew instantly that something bad had happened to them. Inspector Garden made his way to the parked squad car knocked on the window and then saw for himself that they weren't moving.

"Call the station, have CID come out here with crime scene investigators. I suspect foul play."

"Okay Sir!" The call was made and after some twenty minutes waiting and cordoning off the scene to the public, Nathan, DS John and Wavy arrived to examine the site. Nathan jogged over to Inspector Garden for a quick briefing.

"They're two of my best officers here. Do them justice and find their killer for me okay?"

"I shall make that my priority James, don't you worry. Now you have to call their wives and loved ones. I don't envy you." Nathan grabbed the Inspector's waist and held his left elbow with his other hand. The strength of Nathan's grip reassured him. He left James' side and made his way to the two officers lying still in the squad car. "Hey Wavy, anything out of the ordinary?"

Wavy had already dusted the doors of the car for prints and then pointed to the dent on the bonnet. "One of them landed here. When the Coroner's office gets back to us with the extent of their injuries, we'll know which one."

"One of them was dropped or thrown maybe, what about the other one?" Nathan asked. Wavy carefully opened the driver's door. "Curious, Myles usually does the driving, doesn't he?" He remembered them out and about once.

Wavy shrugged, he wouldn't know that, but did point out Callum's throat. DS John nodded to Nathan's question, agreeing with him.

"He was choked by something, something metallic." Wavy ran his gloved hand along the grooves and photographed them.

"His baton is missing. Could it be the thing that choked him?" DS John pointed out.

"We need to find Callum's baton. We're done here, call the Coroner," Nathan turned away to check around the squad car one last time.

"The prints came back from Mrs Dredge's death, a match to Mr Peter Flaws, Guv." Wavy remembered the memo from this morning.

"Great we'll start there then, thanks Wavy." Nathan and DS John decided to drive over to Peter Flaws' address. The news of Myles and Callum passing had filtered through to the ranks very quickly after Sergeant Cole had returned. The mood was very depressing. They had only gone out to question locals and a harmless clergyman, but now they were mysteriously killed and dumped like rubbish out of town. Some of the officers were angry, some were crying, waiting with anxious breath on CID catching their killer.

DS John and Nathan drove to Peter's place without talking. In his mind Nathan kept thinking of the link between all three killings and Fr Peter Flaws. DS John was just upset that his drinking buddies were now dead and resolved to catch the bastard responsible. Shortly they were pulling up in the lane where the Rectory was. Nathan gripped DS John's left arm and spoke.

"Park here. We'll walk the rest and see if we can catch him out." DS John obeyed his boss, parked out of sight and then they walked a few hundred yards further up. As they approached, they saw Peter in the driveway. He was busy hammering large wooden boards to his window frames. "That's the window one of our boys was put through, I'd wager."

"What do you want to do Boss?" DS John crouched below the hedge line concealing his presence. Peter was busy finishing; he didn't notice Nathan standing in the driveway just watching.

Nathan signalled to DS John to join him at his side. "He's big and clumsy. He couldn't hurl a six-foot-tall copper through a window. He's struggling with that board even now."

"Peter, you've got company, so make it look good." said the coat. Peter turned with the last board he was holding. He smiled at the Detectives; it seemed innocent enough.

"Gentlemen! You couldn't help me with this board, could you? Some vandals put my window through last night."

"Did you report it to the police Sir?" asked DS John.

"Hey? No! You boys are far too busy for that sort of trouble."

"If they put your window in, how come there's glass all over the driveway then?" Nathan observed Peter's face change to one of uncertainty. He put the board down; it was starting to get heavy.

"Well, they were inside you see and then threw rocks out, that's why."

"Oh! So where are these rocks?" DS John noticed they were missing.

"In the backyard, on my flower bed."

"Maybe we can see them for ourselves, Sir?" DS John added.

"I would really like to finish this window, then get to a glazier for an estimate on some new glass." Peter was winning this argument with the Detective Sergeant, just like before.

"Alright Father, we'll leave you to it. Sorry to have bothered you." Nathan cut in then and decided to return with a warrant at a more inconvenient time, like when the Priest was sleeping."

"Thank you, gentlemen." Peter picked up the board and continued working.

"They didn't believe you, Peter," the coat chided him for his lack of fibre this time.

"Shut up!" Peter forgot that he had just spoken loudly.

"Excuse me Father, did you say something?" Nathan heard him just as he was walking to the car. Peter shook his head; Nathan turned away and paid it no further attention.

"Let's pile the evidence up on this Priest, come back with a warrant and worry the old bastard into confessing. He's hiding something and we're going to find out what." Nathan promised.

"Right Guv!" DS John didn't like this recent exchange either; the Priest was definitely being sketchy.

They needed to see the head of CID, Detective Superintendent Jean Bascoe to obtain a warrant from the Justice of the Peace at her office. But first thing they needed to do was to stockpile all the evidence, leaning against Peter Flaws, return to the Rectory fully loaded. Nathan loved this part of his job. Results are his specialty.

The report of Myles and Callum being killed had already been in the news by lunchtime. Peri Keeble was watching the tail end of the report.

"And so, the mysterious slaying of two of Maythorne's finest continues, as clues stack against one individual so far, but the name cannot be circulated at this point in time for sensitivity reasons. If you saw anything unusual between 2am and 7am this morning, however trivial you may think it is, call us on the usual Hotline!" The reporter signed off after that. Stuart awoke from his rest to see Peri biting her lip and fretting over something.

"Are you okay?"

"Two policemen have been found dead; they were the ones in yesterday's news about Gail Eldridge being found burnt in her car. I remember that."

"Why are you so worried, Peri?"

"People are dying again, and the count is escalating. That's what happened to Ben and me. I think we should plan to stop Peter, before he takes more lives."

"You think Peter did these coppers in?" Peri nodded repeatedly and bit her thumbnail, just like she used to do when she was a little girl, whenever she felt nervous.

"Get yourself discharged today, you can walk and that's all I need from you to help get that coat away from Peter, that is the thing influencing him."

"I'd like to wear that coat once just to turn the tables on Peter, so he can taste his own medicine."

"Don't say things like that out loud Stuart! She has agents of evil everywhere." Peri crossed herself and went to reception, speeding up his discharge. Stuart felt she was getting edgy, and he felt an overwhelming need to help her. He still had his shotgun at home. When she returned, he was up and dressing.

"You don't really know what you're doing, do you Peri?"

"There is enough resonance of her in me, that I can see her thoughts and what she has planned for us all. Nobody else can stop her, not even you with your gun." Stuart could tell that if Peri knew his plan, then the coat would too. "Any weapon such as a gun or crossbow, she will use against you, her strength is growing greater. each day Peter claims a soul. The last time we had an encounter with her, she was rising inside Ben, and we caught her in time. Now her very essence is competing with Peter and even he can't prevent her rise to Earth. We must do this cleverly." They walked away from the hospital without waiting for the discharge papers. A bus came along just in time, and they rode home to prepare. Stuart walked Peri to her flat and he kissed her cheek.

"Thank you for coming by at the hospital. It hasn't been very easy for me this last month, but you have been a good friend."

"We need each other right now. I have to get some things to help us. I'll call when we have them and free Peter tonight." Peri squeezed Stuart's hands, and they felt purposeful. He watched as Peri went inside, then walked to his own home and rested up.

A couple of hours later Peri summoned a taxi to take her to Boundford the Cabbie honked his horn outside for her to acknowledge him. She stroked the head of Fabian, her pet Myna bird.

"I'll see you tomorrow, Fabian," and with perfect mimicry, Fabian said the same thing back to her. She placed the bird back inside his cage and left for Boundford.

A short trip later she arrived at her old estate. Teresa Keeble, Peri's mother didn't live there anymore. The shame of her husband Max being in prison for murder and her daughter in the sanatorium drove her away. The only person living there from fifteen years ago is John Sobers, the local Clergyman who helped Peri escape the grasp of a Satanic Cult. He had been on a sabbatical in India, but after hearing about Peri's release he cut that short and returned home. His face was a picture when he opened his front door to her.

"You haven't changed one bit Peri Keeble. I only hope the world feels better to you now." He kissed her cheek warmly.

"These are testing times John, that's why I'm here. I need your help." John hurried her in; he didn't want anybody to see her here. The stigma about the Keebles stuck around.

"Can I offer you something to drink?" Peri sat in a tall wooden chair and John came around to the front of her and saw her beauty firsthand. She had grown into a handsome woman, full figured, much taller than he remembered and if he hadn't taken his vows, he would've had her naked in seconds, right there and then. In his mind he quietly reminded himself of it. He checked his expression in a mirror behind her, glancing quickly.

"Whoa mister! You can get me a coffee and for yourself, you should drink something cold," she'd caught him gazing; it was so obvious. The flattery intrigued her, but she didn't want to do anything other than what she came here for, which was to get supplies so she can defeat Lucifer and destroy her hold on Peter. He fixed the drinks and came through holding a large mug and a tall glass of lemonade.

"What do you need from me?" John finally sat down, ready to hear her request.

"You've seen the news about Gail Eldridge and the police officers in Maythorne? Well, I think that Goatskin coat has claimed another agent, or vessel as the cult claimed it to be. Peter Flaws, a Catholic Priest with a conflict of faith." She began to explain.

"We, in our circle call them conduits of evil. If this is so, then first you need proof; that Lucifer is driving him to commit these atrocities. Secondly you need an exorcism kit, containing holy water, a solid gold dagger, and a crucifix that belongs to Peter and most importantly a Bible, strictly from the religion of the fallen Priest. Wait here" John left to find his bag and returned a few seconds later with it. "Then you will need all this." He set the bag down on the floor next to Peri's chair. "I'm coming with you and no arguments alright?" Peri nodded, at the very least, he would know how to perform the exorcism. "Now drink your coffee, and then afterwards, we'll go."

Chapter Six

The challenge ahead.

At Maythorne police station, DI Nathan Joyce, DS John and DC Klein, the rest of uniform on duty, Davy, Scenes of Crimes, Chief Investigator and Emile, the Home Office Coroner, sat waiting for Jean Bascoe to return with the warrant. It was seven in the evening when she finally came back with it. At forty-four, and five feet nine, she was the youngest detective superintendent to ever have represented Maythorne CID, and she was a very pretty lady. She came to the briefing room and addressed everyone.

"Okay then, here's the warrant. You have a good case to search Father Flaws' property. Unusual thing is - do we really believe a sixty-year-old holy man, with health problems, really killed four people?"

Nathan raised his hand.

"Boss, we saw the place for ourselves, a big front window, plate glass by the looks of it and a hole the size of something huge that could've been thrown through it. He was trying to fix the mess when we arrived to speak to him."

"I see, but that doesn't answer my question. Emile, can you tell us anything else about the bodies you've examined thus far?"

"Of course, Jean. In the case of Callum Byford and Myles Gibbons. Myles has two fractured vertebrae, in the lumbar region of his spinal column and glass embedded which was his cause of death. Callum on the other hand was electrocuted with something akin to a taser and strangled with what I can only assume was his own baton. He didn't have it with him, when he was brought to us, neither was Myles' taser." Emile stopped for a moment for the information to carry around the room.

Inspector Garden spoke next. "On our way over to the scene of Myles and Callum, we saw Father Flaws returning to his home. If he did walk from where their bodies were left, the time frame fits perfectly. He has to be our prime suspect Ma'am."

"Very well, we're looking for PC Gibbons' taser, Callum's Baton and anything linking Father Flaws to the two sisters." Jean broke the meeting up and Emile added one more item to the list.

"Please find if you can a fire poker. That is what killed Gail Eldridge, not the fire. Find this and you'll have him for all four murders."

Jean gave the warrant to Nathan, and he slid it inside his jacket pocket. She was given a cute smile. His boss was confident he would bring back what they were looking for, it was what he was best at. Nathan knew that if he solved this case, he would get the carrot of promotion being dangled before him. He placed the thought in his head for a moment; finally, DCI Nathan Joyce, how cool would that be?

Peri and John called over at Stuart's place to discuss practical ways of trapping the evil coat and freeing Peter from it. John knew about pacts and contracts Lucifer had set before and began explaining them. Stuart came through to the lounge and sat listening intently.

"Thank you, Stuart, you have cared for Peri well this past month, now let's get down to business. There are two ways to prise that kind of evil away from Father Flaws; one piece is to complete the Rite of Exorcism. Another is to annul the contract taken by Peter with Lucifer. We find out what that is, then we simply sow the seeds of doubt in Peter's mind, divide and conquer." John opened the canvas bag of tricks he'd brought.

Stuart noticed Peri's body language had changed; she'd sat legs together and pointing away from him and in the line of John's sight. Peri has more faith in John, rather than in him, he thought. This he'd have to correct. "What do you need the gold dagger for?" He queried.

"If Peter and Lucifer don't co-operate, it should be enough to nullify her influence. The dagger is what I went to India for. I knew she would try and rise again, just a precaution."

"By stabbing him? Why a gold dagger and not silver? I thought that was the norm these days?" Stuart added, Peri's legs swung back facing him, he smiled to himself.

"Gold is the purest form of metal on earth, silver stakes and bullets are for werewolves and vampires, but we're not dealing with those. What we're dealing with is something much, much worse. A gold dagger dipped in holy water should do the trick." Stuart's heart sank as Peri swung her legs back over to John's attention.

"How do we separate Peter from her?" Peri couldn't say her name. It would be enough for her to instantly appear before them.

"Easy one Peri, a holy circle around Peter will make them part, then we recite the incantation, and she will be banished, again. I've done this before, remember?" Peri kept her legs in John's direction. Stuart interjected.

"I don't understand how Peter got trapped by the Beast in the first place. Surely it can't cross consecrated ground?" Peri swung over to Stuart briefly then back to John as he answered.

"Good fact Stuart, but obviously the persuasion of the Devil is strong. For her to cross into Peter, she would have to be invited. Once inside, then it will be a slow takeover of the soul, until the contract is fulfilled."

"Think I'll get my gun." He left the lounge to clean and load it, not fully convinced by John's winning arguments. Stuart never realized he felt this strongly for Peri, until now. John and Peri prepared for their conquest.

"It would be wise to bring your Bible! You have an Old Testament I see," noted John.

Back at Maythorne CID, DI Nathan Joyce and his team were assembling uniformed officers to help search Peter's property. Inspector Garden was keen to get involved with this, but not one of these officers knew what they were getting themselves into. They all thought they were just performing a simple task, search and recovery of certain evidence to help bring about a conviction, for the murders of four people. If they weren't careful the body count would rise by the end of tonight. If only they had connected these events to the strange events in Boundford, fifteen years ago, they would alter their strategies. A riot van to collect the officers had been driven into the carpool. Emile came towards Nathan with a sheet of paper.

"DI Joyce, I've just received this fax from the labs. It's fibres collected from each of the bodies Sir. They are all the same and match conclusively."

"What fibres?" Nathan took the fax from Emile.

"They are the hairs of a goat, no question about it."

"Well okay, Peter was wearing a goatskin coat when we spoke with him earlier, let's go get him" Nathan passed the fax back to Emile and then left for Peter's place.

"I think we're dealing with something more than just one man, take care Nathan." Emile called after the van; he tried to warn him.

"So, listen up then folks? We're searching the Rectory for clues to the deaths of Gail Eldridge, Anthea Dredge, Callum Byford and Myles Gibbons. Anything you do find, bag it, tag it and then pass it to either me or DS John, understand?" A murmur of agreement circled the van for a few seconds. One of the officers asked the question everyone else was thinking.

"Guv, what if things get physical and we need to apply reasonable force?"

"If that happens you've all been trained to deal with a situation. Hopefully it won't. The last time we spoke with the Priest, he was meek and mild to say the least, so let's not do something to elicit an angry response, okay?" Nathan's reply hit home, and they all kept quiet from then on. They entered the turn of Quarter Mile Lane and Joyce signalled for the van to pull over halfway up. "We get out and walk. Some of you go around the back in case he tries to get away, understand? Then let's go and do our jobs!"

"I'll start searching the walk from the church to the Rectory, Guv, maybe we'll find clues there too?" DC Klein took two men with him. Nathan always liked the young DC's initiative. He let DC Klein go that way.

"You know Guv, a month ago there were similar mysterious deaths, twelve in all. Do you reckon they tie in with what we're dealing with here?" DS John reminded Nathan.

"Thirteen! I believe. That one young lady was pregnant, if they are connected." Nathan did remember. "Tonight, we find out."

They continued along the lane towards the Rectory and from inside Peter's place the coat constricted and woke Peter. It knew of the imminent threat posed by Joyce and his men.

"Father, you have about fifteen visitors encroaching on your property as we speak."

"You're the only one speaking Devil, let them come. We'll beat them like we did before."

"You think so, do you? Okay you deal with this while I sleep, good night, Peter!" The coat whispered and went quiet. Leaving Peter alone for now. The three usual knocks on the door, all exits covered, and warrant at the ready. The instant he opened the door the warrant was shoved in Peter's face.

"Father Peter Flaws? We have reasonable grounds to search your premises in connection with the murders of four people in and around Maythorne. Please stand aside and let us in" Inspector Garden had a glint in his eye.

"By all means officers, you may search."

Nathan and DS John went in first snapping gloves on before touching anything. Five uniformed men and Inspector Garden; checked further through the house. Not once finding anything incriminating, they became frustrated with Peter.

DC Klein and his two men walked slowly down the lane towards the church. Upon reaching the graveyard, he noticed one had fresh earth over it. He called Nathan on his mobile.

"We have a fresh grave here Guv, Ask the Father if there's been any funerals lately." He waited for Nathan's response.

"So, Father, can you tell me when the last funeral was conducted at your church?"

"Easy, that was three and a half weeks ago, and it was Dr Jessica Fielding. Why?"

"Did you get that Bill?" asked Nathan.

"Yes Guv, we need to open this grave Sir"

"Okay do it, some men are coming with shovels, wait there." Nathan saw Peter's face change; he knew what was in that grave. "Worried Father? I think you should be." An officer approached with a clear bag; it was the fire poker Emile had mentioned. "Take that to the van please Keith. That's one we have you for Father, only a matter of time before we find the rest."

"I haven't touched that poker. It's an ornament. Where did you find it?" Peter knew they wouldn't find his prints on it so, played the innocent card anyway.

At the graveyard the two diggers arrived and started to uncover the earth from the unmarked grave. It took several minutes to dig down, but one officer's shovel hit something two feet down. They spread the earth to find a body; fully clothed in Bishop's attire. DC Klein leaned over and saw with the flashlight and called Nathan again.

"Guv it's the Bishop. He's been buried here but nobody knows."

Nathan kept this quiet for now; he wanted more on the other kills first. Another officer approached with Myles' taser and Callum's baton, it looked mangled and twisted.

"Interesting to find these here. Are you going to tell me you didn't touch these either?" Nathan showed them to Peter who wasn't fazed at all.

"You're right I didn't, you'll find that out when you take them back to the labs." Peter replied. Nathan threw them back to the officer who then took them to the van.

"You play a cool game Father, but soon we'll have something to nail you to." Nathan continued to look around. "Glass from PC Gibbons back matches the windows of this Rectory, meaning he died here, but moving him elsewhere, that will get you a charge."

"I didn't touch him either, you can't prove that."

"Oh, but I can! The fibres on his clothes match your coat; it's goat hair? Try to explain that one away!"

"THAT WOULD BE ME!" Came a great booming voice from Peter's direction. It wasn't male or female, a mixture of the two. This made Nathan and the others stop in their tracks and stare at the Priest. The house began to shake and contort.

"How are you doing that?" Nathan asked, while ushering the others to get out of the house. They were all making for the front door at this point.

"I told you it wasn't me and you wouldn't understand this," Peter said meekly.

"SLEEP NOW PETER, I'LL DEAL WITH THESE NUISANCES!"

Again, the voice was emanating through Peter. Peter dropped to the floor and slept, then began levitating off the ground. The doors slammed in unison and the windows shattered inwardly at the rest of the people inside. Two of the uniformed men caught the brunt of this; they were closest to the windows and glass began slicing through them in huge chards, stabbing them deeply. Both men fell down as DS John shielded himself from more glass behind a wall, moving quickly. Nathan could hardly believe what he was seeing. Inspector Garden tended to his men; one was bleeding heavily, but not quite dead, but the other one was.

"LEAVE THIS PLACE OR I WILL CLAIM ALL YOUR SOULS!" The voice demanded.

"No! I'm not leaving, not without my suspect. I take him or you'll take me, come on? I challenge you whatever you are!" Nathan wasn't scared anymore; he had a defiant streak. "What are you waiting for?"

Chapter Seven

Beating the beast.

The second officer struck by the glass died of his injuries, cradled in the arms of Inspector Garden. On the left elbow of the goatskin coat a numeral began to change, which Inspector Garden and Nathan saw with their own eyes. Their open-mouthed response painting the picture for everyone else to see. The numeral changed from IV to VI, glowing red and the voice boomed out loudly again as the whole house shook violently around them.

"LEAVE THIS PLACE OR PERISH! MY STRENGTH HAS NOW DOUBLED IN CAPACITY; I SHALL DESTROY YOU ALL!" Followed by mocking laughter.

"YOU RECKON? NOT WITHOUT MY SAY SO, CREATURE!"

It was John Sobers. Peri and Stuart, stood directly behind Nathan and Inspector Garden. He squirted holy water at the direction of Peter and the smoke billowed off him and the roar from the coat was ear piercing. Peter fell to the floor and lay still. John pulled Nathan and the Inspector outside. The house ceased to shake at least for now.

"What the hell is that thing in there and what did you do?'

Nathan was more surprised by John than whatever that was in there. Before John could respond to the DI's query, Peri had drawn a circle around them all and then tipped holy water down afterwards.

"That is Hell my friend, Hell on earth if she had her way. We're protected for now in this circle, go outside of it and you may die for sure, let me assure you of this. What we are dealing with is the very core of evil itself. For that is the Devil in there, Lucifer we're calling her, it suits the name because she is female this time around."

"Okay Freaks! Let us out of this circle so that we can do our job," Nathan simply didn't believe this.

"You leave this circle now and we can't save you. Please stay here and let me handle this first? You can arrest Peter afterwards, I promise you." John had that look of honesty about him, impossible for Nathan to mistrust.

"He's telling the truth Sir, I've been inside that coat myself, she's extremely dangerous and volatile."

Peri felt it necessary to back the holy man up. Stuart held his gun behind his back, cocked ready to fire at whatever came his way.

"Stay in this circle and you'll be fine," repeated John before leaping out and returning to the Rectory.

"My men? They're not safe." Inspector Garden was worried for their safety.

"I will control the evil's focus by keeping it interested in me, that should keep the beast contained but I'm afraid it's limitless damage for your men if she attacks. All of you drink from this flask. Peri, help them!" replied John. "Don't worry this is only holy water. It hides your soul from her in there, drink!" Peri passed the flask to Nathan, and he drank, everyone else drank and John disappeared inside the house.

"Everyone in here get out, leave me inside; go now, hurry!"

John gave the instruction, and the police left the house carrying their fallen colleagues with them. DS John immediately called for ambulances.

"Now it's just you and I once more!"

John had more confidence this time. He went towards Peter to see if he was still alive, and he was. Lucifer had kept him in his trance. He went to touch the old man, but a force threw him back way across the other side of the room. A boom from Stuart's gun sounded as John landed at the feet of his friend, the shot stopped in mid-air and was sent back towards Stuart. He turned to dive away, but the shot sprayed into him and sent him against the wall. Stuart lay on the floor motionless, the gun four feet away. John wasn't sure if he was alive or dead at this point.

"Come for me Devil, bring your hate, I challenge you." Peter rose from the floor again, but now he was upside down and star-shaped, the holy water had dried off and its effect had gone. The Devil floated

Peter over John who was prone on the floor, his golden dagger was poised ready to plunge into him, but he wasn't low enough yet. "Peter! Wake up, hear me please. You must wake up. Stop what you are doing!" John shouted very loudly, and the hovering Peter stopped, his eyes opened and suddenly he realized that he was off the ground.

"What is going on? Why am I up here?" Peter was in a state of panic again now.

"NO!" The voice boomed out and the walls cracked from floor to ceiling. Nathan was watching from the circle and saw the walls splitting.

"Look! The house is cracking up we must help that man!" He stepped over the circle and ran towards the house with Inspector Garden closely following. Peri turned to see them disappear inside. The walls were beginning to crumble now.

She finished helping the police and followed them in. "Everyone out, the whole building will collapse!" She called.

Their essence was hidden from Lucifer who didn't notice them inside. Inspector Garden went to see Stuart on the floor. He stayed there with him. Peri saw him and her hands moved to her mouth with shock. She wasn't sure whether he was alive or dead either. Nathan stood underneath Peter; he stared at John, who was looking straight back at Peter, right in his eyes.

"Father Flaws! Remember your faith, the oath you swore to the one and only God, to protect your followers from harm and temptation, the contract cannot be broken. I promise to help you with that, but you must try and be strong now. Can you do that?"

The walls around them were crumbling badly; soon the whole house would collapse, and they'd all be trapped inside, enough souls for the Devil to gather. Then she will become real and ultimately unstoppable.

"I need you to come closer Peter, it's the only way I can help." said the Priest as he collected his thoughts.

Peri rushed forward, quickly squirting more holy water at Peter. This severed his levitation, and he crumpled to the floor just close enough for John to reach. John rolled over and plunged the dagger into

Peter. This had an instant effect. Another huge surge of power and the walls blew outwards, and a gust of wind swirled around the people. It turned to fire and then they finally saw it; the image of the Devil before them.

"Do it again before it's too late!" Peri screamed.

John once more pushed the dagger into the Priest. Following an almighty roar for several seconds. the fiery image drifted off and Peter lay limp in John's arms. From the canvas bag he was carrying, John pulled out a circular box, took the lid off and poured Peri's holy water that was inside it. He dragged the Goatskin coat off Peter and folded it up, closed the lid on it and rolled the box back into his bag. The house teetered dangerously from the previous blast; Nathan looked at the remaining creaking walls.

"We need to go now, it's all over!" Nathan and John both picked up Peter and carried him out. Inspector Garden and Peri had hold of Stuart. "Everyone here move way back now!"

They all struggled to run clear of the Rectory but made it just in time to see the whole house collapse, leaving only the roof recognizable. DC Klein returned in time to see the carnage left before him.

"I missed all the excitement, don't I Guv!" Nathan chuckled and planted a slap on his back.

The relief for everyone was huge. They were reflective, what would they say happened here. Luckily the media had been held off for twenty-four hours by DSI Bascoe, otherwise they would have difficulty containing this. They needed a very good story.

Four ambulances had arrived to collect casualties and The Coroner for Bishop Andrew's body. Nathan climbed into Peter's ambulance, Peri went with Stuart, who was clinging on just, thanks to the help of the Paramedics. John went to join Nathan, but he stopped him.

"He's my suspect John; I must make an arrest."

"He's all yours Detective Inspector, but I still have to exorcise him. Once he's out of surgery I can do this, we'll go together." Nathan agreed as they rode off to the hospital.

They arrived at the hospital and Peter was rushed straight into theatre, the golden dagger had pierced Peter's stomach and left kidney, but he was saved by excellent surgery. He was placed in the recovery ward and Nathan sat waiting for him to wake. John was dressed in his vestments; he was holding a wooden crucifix, which he placed on Peter's chest. He also had the Bible Stuart had loaned him.

"Please excuse me Inspector, but I must perform the Rite of Exorcism, and I must do this piece alone. Peter's soul needs saving."

"I'll be right outside John," Nathan fancied a coffee anyway.

Peri waited for Stuart to recover. His gunshot wounds were only superficial, not life threatening. She prayed for him in the chapel whilst in surgery. Now he was here alive, she was holding his hand for comfort once more. Her feelings for the man had deepened.

The Rite of Exorcism took a few hours; once finished, John came out physically exhausted. Nathan returned to the ward and stood next to Peter's bed. John left for just a few minutes to see Peri and Stuart. Peter woke to find Nathan handcuffing him, unaware of the devastation he had played a part in.

"Good morning, Father Flaws, you've been on quite a journey. Can you remember any of it?" Nathan first asked.

"I only remember putting on a Goatskin coat. It had taken my friend's life and others connected with him. But from then on, my memory is fuzzy."

"Then I'll fill in all the blanks Rev!" This rankled Peter a little, he's a Father of the catholic faith, not a Reverend of Christianity. Nathan took several minutes explaining all the recent occurrences to Peter and that his home was reduced to rubble.

"But I don't remember any of this." How could he? Peter looked a desperately ill man.

"Fuck the rest of this shit. You're under arrest for the murder and disposal of Bishop Andrews of Maythorne and Boundford. When you're well enough you're coming with me."

"The Bishop is Dead?" Peter felt sad.

"Oh, come on, you must remember? It has got you all over it, so you will do time for that even if you don't for the others." Nathan left the Priest cuffed to the bed. A police officer was placed on guard.

A few weeks later, everything had calmed down. The story given for the destruction of the Rectory was a gas explosion. The revelation that the Bishop's body had been found, and the news of Peter's arrest for five murders had finally surfaced. Nathan received his promotion, which meant DI John and DS Klein also rose in rank. Peter had recovered enough to be formally charged with all the murders, but cited insanity. The judge surmised that he was unfit to serve a prison sentence because of his health and he would spend the remainder of his life where Peri Keeble had once stayed, at Boundford Sanatorium.

Stuart and Peri formed a relationship from this latest ordeal and moved in together, but right now, at this moment they were standing, holding hands at the foot of Jessica's grave. John Sobers stood close by waiting for them. He still held on to the round box with the Goatskin coat inside. Stuart crossed himself and laid lilies. Peri kissed her fingertips and pressed them against the headstone. They walked away from Jessica to begin their new life and help John rid themselves of the evil coat once and for all.

"We must cast this out far away from us, any suggestions?" John tapped the bag, and they knew exactly what he meant.

"The sea is a hundred miles from here, throw it in there." Peri recommended, which was not a bad idea.

"Very well then, let's do that right now." added Stuart. All three climbed into Stuart's car and they began to drive to the coast.

Two hours later they arrived and hired a schooner to sail far enough out so they could sink the box down. John had sealed the box tightly and placed heavy rocks inside. He held the box at arm's length and slowly lowered it into the water. Then they stood and watched as the weight of the box sank under. They wanted to be satisfied it was truly gone from their lives. The bubbles rising meant that it hadn't yet reached the bottom. Soon after they had stopped, Stuart spoke up.

"I really hope that's the last we see of that damned thing, I'm tired of fighting it now."

"I'm sure it is my friend." John started the engine of the boat and then turned back to shore.

"Let's all go home then." added Peri and they did precisely that.

The End.

This concludes story three: The Priest.

Story Four
Entitlement.

Foreword

Five years pass and Jonathan Short discovers the Goatskin coat whilst on a holiday at the coast on his boat. He returns home with the jacket and hangs it proudly on the main stair post. During some routine home office filing he stumbles across his wealthy wife's life assurance policy showing a £2.5m payout upon accidental death and payable to him. The jacket works its magic on Jonathan as he plots to acquire this sum of money. The temptation is too strong to resist. But taking the life of the woman you love isn't as easy as it seems.

Chapter One

Life on a wave.

It was 2014; forty-year-old Jonathan Short was a busy man. However, he takes one-week personal leave every year. With that being now, he was more than happy to drive to the coast and sail his yacht; a 45ft schooner, for a couple of days free from the bustle of his humdrum life back at the office, in the Bank that he worked for.

Everybody hates bankers nowadays; ever since company directors awarded themselves fat bonuses. That grated against Jonathan; he was just a middleman. Mortgages and Insurance was about the level he worked with. His wife Karina, on the other hand was higher up. Her father was Chairman of the Bank; Karina at thirty-five, became Chair on the board of shareholders, his right-hand woman.

It was a sunny July day, not so typical of the summer in Britain these days. Carolina's sails were out, and the stiff breeze was sending him out, away from land. The sea chopped a little, and waves became more forceful as he sailed further out. Jonathan was a skilled sailor, had competed at Cowes once; his team claimed the silver prize that year. The clouds closed in, and rain was imminent. Jonathan had his life preserver on and reached for his cagoule, before the rain became heavier. Little steady spits of rain began to fall, and the wind churned at the waves, forcing the yacht up and down on the crest each time. Jonathan never picked good weather to sail in; this was typical of his luck right now. He secured the tether to himself so if he was thrown overboard; at least he was still attached to his pride and joy. If the Coastguard did have to rescue him, they'd have to save his boat as well. Jonathan moved down to the rudder and held the tiller fast, so he could avoid some of the bigger waves being sent up. The prow dipped down and then lurched back up again twice as he steered in; he looked over his shoulder and saw the shoreline had blended in with the clay colour of the sea; he was quite far out now. Then most unexpectedly a bolt of lightning shot down the mainsail and struck the deck. It was literally where Jonathan had stood moments before. He continued to hold the line, and another bolt shot down from the sky, this time it hit the rope he was holding which conducted down and burnt his hands. The jolt sent Jonathan overboard and into the sea. He was conscious for a few seconds and still attached to the boat, which continued to move out towards the ocean. Floating on his back and facing away from the boat he tried to pull himself back on to the deck but one more bolt of lightning had another surprise. It severed the rope when he was halfway up; he hit the water like a plank and this did send him unconscious, sinking down to the bottom of the sea, briefly hitting the bed when his life jacket became buoyant and pulled him to the surface. Something quite heavy had joined him on the rise back up. Jonathan held on tightly to it. When he broke the surface, he held the item attached to him out of the water. It was a round hatbox, a foot in diameter, heavy and sealed tightly. The storm had passed now and calmed seas all around him again. Jonathan swam to the side of the yacht and grabbed for the rope ladder and climbed back on deck. He was pleased not to have bothered the Coastguard this time.

Staring at the box pulled from the seabed, he wondered if this freak storm had led him here and as if by fate he found it. He ignored it for now and turned the yacht towards the chalets on the beach and headed back in. Returning Carolina to the Marina and moored, Jonathan clutched his new find under his arm; he resisted opening it until he was able to get home and share his treasure with Karina.

The near miss sent Jonathan packing a day earlier than he'd liked. He had been driving home for the last hour, the box next to him on the passenger seat. He was curious about it, but his intrigue was short lived thanks to a traffic jam, where he waited for two more hours, shunting forward in first, sometimes second gear. Finally, the sign for Langston, one more mile to his hometown, which is neighboured with Maythorne on the north and west side of the county, Boundford sits at the south and east side. Jonathan signalled for the slip road and drove down to the main route into Langston. Several more minutes and he was turning into his estate, a residential cul-de-sac, with exclusive seven bedroomed detached houses. Karina would be three more hours at work, enough time to prepare supper for when she returns.

He parked up and unpacked his car, placed his salty laundry into his washing machine and put the hatbox on the circular coffee table so that Karina would see it soon as she walked in. Still, he resisted opening it, though the temptation was getting greater, but then the phone rang, and his interest waned. The phone call was from his mother, and they spoke for about an hour about his trip, how she worried while he was away, even though he's forty. He mentioned his accident, she knew something was up and that was the reason for her calling. She liked to think she was psychic, but really, she wasn't. The phone conversation took longer than he'd wanted but shortly after hanging up, he went to the kitchen and began preparations for the surprise dinner.

Two hours later and a waft of Chanel Allure entered his nostrils, telling him Karina was home. He kept quiet until she came to the kitchen.

"Surprised to see me?"

"Mmm! What are you making?" She kissed him and nosed at the recipe. No questions why he was early, it was all about her day as usual. "More shareholders on board this afternoon, that makes four hundred to date, half of them thanks to me!"

"That's terrific Darling." Jonathan whipped up the mayonnaise for the dressing, as he listened to her drone on about how fantastic she'd been. At least his mother was worried about him.

Karina kicked her Jimmy Choo's off and placed them almost OCD like on to the shoe rack. They were expensive and she looked after her possessions very carefully, having worked so hard for them. Nobody could say she didn't deserve these luxuries. She walked past the hatbox, completely ignoring it and fixed herself a drink, then poured an identical one for Jonathan, as he came through with the supper. They sat and ate in silence. He waited patiently for her inquiries into his health in general, having been away from her for almost six days. That's the very least she could've asked, instead she just asked the most annoying of questions.

"Has the home filing been done?"

"Karina Darling, I've just got back three hours ago. I'll do them tomorrow. Do you know I did have an accident yesterday? I don't feel like filing much right now."

"You were going to do them before you went away. I'm sorry about your accident, but we have annual taxes to declare, and they need to be done urgently." She was frowning.

"Well, you do them then!" Jonathan threw down his cutlery and walked out of the room. Their marriage was becoming a strain. These last three years Karina has been a complete nightmare, her job, her success, her Daddy, her this, her that, nothing nice about him. Jonathan almost filed for divorce last year, just to get some peace from it all. Karina followed in with his drink.

"I'm sorry! I've been insensitive, haven't I?"

"Just a little, yeah!" More than he was letting on.

"Okay, do them in the morning then please?" She kissed him again and he calmed down.

This is why he loved her, she would always do this, but it takes an outburst from him for Karina to see. After supper and the dishes, they sat with the television on. Jonathan brought up the subject of his accident and the encounter with the hatbox.

"I went overboard yesterday Karina and almost drowned, then I found this old thing on the bottom of the sea," he went over to it, and she saw it now.

"That old thing? Urrgh, why did you bring it into our home?"

"It could be treasure, it's quite heavy."

"And also, someone's ashes, yuk! It gives me the creeps!"

"I waited for you, so we could open it together!"

"I don't want it opened in here thank you. Do it in the shed. I'm not interested." Karina turned away from him and the hatbox as she continued to watch Emmerdale.

"Okay but if it's gold and worth a lot of money, it's all mine!" Jonathan sighed; he picked up the hatbox and left for the shed.

Karina just sipped her white wine spritzer in complete ignorance. The indifference of the woman incensed him sometimes. Nothing he did seemed worthy of her, as if Daddy had been drumming it into her all this time, since her move upstairs to the big oval table, at the Bank.

In the shed Jonathan laid the hatbox on his workbench, leaned over and took a medium sized chisel from his tool rack. The lid seemed to be sealed with wax, so he chipped it off all the way around the joints. Then using the chisel as a lever, opened the lid right off. To his surprise, it was just a leather coat, with heavy rocks in the pockets and very faint markings. Jonathan had nicked his hand whilst opening the box and some blood got on the collar. Before his very eyes it sizzled on the coat and absorbed every last drop. Jonathan unfolded it and looked at the craftsmanship. It was well made and seemed to fit a well-formed shape of a very large person. On the right elbow a letter J appeared, one standing and the other lying ninety degrees from the standing one. It looked like the coat is going to start all over again. Jonathan was a thin man, thanks to all the stress of his marriage, but nobody really noticed. Because of the size of the coat, he didn't put it on. He would feel dwarfed by it, so instead he took it back into the house and hung it over the balustrade of his stair rail, then joined Karina in bed. She smelled wonderful, the Chanel Allure was a real turn on for him; he had picked it out on one of their rare shopping sprees together. He climbed into bed beside her, but she just turned over and uttered one word.

"Finally!"

She'd been waiting for him to come to bed, put on his favourite perfume, two hours ago, but her interest in sex drained away with each minute he was in the shed with that damned hatbox. Her hand flailed at the lamp switch and turned the room black with night, then instantly fell asleep. Jonathan cursed himself, and lay there for one more hour awake, thinking of that coat downstairs, but not really knowing why. Who did it belong to, why was it cast into the sea. It wasn't fate that he found it, just pure bad luck.

The 6am alarm pipped five times before Karina punched the snooze button, and the coffeemaker began to gurgle. She slipped out of her negligee and went into the en-suite shower; Jonathan was still asleep. She owned the kind of shower that you can program to sense you entering and immediately sets the temperature to your specific needs. How the rich do live their lives! Nine minutes later, the snooze button released; the alarm was louder, and the coffee was done, waking Jonathan with the smell of it and the din of the early morning chirpiness of the disc jockey on the breakfast show. Missing out on a rare moment of passion with Karina last night, made him feel miserable and he knew that a day of tedious filing was ahead of him. He dressed his nakedness in a lazy tracksuit, not even bothering to put on socks or briefs.

He poured two coffees, sugared his and tipped cream in for Katrina's cup. He went down to the kitchen to make breakfast. Sometimes he wished they had a maid or housekeeper; they were rich enough to afford one. Jonathan would feel like a husband then and less like a slave. The shower was programmed to wash Karina for thirty minutes every morning, enough time to prepare for the fried eggs breakfast they have together every weekend. He was finishing the eggs when the creak from the room above told him that Karina had gone straight to the computer and begun her work from home. Jonathan ate his breakfast, and he put a cloche over hers, then set about reading his Daily Telegraph. Karina's father had emailed and requested her to come to the Bank early, so she finished dressing and applied modest make-up, then left the house without a single kiss for Jonathan. He was very much in her bad books. This could now go on for days.

The crossword would have to wait until lunch, there was filing to do. He took his coffee up to the second bedroom, known only as filing hell for dummies, in his mind anyway. He opened the door to a mountain of untouched mail. He sighed again.

By mid-morning Jonathan had finished the Tax Returns and posted those online. Next important bills and official mail. He created four piles, Karina's, Jonathan's, Bills and Correspondences. He took ten minutes out for coffee and custard creams, remembering to refill the coffee maker for tomorrow morning's ritual Sunday. He would have to make tea at lunch and then late afternoon he could have a gin or two, once he'd finished. Back in hell, he began to sort the letters and for six days there were many, mostly for Karina from shareholders, two for him, a card from his aunt who was holidaying indefinitely in Sydney, Australia. The other was an invitation to a Ball, the 25th anniversary school reunion, in September 2014. Great he could show off how rich his wife was and what an under the thumb cretin he is, while the rest swam around, crowing about being a great surgeon, lawyer, supermodel and such. This didn't cheer him up, plus it would take an enormous amount of sweet talking to persuade Karina. He filed it separately under maybe. Next, he turned his attention to Karina's personal mail, a couple from relatives, one from an online shopping site, most likely a receipt for something obscure that he didn't see, or she displayed in silence for him to notice, but failed to. Probably the latter, this receipt went to the Bills pile, next a formal letter. Insurelife, Katrina's life assurance policy; time for its ten yearly review and revision. He opened the envelope and slid out the letter. It was six pages long, explaining the review policy, the amount assured against her life or diminished health capacity, the breakdown on how the money will help in future and on the fifth page a separate policy for payment of £2.5m, to be paid to the client's husband. The breakdown was this: On behalf of Mrs Karina Jane Samson-Short aged 35; Insurelife will pay out £2.5m to Spouse: Jonathan Robert Short, upon **Her Death**. He read the sum again, then the underlined reason. This should enable Jonathan to live a balanced life. Where is the clause page? He thought, that's the last thing of a policy. How do you know when the default comes in? He would have to look into this properly another time. £2.5m, she did love him after all. This is half of her worth, before cashing in her assets. He began wondering what her Will was like, and he would look into this later. He'd already updated his, everything was Karina's, no kids involved. They had careers and they were running out of time to have some. Jonathan had even passed up an opportunity last night. It was now three o'clock in the afternoon, the filing finished, time for the mouth-watering gin he'd been promising himself. He went to the bar and poured a gin and tonic, suddenly a strange voice spoke up, neither male or female but a mix of both and a metallic resonance.

"You have to find that last page Jonathan, it's important!"

He spun around, someone was in the house, who? Did somebody creep in when Karina left? Maybe he should have checked. He sipped the gin and followed where the voice had come from. He stopped at the foot of the stairs.

"Who's there?" He cocked his ear, but he couldn't hear any footsteps.

"I'm right in front of you silly. Now listen, you have to find that last page of the policy!"

"Who the hell are you?" Jonathan's gin arm quivered, the ice clinking - this coat was talking to him! The symbols began to glow, he saw it just briefly, the narrow face of some sort of demon.

Chapter Two

Needles and Haystacks.

"If it makes you feel better, call me your conscience." The mouth on the demon was moving and these words were being said to him.

"Why would I need a conscience like you?"

"Because you're indecisive Jonathan, incapable of making the right choice. You should have made love to your wife last night, but instead you released me from my watery exile."

"How could you know this, you were inside that box?"

"I know quite a lot, Mr Short. Your blood dripped on to me, remember? It gave me a view of your history, when you were married, who to and that recently, you're becoming estranged. Because of this we can work together and get what you're entitled to, £2.5m."

"I love my wife; I couldn't hurt her. Karina is mostly how she is because of her father, Wesley Samson, because she listens to everything he says, even if it sounds like bullshit."

"So, then we start with him, remove these equations. If you learned how he made his millions, would this change your mind?" The demon grinned and knew this would press Jonathan into assisting.

"It would about him, but not Karina. She's lovely and beautiful. I couldn't physically harm her."

"Wesley Short started out as a salesman. He was a shrewd earner, then he encountered a rich widow, befriended her and persuaded the woman into giving her life savings to a phony savings scheme he'd dreamed up. She put up £18m, then she was killed in a mysterious house fire. Her daughter also died trying to help her, so don't shed one single tear over taking his money."

"I read about that fire; the widow was Mrs Gatley. She ran a large chain of department stores. That is wretched if it was Wesley, I wouldn't even know where to begin."

"If you wear me, all you have to do is say what you want to happen, and it will be so. Find that end page of Karina's policy, her father has a nasty accident, and she turns to you for comfort and advice. It's easy, think it over and make your decision. You won't be disappointed; you will be very rich!"

Jonathan drank the rest of his gin, he went to the lounge to pour some more, ignoring the coat for a few hours. Whilst he sat and thought about it, the seeds had already been sown. Wesley deserved to go, then he would begin with this. He would prise the page out of Karina. She would have a secret place to hide it and if she didn't co-operate, then he would have to execute her policy without it. His wife was due home in an hour. He didn't cook, just chose to order an Indian takeaway.

Exactly an hour later Karina entered the house with a slam of the door. Jonathan had dozed off.

"Don't worry Darling, I've paid the delivery boy, he's been waiting half an hour. Did you do the filing?"

"Err, yes all done, thanks Karina."

He lunged with a kiss, but she moved off quickly and hung her coat carefully on the hook and put her shoes on the stand. She went to the lounge for a glass of her customary wine. Jonathan took the bag of takeaway to the kitchen and served it up. Karina was still sour about the lack of attention from Jonathan last night. They had dinner in abject silence. For the rest of the night, every time Jonathan tried to speak, she would either leave the room or shush him during her favourite programs.

Feeling miffed and not thinking straight he decided to carry out the plan on getting his money. He stood up, walked out of the room and pulled the door to. He whispered to the coat.

"I agree, we have to do something, but tomorrow okay?"

"You won't regret this Jonathan, good man!"

He retired to bed. His thoughts were about to whom Karina would leave this page, probably a lawyer, her insurance company could still have it; it could even be in the house, but most likely of all she left it with a colleague at work. Who did she trust? Of course that would be

Olivia Hansen, one of her best friends and closest colleagues. Olivia had taken a fancy to Jonathan, although she was thirteen years older. An attraction had built up between them, because he wasn't achieving fulfilment from Karina. At last year's Christmas party, they shared a kiss, but an interruption prevented any further action. The hall they had hired flooded, thus averting something a bit more substantial. Awkward moments between the two have followed them ever since. Nobody else knew about it and Karina was totally oblivious. He drifted off to sleep with Olivia on his mind.

The following morning, Jonathan woke and looked to his right. There she was, crept into bed without a word of affection. He got out of bed and went downstairs, the clock in the kitchen pointed at four fifteen. The coffee machine will wake Karina at six; he halved a grapefruit and poured orange juice, toasted bread for himself and ate his breakfast alone.

He washed up after himself and went back to his room, to dress for his first day back at work; he put on a charcoal two-piece suit, pale blue shirt and a champagne toned tie. He gave his loafers a polish, put them on. He came back downstairs and hung his suit jacket on a kitchen chair.

"Good morning, Jonathan." came a voice from behind him. It was that coat again.

"Hi, listen? I don't want to hurt Karina." He whispered and then sat at the third from bottom step so he could listen to some more advice.

"We're not going to hurt Karina today. Leave your suit jacket here and put me on instead. We will focus on Wesley, then see if Olivia has that last page." How could the coat know of this? He was only thinking of this last night and then he remembered that he dripped his blood on to it. "All you have to do is drop a little bit of Olivia's blood on to me, I can do the rest. There is little point going after your wife at this stage. You need her wanting you and the only way of doing that is by sorting out Wesley." Jonathan liked this plan.

"Fine, I'll wear you, but only to take out her precious Daddy."

"Suits me!"

The coat went quiet again. So, Jonathan left the house to buy his morning paper from the newsagent. On the way over he was thinking;

how could he possibly collect Olivia's blood? She worked on the same floor as Karina; the only way was to see her in the canteen before they started work. He bought his paper and returned to the house and swirled the coat around his shoulders, sliding his arms in, leaving his suit jacket behind. The coat immediately accommodated his frame. The shoulders narrowed and fit snugly, the sleeves shrank to meet his wrists, at last another plaything for the Devil. Jonathan had no idea what he'd let himself in for. He locked the house and clicked the central locking on his car to open. He drove for ten minutes to the bank and parked. He saw Olivia's car parked in the executives' bay and with her in mind, he went to find her in the bank. Straight to the canteen and there she was, but so was Karina. They were sitting together; Jonathan bought a coffee and sat at a separate table. A few minutes later Karina left the table and walked towards Jonathan, she seemed less angry with him, or maybe it was because she was at the bank.

"See you for lunch?" She smiled, not even noticing that he was wearing the coat.

"Of course." He kissed her and she left for upstairs. Hesitantly he moved to Olivia's table. "How are you today?" Olivia smiled at his inquiry.

"I'm okay Jonathan, thank you." She was shy and tilted her head to the side; she smiled and gazed at him. When speaking on the phone she had a very confident voice, but to see her here now, you wouldn't place the two together as the same person.

"Can I get you another coffee?"

"That would be nice, thank you."

Jonathan moved quickly. He always kept an emergency sewing kit with him; he took Olivia's cup to the dispenser, he poured a coffee, then dropped a small needle from the sewing kit into the cup and then filled the rest with milk. A trick he once played on a bully at school; he drank the needle, and it pricked the bully's throat when he tried to swallow it. The blood frothed out and everyone laughed at him. He didn't bully Jonathan after that. This was how he would catch Olivia; he poured one coffee for himself and carried some napkins back to the table, pretending that the coffees were hot. Olivia drained her old one and took the fresh cup from Jonathan. He sipped his and anticipated

Olivia drinking hers. She gulped in a mouthful and the needle went in. It jabbed her cheek, and she held her mouth with her hand. Acting surprised, Jonathan assisted her.

"What's wrong Olivia? Can I help?"

She spluttered and coughed. She hadn't swallowed the needle, but there was enough blood to see. Jonathan held out the napkin, she dabbed the blood onto it and Jonathan led her to the restroom to help clean her up. The napkin went into the coat pocket. He knew the coat would analyse this whilst he was helping her. In the restroom, Olivia ran the cold water and drank some more, stemming the bleeding.

"There was a needle in that coffee. That was close, I could have swallowed it."

"Yes, it was close." Jonathan seized his opportunity to get closer to Olivia; he cupped her face with his hands. "Let's have a look inside your mouth?" She opened up and he looked inside. "You're fine, the cold water seems to have done the trick."

Olivia brushed her teeth to remove the taste of blood. Jonathan moved away from her. They had a desire for one another, but Jonathan didn't want to take advantage so soon. He left the rest room first and Olivia a couple of minutes after. He went to his desk and set about doing some work. Olivia took the elevator up to the executive floor; she walked quickly into her office before Karina could see.

Jonathan sat at his desk, thinking about Olivia when Wesley Samson decided to make an impromptu foray on to their floor. He passed Jonathan's desk and just stared through him again, just like he always did. . Then he spoke.

"This year's figures have come down from The Treasury. They are promising after such a shaky start. You will receive a bonus this Christmas. As directed by the Chancellor of the Exchequer, all the Executives' bonuses have been frozen pending an independent inquiry; so well done everyone, please continue the good work." Then he waved Jonathan out of his chair. "Mr Short, I'd like a word with you!" Wesley then left the floor with Jonathan following behind.

They got into the elevator, Wesley pressed for the top floor. Why was he being taken to the Execs' floor? He strode out after reaching the top floor and into his office, the PA and Jonathan barely keeping up, it was a different pace up here he thought to himself. The PA continued through to her area of the office and Wesley slunk down into his leather chair, inviting Jonathan in. Wesley opened a brown file on his desk and summoned Jonathan to sit down.

"Before your vacation, I distinctly asked you to close your Mortgages, that were nearing completion. Why wasn't this done?"

"Stubbornness Mr Samson, the lady at Sunningdown Farm; Mrs Hawkes, would not foreclose. She said she needed the money to repair a farm building." His excuse worked on Wesley. "Maybe you could come yourself and persuade her to pay. The other ones I will close this very week. They have promised to pay me."

"Where is this farm then Jonathan?"

"I can take you, if you fancy a jaunt with your son-in-law."

Jonathan knew he would not relish another lecture session, on how to treat his daughter. Karina probably complained about the other night, but Jonathan wanted to unleash his frustrations on Olivia and oh god he would be doing that very soon.

"After lunch then, you can take me there, I'll tell the PA, to cancel any appointments. Right, get out and close some deals!"

Wesley went out onto his balcony for a cigar. The PA opened the door and ushered Jonathan out. He returned to his own desk and sat thinking about how he could dispose of Wesley Samson.

"Olivia doesn't have the paperwork, but you wanted to nail her good, yes?"

"She is amazing, I wouldn't be able to help myself."

"Never mind that, somebody else has it here though. Olivia was present at the insurance company with Karina, when she renewed it, Olivia knows that Wesley Samson's PA holds the complete policy. Karina has all six pages inside her safe in the office." The coat gleaned all this from just a few drops of blood.

"So, I need to get the combination and take a look?" He whispered.

"Or seduce the PA."

"That will have to wait until another time. I have an arrangement with Wesley this afternoon."

"Good move, now remember whatever you want to happen, it will be so."

The coat went quiet again; some of Jonathan's co-workers were staring at him strangely. Had he been talking to himself? He typed into his computer to log on, began to address his workload.

At lunch he met with Karina, and they ate together but didn't really speak. She really wouldn't give up this until Jonathan apologized. But he never will; not while he's wearing the coat. The wedge would be driven further between them and an irreparable distance would be built. But she did speak about business and work things, much to his annoyance, making him want Olivia's company more and more.

"Daddy says you're going to visit a client of ours, because she refused to foreclose on her mortgage." She probed.

"Yeah, that's right. He can see how stubborn she is then, can't he?"

"Be careful of Daddy, Jonathan. He doesn't suffer fools gladly."

"So suddenly you're married to a fool, are you?" This was the wrong response Karina was looking for. Jonathan left the table and walked away, then called back. "I'll see you at home!"

It was approaching two o'clock and time to collect Wesley for their trip to Sunningdown Farm. In the back of his mind, he was thinking that Karina knows they are going together, but the man irked Jonathan so much. With him out of the way, he would finally become the male influence on Karina that he always should have been. He could easily convince her that it was an accident. Wesley was waiting in the car park for Jonathan who unlocked his car and opened the door for Wesley to get in.

"Right on time Short, that's an improvement." Jonathan resisted his jive talk and drove out to Mrs Hawkes farm. Then just to provoke Wesley a little, Jonathan brought up his not so innocent origins.

"I learned a little about how you earned your first £18m."

"There's nothing secret about it Short. Just very wise investment plans are all you need to know."

"But I know a little bit more, like how you started the fire that killed Mrs Gatley and her daughter. Not very shrewd. I bet the police don't know" He was enjoying this, as Wesley squirmed in his seat.

"Your job isn't very secure right now Short, redundancies are imminent, but if you'd like to still have yours, then keep your mouth shut!"

"Relax Mr S, I won't tell a soul. You should know though, that if I want to move up the company, then I would have this in my locker, should you refuse."

"You can't prove that I did start that fire, therefore you don't have much to blackmail me with."

They were approaching the farm at this point, so the conversation stopped while they visited Mrs Hawkes. Jonathan looked to his left and saw the derelict building. It was indeed in a desperate need of repair. He parked and let Wesley out, Mrs Hawkes noticed them parking and came out to greet them.

"Good afternoon, Mr Samson, Mr Short. How can I be of service?"

"Come now Mrs Hawkes, you know why we're here. The rest of your mortgage must be paid; you really should foreclose." Wesley announced almost instantly, no messing around with him when it comes to business.

"Yes, I understand Mr Samson. Please I need an extension, the building I mentioned to Mr Short needs fixing, rather urgently. It is graded so I can't knock it down without permission and that costs money."

"Mrs Hawkes I can't extend your mortgage, you must pay the rest, then we can negotiate a new mortgage and then you can save this old barn."

"It is more than that Mr Samson, come with me. I want to show you something."

Mrs Hawkes and Wesley walked over to the building. It was huge, had tarpaulins covering the roof, the windows had been smashed, and Jonathan was walking three metres behind. What were they going to see inside? They reached the building and inside were thousands of stacks of hay bales, piled from floor to ceiling. Jonathan looked through the window as Wesley and Mrs Hawkes entered the building. Jonathan then thought to himself, what if those haystacks fell onto

Wesley; they'd crush him wouldn't they? The coat glowed and seemed to like this idea.

"Where am I going to put all this hay if I don't have a building Mr Samson?"

"I sympathize Mrs Hawkes, I really do, but you signed a contract with us to foreclose by the end of August. That has passed." Wesley didn't budge.

"Now!" shouted Jonathan.

No sooner had he done this, there was a rumbling sound and then hundreds of hay bales burst out, fell and began to roll towards Wesley and Mrs Hawkes. The looks on their faces as they moved backwards, was one of horror as the stacks continued to fall like chimneys being demolished. Wesley ended up against the wall and couldn't go any further and the rest just quickly rolled along and then slammed into him plus a few hundred more behind them. Mrs Hawkes used her sense and lay on the floor allowing the bales to roll over her, this saved her life, although she was buried and a little dazed. Jonathan helped Mrs Hawkes out first and then began to look for Wesley. His arm was sticking out, but it wasn't moving. Jonathan checked for a pulse, but there wasn't one. Mrs Hawkes dashed to call for an ambulance and Jonathan telephoned Karina at the Bank. The ambulance came and the fire rescue team helped lift the heavy bales off Wesley. When they finally recovered him, his ribs had been shattered and they had punctured a lung, blasting the wind out of him and killing him instantly. He was pronounced dead on arrival at the hospital. Jonathan would need to explain to Karina, what happened. The coat had collected its first soul, eleven more to go and just for show, a numeral I, appeared on Jonathan's left elbow.

Chapter Three

Queen of the Bank.

The next morning, Karina sat with Jonathan, waiting to be driven home from the hospital and for an explanation. Exactly how did her father end up getting squashed by thousands of hay bales? It could be up to a few weeks before the Coroner would release Wesley's body for a funeral.

"So, tell me, why weren't you injured from this accident?"

"Because it was a derelict building, it wasn't worth the risk going in. Wesley entered with Mrs Hawkes and the rest you know. I was at the window, there wasn't enough time to warn him, let alone get to him." From the look in his eyes, she knew he was making some of it up.

"He shouldn't have been there; it was your mess to clear up."

"I did say I would handle it alone, he insisted on coming along to finalize things."

"Just drive me home Jonathan!"

This didn't seem like they were getting any closer, more distant and her anger was being vented on him, not at her father for dying. He drove home and gave Karina some space to calm down but was there for her if she needed him. Karina called Selena, her sister; she'd be devastated. Jonathan stood in the garden and peered out at the ornamental fishpond, then that voice from the coat chimed in again.

"Jonathan don't waste any time feeling bad about Wesley. You must find that page, do it quickly too. Karina is getting suspicious of us."

"I don't feel bad. Yes, you're right, I'll go to the bank in a bit." He drank his juice and placed the glass in the sink. He went through to Karina in the lounge. She was still speaking with Selena, and it seemed they were both upset.

"I have to go back to the bank, will you be okay?" She waved him off dismissively and he took that as permission. Olivia would be there, his chance to catch up with her, to make sure her mouth was okay.

As he parked at the bank, the voice from the coat spoke once more. "Forget about Olivia, find that document, the P.A has it remember, focus on that."

"Okay! Not so loud, people will hear." Jonathan rebuked the coat; he hated to be rushed on things.

"Sorry Jonathan, you're the only one who can hear me. Now do your work!" The coat replied coldly.

Jonathan entered the bank, placed his case at his workstation and headed for the lobby lift. Pressed the button in for the top floor, but just before the doors closed a lady entered the lift with him. She was in her mid-thirties, had brown bobbed hair. She was tall and smelled wonderful. Her tapered blouse was tantalizingly unbuttoned to her midriff, showing a steep plunging cleavage. The skirt she was hardly wearing showed off her shapely behind. Jonathan liked what he saw.

"I'm going to see my mother, I'm Amy Hansen." She introduced herself.

"Oh yes of course, Olivia, she's your mother, she talks a lot about you actually, though I've never seen you before." Jonathan stared ahead at the mirrored lift walls, admiring her beauty, without her noticing.

"That's a very nice jacket." She didn't seem to remember it. It had been nineteen years, enough time to forget.

"Thanks!" Jonathan was perplexed why she was the first person to mention it. Nobody else commented so far, unless they didn't like it.

They reached the top floor and disembarked, heading in different directions. Amy went to Olivia's office; everyone could hear shrieks of joy as she went in. Jonathan on the other hand went to the P A's office to find that page. He entered and Louise Garfield questioned his presence here.

"Shouldn't you be at your workstation Mr Short?"

"Yes, you're so right Louise, but before the untimely passing of Wesley Samson, he asked me to gather some files that he was reading on my behalf."

"Oh really? He didn't mention it, where are they?"

"They are in his safe, you're the only one who has the combination. Why, don't you help me?"

"Not really Jonathan, no!"

This remark made him think negatively for a few seconds that filing cabinet you're standing next to is going to fling open and cut your right arm. That very thing happened; the cabinet did exactly that and sprang out so quickly, it knocked Louise over and across the floor.

"Good lord Louise are you okay?" Her arm was bleeding badly. "I'll get the first aid box, wait there." He moved quickly to the cupboard and grabbed the green box, his opportunity to get that combination without anyone knowing. Collect the blood and allow the coat to analyse it. He rolled her sleeve up and tended her wound, pressing a cold sterile patch to stem the blood. She winced but was pleased that it took the edge off her pain for a few moments. Afterwards Jonathan slipped it into the pocket of the coat. He rolled out a bandage and applied it to Louise's arm. All wrapped up, he replaced the box.

"You're good at that, thank you. That looks tidy."

The distraction allowed them to feel more at ease with each other. Little knowing that Jonathan was the cause of it all. He left the office and returned to his own desk.

"That was clever Jonathan. You're accepting that it could be easy to take care of your wife in the same manner."

"You're mistaken, I love her, despite her flaws. I couldn't hurt her."

"But you won't be hurting her, the forces of nature will take care of it for you." The coat left that point hanging, but Jonathan didn't respond to it.

"Just work out the combination and we'll have that copy. Once we know the terms and conditions, I'll decide what to do with her."

Jonathan worked for two hours and then he saw Karina walking in and a black man in his early sixties. It was the Treasury Director, Floyd Gant. He spoke to the senior staff on the floor and an announcement was made.

"Ladies and Gentlemen, fellow workers! Following the sad news of your Chairman, Wesley Samson's passing I can tell you that Karina

Short will be Temporary Chairperson for the interim period, until we can elect one in a fair Ballot to be held at the end of August. So please continue the good work and make Karina as welcome as you did her father. That's all, return to your desks!"

Oh great! Thought Jonathan. She's in charge here as well as at home now, this will be unbearable. Floyd and Karina left the sales floor for the comfort of the upper offices. Then the coat interrupted his train of thought.

"The combination to the safe is 32 west, 23 east, 5 east followed by 10 west. Now all you need to do is get up there and get it."

"If I go up there whilst Karina's up there, she'll kind of know what I'm looking for, won't she. I'll wait for Floyd to leave."

"Be wary of that man Jonathan, his motives with Karina are impure."

"You mean he wants to fuck her, don't you? Old news, every man here wants to do that, but I'm the one who gets to take her home."

"Not for much longer if you don't get a move on with your plan. She'll be too powerful for you to control."

This made Jonathan jolt out of his chair and check upstairs. He crossed paths with Olivia and Amy, heading for lunch on the way up. She smiled coyly and Jonathan grabbed another lurid look at Amy by way of a reflection. He seemed to fancy her daughter more than he did Olivia now. The lift shut on all three of them and Jonathan focused on what he wanted to achieve this afternoon, get that last page from Karina's safe. He could hear talking and laughing coming from his wife's office, the door was shut, and Louise was strangely outside, when her office was situated right next to Karina's. Now Jonathan was curious. He headed to the office door and leaned his ear to listen. He heard ice rolling into two glasses and liquid being poured.

"So sorry that my friend Wesley has left to do St Peter's accounts." Floyd toasted and Karina clinked his glass and replied.

"I still don't get how he died and the other two were unharmed. If that building was as dangerous as Jonathan says, how come he allowed him to go in?"

"It is odd, but wait until the accident report comes through, then you'll know more."

Floyd touched her shoulder and rubbed it gently. Karina felt an immediate attraction to Floyd. She didn't move away, and his thumb followed up that caress with a journey south to her left breast. Again, she stood and allowed this, his whole hand cupped under and gently squeezed, she bit her lip. This is the kind of attention that Jonathan should be giving her, she thought. Floyd's other hand joined the party with the other breast, his skilful thumbs hitched down her top and scooped out her breasts to look at. She sighed as he paid attention to them. Karina moved her own hand to Floyd's trousers. She felt him through the cloth, his was at least ten inches long. Then Jonathan knocked and entered, catching them in mid foreplay.

"Fucking unbelievable, you're groping my wife you Sleazeball!" Karina lifted her assets back into her top and stepped away from Floyd. The office door shut and the three stood looking at each other. "Well! What are we going to do about this?"

"Look Mr Short, I got carried away in the moment of it all. If you'd like to keep this quiet, then there's a corner office on this floor for you."

"No, it's okay, you can have my wife. I'll get my stuff and go. As for you Darling, I'll go home and pack a case until you decide what it is you want from our fucked-up marriage!" Jonathan left the office and strode back towards the lift. "Floyd should be thrown from the window and fall to his death."

Jonathan made the merest of mumbles and then heard a crashing noise, Floyd had instantly dived headfirst, smashing into the window and down to the pavement below. There was a loud thump as his body landed. Karina screamed as she saw him from her floor, lying still, his blood escaping from a very large gash. Floyd breathed heavily. Jonathan's coat showed a second notch on the sleeve, now it read II. Two souls down, ten more to be found.

"Jonathan, if it's any consolation he's the biggest womanizer in Langston, his death was necessary. Karina won't thank you for killing him, but at least he can't touch her anymore!" The coat made some sense, but Jonathan wasn't worried about Floyd. He wanted Amy now and he was even more determined to take her. Karina had dug her own grave with this, 'act of betrayal'. If he hadn't entered at the point he did, Floyd and Karina would have been making love right there in that office.

"I still need to find that policy page and now I've resigned from the bank. How will I succeed now?"

"Karina's solicitor has another copy; you could go there."

The siren of the ambulance could be heard coming to collect Floyd's body. A crowd had formed around him. Jonathan went over to look. Floyd was a mess, this was what he wished for, he looked up and saw Karina staring down from up there like some sort of overseeing god. Her face had regret written all over it, but he didn't care right now. He averted his gaze and walked over to his car.

"Okay then, let's go to her Lawyer's office, I'll get that policy."

"Now were talking!"

Jonathan drove from the bank to the Lawyer's office. Having now taken two lives, his power of persuasion would double, and other skills were about to develop. The building of Francis, Kelly and Vale Associates is a big hunk of marble placed in the middle of Langston, a gift from the Arabian Sheikhs who were once a client of theirs. Jonathan entered reception and rang the bell. A lady came to the window. She was small in stature and looked old, nearly seventy years of age, but very humble and kind.

"Can I be of service to you Mr?"

"Short, Jonathan, I'm Karina's husband. She has left a policy with you, and I am eager to look at it briefly. You see the one at home is incomplete and I need the whole policy so that my own Lawyers can peruse it. Can I speak to someone please?"

The lady dialled the phone and relayed the same request to whoever she was talking to upstairs. Jonathan felt like some kind of Jedi and looked forward to seeing Karina's Lawyer.

He wasn't disappointed either. She was confident, sexy, striding towards him and the rise and fall of her clothing was turning him on.

"I'm Janice Vale, Mrs Samson-Short's brief. Please come to my office, we can talk more privately there." Jonathan followed her through and sat down at her invitation.

"You have a life assurance policy held here on behalf of Karina; I would like to take a look at it please." She obeyed his request and went to her files, pulled out the policy and laid it on the desk, then slid it across.

"What did you want to look for in particular?"

Jonathan went immediately to the back and discovered that this one was incomplete too. He frowned and Janice asked again.

"Is it all there?"

"No, it's not. Where would the last page be, if you don't have it?"

"Her father perhaps, I don't know; he was here when they filed it with us."

"Of course he was, he's always been in the way! Thank you for your time, Janice, I'll leave now."

Frustration filled his mind, and he was about to have an outburst of anger, but the coat stopped him in his tracks.

"Don't do that here, you can't hurt innocent people. She was telling the truth back there. Wesley does have a copy; he took it after they filed it."

"That's lovely, where do we begin to look. He's dead, isn't he?"

"He's still at the hospital; he will still have a small amount of blood in him. We go there and take some, you'll have your answer."

"That's a better plan than mine. We'll do that now."

"Good, we won't fail this, I promise." Jonathan drove to the hospital.

⊷⊶⊷◄◆►⊶⊷⊶

Chapter Four

On with the Plan.

Jonathan reached the hospital and requested to see Wesley Samson's body. The receptionist didn't even argue, she just called for an Orderly to show him the way. They caught the lift down to the depths of the hospital and along a tiled corridor with black rubber doors at the end. Once inside the room, the Orderly stood by Wesley's body and rolled the sheet back. His pale face sleeping peacefully, Jonathan ushered the Orderly away.

"Can I get some privacy please?" And away the Orderly went.

Once again Jonathan took out the pin from his sewing kit and probed it into Wesley's cheek. A bead of blood emerged after a couple of seconds, he dabbed a cloth with it and placed it into the pocket of the coat. He then cleaned away his activities and placed the sheet back over Wesley's face. Then pretending to be overcome with grief, he rushed out, pinching his nose, which fooled the Orderly completely. He wasn't aware of anything odd about it.

"Well done, Jonathan, you're improving your technique." Congratulated the coat.

"Thanks!"

The coat would take a few minutes analysing the blood, to find out where Wesley would hide the complete policy. Jonathan went home to pack a small case of clothes. Now he needed somewhere to go. He remembered that Olivia and Amy went home for lunch; he was hoping they could still be there. He drove to Olivia's house and parked outside. Why was he hesitating? It was over between Karina and him; the path was clear. Amy came to the window and saw Jonathan. She waved and then spoke to her mother, who looked out and smiled at him. That was all the invitation he needed. He left the car and knocked on Olivia's door.

"I heard that you walked out. Secretly I hoped you'd come here first."

"Can you believe the nerve of that man? Going after my wife like that, he must be unhinged or something, but she didn't protest about it either," explained Jonathan.

"You can stay with us until you find somewhere if you like. Amy won't mind, will you?" She looked at her daughter.

"No, you're welcome to stay." Getting the seal of approval from both made Jonathan glad.

"I'll set up a bed in the spare room for now. We don't want to rush things, do we?" offered Olivia.

Jonathan was happy with that, because he lusted for Amy more. She showed the room, and Jonathan dropped his bag down and stood inside for just a few moments.

"I'll give you time to clean yourself up. I've taken the rest of the day off. We'll have an early tea, then a few drinks perhaps. I'm so happy I feel like celebrating!"

Olivia left to prepare tea for them and Jonathan began to change out of his suit. It was at this juncture that the coat intervened.

"Wesley has the full copy of the policy at his house in Maythorne. You'll have to go there and retrieve it."

"Well seeing as it's a drive to the neighbouring town, I'll do this tomorrow. At this point in time, I'd like some alternative company other than yours."

"Who is it you're talking to?" asked Amy, whilst standing in the doorway, looking at him in his half naked condition.

"Err! Nobody, just a reflection to myself that's all."

"Sounded more than just a reflection to me." She stepped inside the room and closed the door behind them.

Jonathan had taken off the coat to change, so without it he was just a normal man. Amy had some contact with the coat several years ago and instantly recognised it as it hung on the chair before her.

"I've seen that before. I've even worn it; how did you get it? I'd never thought I'd see it again."

"I found it whilst sailing. It's been with me ever since. How do you know about it, when nobody else can see it?"

"My Mom's vile, abusive ex-partner tried to have sex with me when I was fifteen. He tried several times to do it. When I turned him down, he drugged me and did it anyway. Then I met a kind man named Fabian Le Vor, who guided me away from that evil man and I was allowed into a group that he ran. I wore the coat and made an accident happen which made sure my future stepfather could never do that again. He died of his injuries when infection set in. I'm not sorry, he deserved it." She told him.

"Well, that's been happening to me lately. Everything I think of will happen when I wear it."

"Wear it now and show me, please?" Amy asked.

As soon as Jonathan put it on, Amy couldn't see the coat anymore and so he made one suggestion.

"You don't know anything about this coat Amy, or what it can do, unless I take it off again."

"Oh, I'm so sorry, I don't know why I'm here I'll just go!" Amy felt embarrassed and left the room, afterwards the coat spoke.

"She is the only one who knows about us. If you take me off again, she'll end up stopping you from doing what we've planned."

"Okay, I won't do that again." promised Jonathan and went out to have tea with Olivia. He still had a desire for Amy though; he would seize that chance soon.

Everything else went as normally as it could do until they retired to bed, a bit tipsy and glowing from each other's company. Olivia wasn't going to take advantage so soon, pecked Jonathan's cheek and he went toward his own bedroom. On his way, he walked past Amy's room and looked in. She was asleep, but her bedclothes had ridden back to reveal most of her sexy body clad in a negligee. Even on her back her breasts looked full and lovely, the rise and fall of her chest so sexy, but though he had the power, he didn't impose any further; he would wait for an invitation. He quickly went to his own room and slept off his drunkenness.

Olivia lay in her bed thinking of Jonathan. How lucky she was that he and Karina had fallen out. Her opportunity to get closer to him had arrived. Now all she wanted was to savour every moment, but only when she was ready.

Next morning Jonathan prepared himself for a drive to Maythorne. He researched on his laptop for the address to Wesley's mansion. He crept out without disturbing Olivia and Amy, began his drive to Maythorne. The journey took thirty minutes and on reaching Maythorne, he noticed that the rush hour had started, as it was an artery to the motorway. It was utterly unbearable. As the rush hour began to fade, the coat had something to say.

"We haven't long until we reach the mansion. Wesley employs a crew of workers who may pose threats to what our goal is."

"No problem, we'll deal with them all."

"Even if that means harming someone?"

"We'll take care of it." Jonathan's well ironed scruples had completely disappeared now.

"Very well then, in that case, drive on!"

He stopped his car just outside the Mansion ground and walked the rest of the way; the estate was huge, gated at the front and tall conifer trees planted around the perimeter. This was okay; Jonathan could find a way in without drawing attention to what he was doing. On this day Karina and Selena had invited the whole family over to discuss the will their father had left for them. Jonathan didn't know this. He had his work cut out if he wanted to reach that final clause he'd been searching for. As predicted by the coat there was a larger than usual squad of security on duty today.

"Something big is happening."

"I can only tell you what it is if we have some blood to analyse." mentioned the coat.

"No need, I can see Karina's car here. They'll be sharing out Pappa's estate, no doubt, fucking group of hawks the whole family are." The coat was relishing this newfound bitterness; but this made Jonathan unpredictable.

"You'll still need to bypass the security."

"Watch this!"

Jonathan's new bravery now held him in good stead after his handling of Floyd at the bank. He now knew whatever he says will happen, if only he'd ask for it. He walked out of his hiding place and walked quietly towards the guards. They saw him walking over and, in a pincer shape moved to intercept him.

"Don't worry boys, I'm not here for trouble. I've come to see Karina. I know she's here; I can see her car." He shouted to them.

One guard shouted back on behalf of the others.

"Mr Short we were told to keep you away from the mansion whilst you are separated from Mrs Samson-Short. Sorry you'll have to leave." Jonathan didn't realize that the coat only worked within one hundred feet of the victim.

"You'll need to get closer." The coat urged him.

Jonathan beckoned the first one over and he stepped forward. The other five stayed behind a few yards. He had to think quickly, speak clearly so they could hear his suggestions. They were holding billy clubs and bats; any gunshots would have alerted the family in the mansion.

"Hey Mike! Look, you're a nice guy but you can't go beating your friends up here with your bat, you could hurt someone." implied Jonathan. Straight after, Mike began swinging his bat at his colleagues, hitting two in the back and battering them both in the head and neck repeatedly. They were lying still on the grass, blood oozing from them. Jonathan stooped and touched some blood. He continued. "Well defend yourselves, don't let him get all the glory!" The rest of the men piled in and began to respond by kicking and hitting Mike back again. He fell to his knees; as one of them cracked his skull for the final time, he collapsed to the ground. Jonathan looked at his coat sleeve, and the numerals instantly changed from II to V, his power was three times stronger than before.

"Okay enough, you have kidney failure." The fourth man grabbed for his sides and crumbled to the floor. He vomited and then gurgled blood, but that was all he did, because now he was lying still and quite dead. "And you are quite unfit, so why don't you have a nice quiet aneurysm?" The fifth man clutched his head in obvious pain and Jonathan strode away, leaving him writhing in agony. Soon after the sleeve changed again to VII as he reached the mansion entrance. Jonathan smiled to himself; he liked this power now.

Once inside the mansion, he knew that the ladies would be in the front lounge and the study is to the right of the main hall. He crept in quickly and found the safe with ease. No combination needed; it would be Karina's birthday. He opened it and found the policy, and as quickly made his retreat. Running back to his car and racing home to Olivia's house, he knew that by now she had left for work. Only Amy was at home and probably still sleeping. He wasn't wrong. He crept back in and straight to his own room. He opened the envelope and peered at the last page, the clause. It clearly read that for Jonathan to claim his 2.5 million, he would have to stay married to Karina. Any foul play or random acts of violence that could potentially end her life would void the contract. She would have to die of natural causes.

"Bloody perfect, I can't even touch her now!" He threw them in the air, the six pages fluttered about in a mess.

"You can't touch her, but you can easily get someone else to do it. Like one of these girls?" The coat suggested.

"Yes, I see what you're getting at, I'll try it with Amy. She looks suggestible."

"Try what with me?" Amy announced, startling the hell out of Jonathan.

"Shit! Sorry didn't see you there" He quickly thought it over. "Would you like to go to a reunion ball with me this September? I'll pay you for just coming with me?"

"Okay I'd like that, what about Mum?"

"Oh! Don't worry, she'll be busy, helping Karina probably."

"Very well, it's a deal. Just tell me when and I'll be ready."

"Brilliant, now take off your night gown and show me your body?"

"Here, now?"

"Please? I wanted you the minute I saw you."

"Okay!"

Amy dropped the night gown down to the floor and Jonathan unzipped his trousers and took out his penis. She walked toward him, reached out and held it in her hand. She marvelled at how excited it made him. She knelt down and fed it into her mouth, moving her head back and forth. Jonathan had to leave the coat on, or the effects wouldn't work. He fondled her breasts while she sucked him with her mouth. He pushed his door shut and lifted her up, then he began to make love with Amy on the bed. She relished it all, getting on top and riding him quite well. They lasted a whole hour, and the coat remained absolutely quiet for once. After they climaxed together, they stayed spooning together in the bed. She turned on her back and lay still; he was stroking her hair and gazing at her perfect body. Jonathan was quite pleased with himself. He'd got what he wanted, didn't really feel guilty.

Chapter Five

Building an army.

Jonathan was happy, he'd successfully seduced Amy, found the clause page of Karina's will and killed five more men for the coat. He was lying next to Amy, the sheets were strewn everywhere, and he was gently caressing her shapely bottom, while she slept on her front. Then his mobile phone rang, and he could see it was Karina's mobile.

"What?" His voice sounding frustrated.

"Were you at Daddy's, yesterday?"

"I came by, but your goons prevented me from seeing you."

"Well, they're dead Jonathan, all of them. Did you do that?"

"Do you think I could do that? Come on Karina, I'm pissed off with you, but not to that extent."

"No course, I don't; but it's a mess here. Some papers are stolen from the study too. I'll have to stay here for a day or two, but can we meet to talk things through?"

"What's to talk about? I caught you with your tits out, being groped by our director! Any longer and you'd be fucking him!"

"I know that; it was a terrible mistake, and I was frustrated because we were supposed to have sex the other night. Please pick a day and time I'm sure we can straighten this out."

"Meet with her and play along, just long enough for you to get your money." The coat was alert again, after a ten-hour sabbatical.

"Okay Karina, I'll come to the bank at lunchtime. We'll talk there; my severance is due, and I need it."

"So, you're definitely leaving?"

"I think it's for the best; I have a business idea, and I want to set it up soon. We'll talk this afternoon." He clicked off the phone, without hearing Karina say, 'I love you,' He didn't care.

Amy stirred awake and clutched at her nakedness with the sheet. She became extremely embarrassed. Now she was shy and wanted nothing more than to get the hell away from Jonathan to her room quickly.

"Don't tell Mom about this, please?" She begged.

"You were lovely Amy, of course I won't tell her and thanks."

Jonathan smiled and rested on his hands behind his head, with a smug expression on his face. Amy left quickly to dress. Now he and the coat were able to converse.

"That sample of blood we took from the goon, well he was listening in on the first conversation with Karina. She plans to divorce you and nullify that will."

"Bet it was that horrid mother of hers and that hawkish sister, trying to convince her?"

"Yes, Mom was the influence, but if Karina rang you, maybe she's doubting that. Smooth things over with her, don't risk it. If you need my help, just say so."

"Right, I will try."

"You will succeed" The coat went quiet again.

Jonathan felt he needed to wash and pleaded for the coat to allow him to shower, he smelt awful. . The coat conceded and let him do this; smelling good, to remind Karina that he hasn't lost his charm, will help. He stripped, grabbed a towel and wash bag, went for a much-needed shower.

Amy was dressed and left her bedroom. She went to see Jonathan. His room was open, but he wasn't in and she could see the goatskin coat draped over the chair. She instantly knew that Jonathan had tricked her into sex last night. She was very cross and now he was no better than her mom's perverted boyfriend. She quickly left the house in disgust, and she planned to keep away for a while. She found a cafe and ordered coffee. The TV was on, the news headline reporting about the five men killed at Samson's Mansion. She knew that Jonathan was involved in that too. From what her Mom told her about Floyd Gant and Mr Samson, maybe he had something to do with those people too. She needed to tell her mother everything and quickly.

Back at Olivia's place, Jonathan was unaware of Amy's realization, as he towelled himself dry.

"Amy noticed me again, and now she's gone, you need to stop her, or she'll spoil everything." revealed the coat.

Jonathan seethed and dragged his clothes on and the coat, hurried to his car, headed to the bank, hoping he could intercept Amy, before she got there. Amy resisted going to the bank though and was being patched through to Olivia's extension from her mobile.

"Olivia Hansen!"

"Oh, Mom I need to tell you something about last night and please you've got to believe me" Amy began

"Okay, I'll try, what happened darling?"

"Jonathan seduced me last night and he's wearing that evil coat I told you about. Remember what it could do while you wear it? Well, Jonathan has it now. It was on the news that five men were attacked at Karina's father's place. Look what happened to Floyd and her father."

"Jonathan wouldn't seduce you; he's a gentleman."

"Not with that coat on; he's not. It makes you do strange shit, remember what happened to Gerald. Fabian let me wear it and look what I did to him. What about all those bodies turning up in strange circumstances, a few years back, in Maythorne and Boundford?"

Olivia did remember and gave her daughter some advice.

"Don't come to the bank, stay away, I know somebody in Boundford who helped in two of those cases. Try to find Peri Keeble; she's dealt with it all before."

"I will Mom, and I'm sorry, I couldn't control it. I'll call once I've found her."

Amy hung up and left to find a bus to Boundford. Olivia felt apprehensive and hurt by Jonathan's antics. Amy always told the truth.

Twenty minutes later, Jonathan arrived at the bank. He scouted everywhere for Amy but soon realized upon reaching Olivia's floor, that Amy didn't go there. Olivia stood with her eyes shut, before the ping of the elevator announced Jonathan's arrival.

"Jonathan, what are you doing here? You left, remember?" Olivia tried to play it cool.

"Where is Amy and what did she tell you?"

"Plenty, but it's okay, Amy has always attracted men sexually. It's her way, but I want things to be okay with us because, Karina and I work together. So are you going to probe me with your Jedi mind-meld thing, or don't you respect me enough to believe me when I say, I don't know where Amy is."

Jonathan knew Olivia had some idea about the coat he's wearing, so simply answered her question. "Of course I do."

Olivia stepped back three paces and slammed her office door, turned the lock, securing herself inside. She recalled Amy telling her, that the magic doesn't work indirectly, so with the door shut she felt safe, but if Jonathan wished it, he could have anyone kick the door in.

"Did you push Floyd from his window? Have you seen the news about those men?" Olivia called from behind her solace.

"Come on Olivia why would I? Floyd jumped out of guilt, and I never attacked those men."

She didn't say attack, so knew he was involved somehow. She knew that Amy would be safe from Jonathan for a while, until she could find Peri.

"I think you should go Jonathan; Karina will be here soon."

"Don't worry about it. I'm not going to hurt Amy. She's just a fleeting distraction from the grand scheme of things. I hope you can forgive me, Olivia."

Jonathan left the bank and headed for his car; Olivia checked he was leaving from her office window. She felt hurt and betrayed, began to cry a little. But at least she and Amy were unharmed.

Karina's voicemail told her not to meet him at the bank and that he would come to their house later tonight. Karina heard it and made preparations for it. Olivia had plans to tell Karina everything, when she arrived for work, now that Jonathan would not know.

Jonathan couldn't go back to Olivia's after what he'd done, so took the afternoon driving about in Langston, looking for alternative accommodation…

… Meanwhile Olivia and Karina were chitchatting in her office.

"Karina, you should realize that Jonathan has been staying with me and has taken it upon himself to seduce my daughter. Now she doesn't lie and if she says he did the seducing, then that's true." Karina looked sternly into Olivia's eyes as she revealed this. "Something else is troubling me too; he's wearing a coat, and it makes you do horrible things to people. Amy has firsthand experience of this, and Floyd knew this too when I told him. I reckon that Jonathan is involved in all the strange deaths around here; if that is the case than you are in danger." Olivia wasn't angry with Jonathan for this, she felt sorry.

"He's been acting odd since his holiday. He brought an old box back with him and everything has gone bad since." Karina had her suspicions, now they were confirmed by Amy and Olivia. "Don't worry about it now, he's meeting me later and my sister is fetching some people she knows over. We're going to intervene."

"It's that damned coat he's got on, if we can somehow get it away from him, then it will all stop." Olivia sipped at her tea and her tears rolled again.

"Come by my place later then, you'll be safe just in case he decides some sort of retribution is due to you?" Karina offered.

"I will, after Amy has found Peri Keeble, she can help us solve this." The two women smiled, and they returned to work.

Amy stopped the bus at Boundford and asked nearly everyone she saw if they knew Peri Keeble. Only one man answered her. It was Leon Wilkes. He was coming along with a white cane, swishing from left to right.

"Excuse me Sir, do you know a person called Peri Keeble?"

"I did know her once, she used to be a good girl, but she's a bad seed now; you'll find her living in Maythorne though. Boundford is too painful for her to live in. Hope that helps?"

Leon shuffled away and Amy returned to the bus station, so she could get on a bus to Maythorne. Amy felt a little worried now. Who was she going to meet and what did he mean by bad seed? Not long after she arrived in Maythorne, she found a taxi rank and questioned the controller.

"Hello, I was wondering if you know a woman called Peri Keeble, I'm told she lives here. Can you help?" An Asian man came to the window; he was the one ordered by Ben to take him to Peri's once. He had never forgotten that.

"She lives in Cortez Street; I'll take you there." the Cabbie offered and away they went. Ten minutes later they pulled up alongside a block of flats. "She lives in the first ground floor flat, see ya!" The Cabbie hurried away; he knew everything that went on in there. But didn't reveal anything to Amy. Amy walked to the flats and called flat 50, P Keeble on the intercom button.

"Hello?"

"I'm Amy Hansen, I once was like you, but I managed to escape from Fabian. I must talk to you; it's extremely important to us all."

"Yes of course, wait there I must do something first." Amy waited while Peri prepared a circle for them to sit in and talk safely. If Amy was with Fabian, then it meant she had been in contact with the coat again. Soon after her call Peri unlocked the door to allow entrance and finally the two girls met again. "Come in Amy and go to the circle, we'll light the candles in just a second." Peri was very clear in her instructions. Amy took off her shoes and went to the circle, Peri came too and then lit the candles, added some holy water for safe measure. "We'll be safe for a while." She smiled at Amy, finally somebody else who knows as much as she does about Fabian, her mind raced for a few seconds. But soon settled.

"Why is your visit so urgent?

"A man called Jonathan Short, has got his hands on the goatskin coat. Now he's using it to destroy people's lives. Last night he seduced me, but I saw the coat while it was off him."

"If it is off him, he isn't overwhelmed by her yet and we can stop them. I'll call John and Stuart, but we must act quickly." Peri dialled her mobile.

Chapter Six

Jonathan versus the world.

John and Stuart arrived fifteen minutes after Peri's call. John had his familiar bag of tricks with him and Stuart charged his shotgun this time with holy water. They waited in the car whilst Peri prepared her own ingredients. Amy bit her nails nervously in the circle of light, keeping the coat from not knowing what she had planned. Peri made Amy drink holy water. This would at least cloud her mind and dull her thoughts during the journey and now they were ready.

"Right Amy, where do we need to be? But be quick before Lucifer discovers us."

"Oh, I didn't plan a meeting place I'll call my mother, she might know." Amy ransacked her bag for her phone and called Olivia. She answered straight away.

"Darling, thank god, did you find her?"

"More, there are two others. What else did you find out?"

"We go to Karina's house; she's got people too. You remember the address, don't you?"

"Yes of course. You go straight there now, and we'll see you there." Amy cancelled the call, then she and Peri ran to the car.

"Can we get going now?" Stuart as always impatient. "I told you - you didn't bury that coat far enough away; this time get it off him and burn it to ashes." Stuart stated as they climbed in the car, "Where are we going?" Stuart stared at Amy through the rear-view mirror.

"Langston, I can direct you to the address once we get there. There are more people coming." Amy replied, then folded her arms; she sat grumpily looking back at Stuart.

"Let's get this done once and for all." John gave the order, and they started to drive towards Langston.

Olivia arrived at Karina's house, and she answered the door. In the sitting room were her sister Selena and husband Nathan Joyce from Maythorne CID, they were here to protect Karina from Jonathan. Nathan as you know dealt with Peter Flaws and put him away, after his killing spree.

"I'll get us some coffee now we're here. Any news of Peri?" Karina fired her question at Olivia whilst the others were waiting.

"Yes, Amy found her and called upon two others and they're heading here now. How long before Jonathan arrives?" Olivia was scared he'd come, and they wouldn't be protected."

Karina poured the coffees and Olivia helped carry them through.

"He'll be here at eight, that gives us an hour and a half to prepare." The coffee was handed round and everyone started getting to know one another and describing their encounters with the coat.

Whilst this was going on, Jonathan had secured some accommodation easily enough with the coat he was wearing and his ever-increasing power. He had convinced a lovely lady by the name of Eileen Dailey to allow him to stay. After seducing her and leaving her to get dressed again, he decided to gather his belongings from Olivia's, and it wasn't long until he realized Amy or Olivia hadn't been home since this morning. He drove back to his temporary abode and began formulating plans for his final grab of that money.

"You know by now, Olivia and Amy have begun to gather an intervention, whilst you decided to waste your time screwing gullible ladies. You should have eliminated them and got them out of the way!" The coat scolded Jonathan for failing.

"I can't kill innocents; you said that and anyway we can deal with all of it tonight." Jonathan countered.

"Amy is far from innocent; she killed a man through me using this very coat. And I can't foresee what they have planned, you need to recruit people you can trust and organize them, or you'll fail." The coat warned.

"I don't need people I've got you and my power." Jonathan seemed very confident now and reasoned he'd get through to Karina, just the same as Amy and Mrs Dailey. Talking women into things, was his newfound hobby.

"You need to be careful and keep your temptations down; they'll weaken you unless you take another soul. Oh, and you need to find some brimstone; it's flammable and a good counter against holy water. There's a shop down this way where you can buy it." The coat went quiet again so Jonathan could get ready for his meeting with Karina.

Amy and her new friends arrived at Karina's house. Stuart chose to park out of the way and John then made strategies for each of them.

"Amy and Peri, you go inside. When Karina answers, get everybody in there to drink from this flask of holy water. This will shroud you from Lucifer's thoughts; then go around the outside of the house, sprinkle this." He handed Peri a gold box. "It is hallowed dust; you must make sure the circle isn't broken. We'll wait here until we see this Jonathan, just so we know what we're up against."

"Okay, we're going inside now." Peri kissed Stuart and they hurried toward Karina's front porch.

Karina answered the door with Olivia; all four women hugged and went inside. Peri immediately laid out John's instructions. Everyone was now introduced and ready for Jonathan.

John sat in the car sifting through his bag; first he held out a small crossbow, the little arrows were shaped like crucifixes and solid gold. Eight arrows were neatly slotted into the rotating barrel. Next, he primed the trigger and latched down the safety catch. He placed it on the dashboard and fetched out the familiar golden dagger. He poured holy water on to it.

"Are you going to get close enough to shoot that thing?" asked Stuart, not really focusing on priming anything of his.

"If I don't get close, you need to, or one of them in there needs to. We need to kill the force compelling the man. All the coat has to do is gather five more souls, then Jonathan is dead, and that evil is out there and nobody can stop her." John had a stern look on his face, making Stuart check his gun, just one more time, for luck.

A few minutes later Peri came back out and began to sprinkle the dust around as previously explained. Inside, the guests were drawing a chalk circle completely around them and lighting candles. Neither John nor Stuart knew that Nathan Joyce was inside, a potential ticking bomb. If he sees that coat again, there is no telling what he would do. Peri finished with her circle and went back inside the house to safety.

"Don't forget the holy water or all this is of no use." Peri needed to remind the guests that it was the most important thing. They all swigged from the flask except for Selena who pretended to and now it was a quarter to eight, nearly time for Jonathan to arrive; he was always on time.

Jonathan drove to the entrance of the cul-de-sac, slowly and warily parked his car across the street; John and Stuart shrunk back in their seats, concealing their presence. Karina peeped out the kitchen window and made everyone leap into their circle. They all kept quiet.

"Can you sense anything unusual here?" Jonathan quizzed the coat.

"There is a heavy presence of holy water here, can't get exact numbers, but there is a sceptic sitting inside and I can tune into her." replied the coat. It was Selena, she'd been quietly disbelieving all this. Always the agnostic, but she was going to be in for one hell of a show tonight. "Go to the door but wait for Karina to invite you in, no invite no entry. Then use the brimstone." The coat guided Jonathan briefly, then left him to his own devices.

John watched quietly from his car to see what happened next; Stuart fidgeted, he had already seen what the coat could do; only John has defeated it twice. Karina saw it was eight o'clock and went to the door. She stepped over the threshold and down the driveway, knowing the dust circle wasn't too far. Johnathan approached cautiously, then Karina stood still.

"I know you have some friends in there. I don't want anyone to get hurt, so please can we talk civilly?" Johnathan broke the ice.

"Tell me the truth first. Did you really sleep with Amy? Did you kill Daddy and all those other men?" Karina felt safe enough so far.

"You know that already, so there's no use in denying it, but you can't claim the moral high ground here and okay, I did wish for them to be harmed, but it wasn't me entirely, plus your ruthless Father deserved it and those other men got in the way. Now can I come in?"

Jonathan was not sounding like his usual demure self, according to Karina.

"But you killed Daddy!" She wanted him to admit it entirely, before letting him in.

"Karina love, you won't coerce me into a confession, now let me in or I'll come in and take my things."

"You can't without an invite, sorry." Karina turned on her heels and went to go back indoors. His influence over her was weak, as predicted by the coat. "Holy water." He said in a lowered voice.

"Call someone who hasn't drunk any then?" The coat suggested.

"SELENA, COME OUT HERE AND INVITE ME IN PLEASE"

Jonathan yelled at the top of his voice. The coat had no influence over Selena directly, but she was protective of Karina and would definitely fight for her. Selena stood and left the circle, walking out to the front door. Nathan also felt protective all of a sudden and he broke the circle too. He followed out at almost the same time.

"You and that jacket aren't coming anywhere near us here. Stay the hell back or I'll be forced to take you down." He held Selena's shoulders, and the coat began to glow, that was the signal for John and Stuart to react. Seeing the symbols would force a violent reaction from Nathan.

"DCI Joyce, go back inside with your wife. Let us handle this." John said as he strode toward Jonathan, then stood sideways on holding the crossbow. "Mr Short, if you move, I'll fire this." threatened John.

"That won't work."

He grabbed a handful of brimstone from his pocket and blew it in John's direction. The pungent smell in the air caused everyone but Jonathan to heave and cough. The brimstone settled on the crossbow, and it couldn't fire. Nathan stumbled and broke the dust line surrounding them, then Jonathan raced toward the house to confront Karina. Nathan tackled Jonathan to the ground still coughing on the brimstone,

"Selena, drop that slab on to your husband's head."

He looked at Selena and she picked up the heavy slab and held it over Nathan, it landed on the back of his head. He was out cold and bleeding, Stuart raced to help Nathan, as Jonathan took Selena by the hand and they both went indoors. Selena hated Jonathan and adored her husband. "So how could I be controlled like this?" she thought as she was being towed behind him. The brimstone wore off a little and John poured more water onto the crossbow, which released an arrow, and it pierced the coat, plunging into Jonathan's back and he stumbled inside with Selena and John followed in.

"Only seven more arrows to go." said John.

The numeral VIII appeared on Jonathan's sleeve, and he felt a surge of power once more, the coat had absorbed Nathan's soul as he lay dying. As Jonathan entered the lounge all the people in the circle, cowered in fear. The flames around the circle rose and shone brightly, to protect the four women in there. John came in behind Selena and Jonathan, but he was looking at Peri.

"Throw me the box and stay still in there, you'll be safe." He said quietly.

Peri did so as John raced back outside to re-form the dust circle. Now everyone inside was sealed in. Nobody was going anywhere, and he was determined to finish this tonight.

"I address Lucifer, not Jonathan, cease this quest for domination and come quietly with me, or I will destroy you entirely."

He shot one more arrow at Jonathan and it pierced his leg, but there wasn't any reaction from Jonathan.

Chapter Seven

The Devil you don't!

Jonathan suddenly couldn't move, and the coat tightened around him, constricting the air to his lungs. Now the coat could speak loudly. And it did so.

"You will try, and you will perish, all of you. I control this vessel now and I will consume you all." There was a loud, shrill laugh and the whole house shook, the flames on the candles burned bright red and heated up, frightening the women.

It was then that the symbols on the coat shone brightly, orange in colour and everyone in the room could see it. A face appeared on the front chest piece, bright orange too and it was speaking. Jonathan's limp body hung, inches off the ground, still unable to move.

"It's the Devil!" gasped Selena.

Amy quickly passed the flask of water to Selena, and she drank several gulps, now the influence of Jonathan started to wash away. She remembered that she'd just killed Nathan outside. She was sobbing in the circle, and Amy was hugging her tightly.

Karina suddenly felt afraid for her husband and now knew who really killed her father. He had been acting strangely for days now; she could now see the reason why and wanted to help John in any way possible. Brimstone started to pass through the coat and out, into the air, causing everyone there to cough and splutter. Once again, the pungent smell filled the room and cancelled out the holy water as it landed on the protective circle. All except John who covered his mouth with a silk cloth. He fired one more arrow into Jonathan, and it pierced his shoulder. John rushed forward when the coat reached for Karina; she moved away and the brimstone landed on the candles and they raged into a huge fire, making everyone scatter around the room.

Fire was starting to burn in the middle of the room with Jonathan just hovering over it. Olivia made for the patio doors to escape, with Amy and Peri close behind her. As they left, Stuart ran in from the opposite direction, his gun hadn't been affected by the brimstone, and he shot at the smiling face on the coat, sending Jonathan four feet backwards. John shot another arrow, the fourth in total. These shots were going into Jonathan but not stopping the coat or the fire. Karina was still holding the flask of holy water, and she shook some of that at the coat. A huge yell came from it and the face contorted as if in pain. It looked crossly at Karina and once again made for her, grabbing her jacket; she struggled with the coat for a bit and shook more holy water.

"Fire another one now!" She called to John.

He did just that. The fifth arrow landed square between the eyes of the face, and suddenly the coat became loose, Karina sprayed more holy water, but the flask was now empty, and Jonathan's limp body tumbled forward out of the coat. The coat landed on the floor in a smoking heap. Stuart and John reached for Jonathan and held him up so they could leave the house.

"Mrs Short let's go. Don't worry about the house. Let it burn, we need to destroy the coat."

John saw that the coat was in the circle of light, and they all moved quickly out of the house. Selena landed at what was left of her husband; she was cradling his limp body and wailing, because she'd killed him.

The house raged into an enormous blaze, as the remaining seven people ran to safety. They stood to watch it burn. One of the neighbours had called for the fire brigade which could be heard arriving. As it pulled into the estate, the house exploded making everyone watching, duck for cover. The fire engine stopped fast and turned off the siren. The fire crew stood looking at the debris all over the place and at least eight or nine people lying flat on the ground. Was anyone alive? The crew of the engine scrambled to assist.

At the epicentre of the blaze, a red flame was burning. Inside that was the last piece of the coat, but it wasn't long before that had burned completely away. Not long after, the red flame petered out and the fire crew had controlled what was left of the house. John was talking to the chief about the explosion; the chief called for ambulances, to attend to the injured.

Whilst waiting, John was worried that they wouldn't be able to explain why Jonathan had arrows in him and a gunshot wound. He knelt by his side and pulled each one out, hiding them in his bag; he wasn't even sure if Jonathan was still alive. Karina was crouching next to John and saw some paper poking out of Jonathan's inside jacket pocket. She reached for it and pulled it out.

"It's the insurance policy; it went missing from Daddy's office yesterday." She pointed out. "I knew he'd bloody taken it, even though he denied it."

"There's your reason for them attacking you, money and power, they go hand in hand." said John.

Karina rolled the policy up and took it with her; she now felt the need to change it again. Jonathan won't get a penny now, certainly not if he survives this.

"Jonathan would never hurt me; it's the coat that made him."

"In the beginning maybe, but as his power grew, he was making those choices and don't forget he seduced your best friend's daughter. I'm sure Lucifer never helped him with that." John hugged Karina, then she sat by Jonathan's side, waiting for the ambulances.

John went over to where the coat was last seen, all he saw was nothing but ash. In his bag was a gold container. He took it out and opened the lid, poured holy water in and swept all the ash inside, closed the lid and placed it back in his bag. He looked over at Selena and saw she was in so much despair, so he went to comfort her, until the ambulance came.

Peri, Amy and Olivia stood together, and Stuart sat on the bonnet of his car, there wasn't anything wrong with him this time. He was proud of himself for saving the day and glad that the whole thing was over. He looked towards Peri, who immediately acknowledged him. She embraced Amy and Olivia, then went to be with her lover.

"You know Honey, I'm pretty sure your dad would want to know, that shitty thing is now gone forever." He put his arm around Peri, and she kissed his cheek.

"Thanks to you, we're all safe, you're my hero; we'll go see him at the weekend, if you'd like." She suggested.

"Sounds good."

They didn't wait for the ambulance and got into the car and drove back to Maythorne. As they left, they waved to John, who in return waved back.

Selena entered the ambulance with her husband and admitted to killing him, although she couldn't think why. Even harder was how to explain what went on here. Amy and Olivia only had a few scratches, they were treated at the scene and allowed to go home, leaving just John and Karina with an unconscious Jonathan, who neither thought would pull through. They boarded the last ambulance to Langston Hospital.

"Hey! Care to explain what happened here tonight?" asked the attending Paramedic.

"Not really sure exactly. Could have even been a bomb or something; it all happened fast. I'm glad most of us got away from there."

John's answer sounded plausible to Karina, and she decided to go along with that. For insurance purposes, that was the story she was going to feed her policy holders.

Who would believe her anyway if she started to rant about Devils and plans to get her money? One thing was for certain, she couldn't be married to Jonathan anymore, his adultery with Amy and other misdeeds over the last month had taken its toll on their already fragile marriage. John looked very capable of looking after himself, so she turned her attention toward him. Having seen his fair share of evil over the last twenty years, maybe it was time for him to settle down too. Karina and John gazed at each other over the prone form of Jonathan Short, as the ambulance arrived at the hospital. Their passion for one another simmered underneath.

Jonathan was taken to surgery and operated on for three hours. The gunshot had damaged his lungs, but he never really recovered from his wounds, he went into a coma and died three days later, saving the need for an acrimonious divorce.

Jonathan was laid to rest two weeks after his death. Karina and John did start a relationship. After that the gold box with the ashes in were interred at the Vatican, sealing it in forever. Karina and John moved away from Langston, forgetting everything that went on there. They lived happy lives together and no evil befell them again.

Stuart and Peri married, five years later. They have a child now called Maxine; they also never faced a day of evil for the remainder of their lives. They emigrated and stayed right away from Boundford and Maythorne.

Olivia became the chairperson of the bank by a popular vote, Amy continued to pursue her Arts with rich rewards. Selena was placed in a psychiatric unit, after the court ruled that she was not in control of her mind, the night she killed her husband. Nathan Joyce received a good send off from his colleagues at Maythorne Police Department.

It was all explained away and swept up neatly by all parties involved at Langston. The house got rebuilt, a new family lives there now. After discussing the incident with some Cardinals, since John took the ashes to Rome, a company of Catholic Priests were sent to seal the evil in that took place there, making absolutely sure that it couldn't rise again....

.... At a reunion party ten years later, Peri, Stuart, Karina, John, Olivia, Amy and a heavily sedated Selena gathered to celebrate ridding themselves of that evil old coat. As they were the only ones who saw it, they met secretly far away from Langston, Maythorne and Boundford. Having lost so much in the past it was necessary to reflect back to those awful days.

They were drinking, eating and chatting but didn't notice in the corner, a middle-aged man, wearing a tan goatskin coat, without strange ancient symbols on it, who had decided to come in from the cold and join the celebrations. He stood up at his table and walked over to the party and stood still, cleared his throat and they all turned their heads. They looked at him, in shock, but relaxed when they saw it was just an ordinary, plain tan jacket.

"Hi, I'm Fabian, mind if I join you?" The man said.

"What the hell are you wearing?" asked John.

"Oh this, it's just a coat, don't worry, nothing's going to happen." Fabian smiled and they all felt at ease, laughing at one another.

"Well in that case, sure, why don't you join us?" They continued to celebrate late into the night. Everyone laughed wholeheartedly and continued to celebrate....

This ends story four: Entitlement:

And completes the story of:

The Goatskin Coat.